Sins of Midnight

Connor nipped at the flesh just above her collar, then soothed the small sting with a flick of his tongue.

"Stop me, Jillian," he murmured against her skin, wringing a shiver from her. "Say no now or it's going to be too late."

As if to emphasize the truth of his warning, the hand that had been at her waist lifted—and unexpectedly cupped her breast.

She released a trembling moan. Even through the material of her pelisse, she could feel the heat of his touch, scorching her.

She swallowed convulsively and made a restless movement. "Connor . . ." Her voice was a whisper. "Connor, please . . ."

She had no idea what she was begging him for . . .

Other **AVON ROMANCES**

ANGEL IN MY BED *by Melody Thomas*
BE MINE TONIGHT *by Kathryn Smith*
HOW TO SEDUCE A BRIDE *by Edith Layton*
SINFUL PLEASURES *by Mary Reed McCall*
THE VISCOUNT'S WICKED WAYS *by Anne Mallory*
WHAT TO WEAR TO A SEDUCTION *by Sari Robins*
WINDS OF THE STORM *by Beverly Jenkins*

Coming Soon

FROM LONDON WITH LOVE *by Jenna Petersen*
ONCE UPON A WEDDING NIGHT *by Sophie Jordan*

And Don't Miss These
ROMANTIC TREASURES
from Avon Books

THE DUKE IN DISGUISE *by Gayle Callen*
DUKE OF SCANDAL *by Adele Ashworth*
SHE'S NO PRINCESS *by Laura Lee Guhrke*

Kimberly Logan

Sins of Midnight

AVON BOOKS
An Imprint of HarperCollinsPublishers

This is a work of fiction. Names, characters, places, and incidents are products of the author's imagination or are used fictitiously and are not to be construed as real. Any resemblance to actual events, locales, organizations, or persons, living or dead, is entirely coincidental.

AVON BOOKS
An Imprint of HarperCollins*Publishers*
10 East 53rd Street
New York, New York 10022-5299

Copyright © 2006 by Kimberly Snoke
ISBN-13: 978-0-06-079256-5
ISBN-10: 0-06-079256-6
www.avonromance.com

First Avon Books paperback printing: July 2006

Avon Trademark Reg. U.S. Pat. Off. and in Other Countries, Marca Registrada, Hecho en U.S.A.
HarperCollins® is a registered trademark of HarperCollins Publishers Inc.

Printed in the U.S.A.

10 9 8 7 6 5 4 3 2 1

To the Avon Ladies—both past and present—who have touched and inspired me through the years with your wonderful romance novels. I'm honored to finally be one of you.

And to my mother, for being the best brainstorming partner a gal could ask for, and for always being there when I need you. I love you, Mom!

Prologue

Not everything is always as it seems, and a crime is never solved until the last clue is uncovered.

A Compendium of Basic Investigative Techniques
Lord Philip Daventry, 1807

London, 1813

*S*omething bad is going to happen.
The thought jolted seventeen-year-old Lady Jillian Daventry from a sound sleep with the force of a shout.

Her eyes flew open in alarm, just as a clap of thunder shook the town house, sending her heart flying into her throat. A few seconds later, a flash of lightning illuminated her bedchamber with an unearthly radiance.

Something bad is going to happen.

1

It was a persistent whisper in the corner of her mind, insidious and undeniable. She had no idea where the feeling of dread had come from or why it was so strong, but she couldn't ignore the sharp stab of fear it brought with it, causing her breath to seize in her lungs and her hands to bunch into white-knuckled fists in the bedclothes. The very air around her seemed weighted down by an aura of impending doom.

Quickly sitting up against the pillows, Jillian clutched the silk coverlet to her chest as her gaze traveled over her surroundings, struggling to penetrate the shadows, to search out the source of the threat. But nothing moved. All was still except for the quiet patter of rain as it pelted her window.

Perhaps she had been dreaming, she mused, making an effort to steady her wildly racing pulse. Having some sort of nightmare. It would certainly be understandable in the circumstances. After the events that had transpired at Lord and Lady Briarwood's annual ball earlier that evening, she was surprised she had managed to sleep at all. The last thing she could remember before she must have drifted off was the sound of Mama and Papa arguing in their room just down the hallway, their angry words hushed, but distinct.

"Damn it, Elise! Must you create a scene wherever you go? Flirting with Lanscombe and Bedford in such a brazen manner. Throwing yourself at Hawksley, and right in front of the man's poor wife. You are the

Marchioness of Albright, yet you carry on like some dockside strumpet!"

"I don't know why you're so angry, Philip. It's not as if you're jealous. I could parade about naked in front of every man in London and the only thing you would care about is the gossip it would stir."

"That's not true."

"It is true. You never kiss or touch me anymore. You don't even look at me unless you're berating me about something. How else am I to get your attention?"

"That's no excuse for the way you behaved tonight. This was to have been the last event of Jillian's first Season, and you ruined it with your outrageous conduct. I'm certain that Shipton's heir was prepared to make an offer for her hand, but now—"

"That silly boy? Come now, Philip, do you truly believe he could ever hope to make her happy? She's far too independent and strong-willed for the likes of him."

"By damn, this is not one of your Covent Garden dramas! Need I remind you—"

"You need remind me of nothing. Lady Olivia takes great delight in pointing out to me on a frequent basis just how unsuitable a former stage actress is for the role of marchioness."

"My sister cares about the welfare of this family. If you will not think of our daughters, someone must."

"How dare you accuse me of not thinking of our daughters? Are you thinking of them when you close yourself away in the library with your books and papers and spend all of your time conferring with that Bow Street Runner? And what about Jillian? You profess *your concern for her well-being, yet you encourage her unseemly interest in your research. I somehow doubt that society would approve."*

"My work with Bow Street does not encourage the speculation of the ton. *Your behavior, however, does."*

"You knew what I was when you married me, and you said you loved me anyway. Has that changed?"

"Dear God, Elise, but I am so tired of these endless battles. Tell me what's happened to us . . . ?"

With her father's agonized query still echoing in her head, Jillian sighed and reached up to tuck a stray strand of ebony hair back behind her ear. Sometimes she wondered if she would ever understand either of her parents. She could remember a time, before her grandfather had died, when the two of them had loved each other passionately. But since Papa had taken over the title of Marquis of Albright four years before, their relationship had grown more and more volatile, and their verbal skirmishes had become an almost daily occurrence.

"Jilly?"

The voice that pulled her from her musings was soft and hesitant, barely audible even in the stillness, and at first Jillian was certain she must be imagining it. But at that moment, another convenient flare of lightning revealed the shivering, white-clad figure huddled in the doorway, tousled black curls covered by a lace-edged nightcap. A figure Jillian recognized as her fourteen-year-old sister, Maura.

"Maura? What is it? What's wrong?"

Arms wrapped about her thin frame in a defensive posture, the younger girl took a step into the chamber. Her blue eyes were wide with fright. "I d-don't know. I—I think I heard something. Something strange. And I can't find Aimee."

Jillian was instantly concerned. It wasn't like their timid, nine-year-old sibling to wander about the house alone at night, especially during a thunderstorm. Her apprehension returned with a vengeance.

Something bad is going to happen.

Tossing aside the blankets, she rose from the bed and slipped into her dressing gown before moving to light the candle on her nightstand with swift efficiency. Then, holding it aloft, she joined Maura.

"I'll come with you to look for her," she said in a soothing tone, praying that her expression betrayed none of her disquiet. "She more than likely just couldn't sleep and went down to the library to look for something to read. I'm sure we'll find her curled up in Papa's favorite chair with her nose buried in a book."

Please, God, let that be the case!

Taking a deep breath, Jillian led the way out into the quiet, dimly lit corridor and started toward the staircase at the far end, Maura's cold, trembling hand clasped in hers. The silence that closed in around them was fraught with a tension that was unnerving in its intensity, and Jillian's worry only increased when she noted in passing that the door to her parents' room stood ajar, exposing the empty chamber within. The big, four-poster bed looked untouched, as if the marquis and marchioness had never retired for the night.

What on earth was going on? Where were Mama and Papa?

They had just reached the landing when a sudden banging from the ground floor froze both girls in their tracks.

"W-what was that?" Maura hissed, her grip tightening on Jillian's hand until it was almost painful.

She shook her head in answer, peering over the railing into the inky blackness below. "I don't know."

For what seemed like a small eternity, they remained unmoving, ears pricked, as they tried to discern the source of the noise. And when an abrupt burst of rain-scented air swept up the stairs, ruffling the hem of Jillian's dressing gown, realization dawned.

The front door.

Without any further hesitation, she tugged Maura with her down the steps to the foyer.

Sure enough, the heavy oak entrance portal was flung wide to the elements, the gusting wind sending it slamming against the wall with loud, intermittent thumps. Rain slashed in through the opening, wetting the parquet floor.

Maura gasped. "Jilly, you don't think Aimee is sleepwalking again, do you?"

Jillian didn't reply, lifting the flickering flame

of her candle high to stare through the gloom. It was much darker here than it had been upstairs, for the sconces that were usually left lit in the entryway had obviously been extinguished by the damp air.

But a thin strip of light seeped out from underneath the closed door of the library.

A strange sense of foreboding crept over Jillian, and for a moment she was tempted to run for help, to awaken the servants in a panic. But she reined herself in and started forward with determined strides.

You're being ridiculous, she tried to tell herself firmly. *Aimee was simply frightened by the storm and woke Mama and Papa. They'll all be in the library, safe and sound. Everything is fine.*

But even before she pushed open the door and stepped into the room, she knew everything was not fine.

A lamp had been left burning on one of the sideboards, and it cast its muted gleam over the chamber, bathing the masculine furniture and the mahogany bookshelves that lined the paneled walls in a pale glow.

And illuminating the lean, broad-shouldered form that lay stretched out on the floor, facedown, a few feet away.

The Marquis of Albright.

"Papa!"

Setting her candle on a nearby table, Jillian rushed to her father and dropped to her knees next to him, exerting every bit of strength she possessed to roll him onto his side. He was still dressed in the elegant, dark evening clothes he had worn to the Briarwood ball. His eyes were closed, his breathing ragged and shallow, his thick, golden-brown hair matted to his skull with something that gleamed dark and wet in the dimness.

Blood.

Frantic, Jillian loosened his cravat, feeling for a pulse. Faint, but steady. Thank God.

It was as she breathed a sigh of relief that she noticed the fingers of his right hand were closed almost convulsively about a crumpled piece of paper. Prying it from his grasp, she unfolded it, struggling to decipher the spidery handwriting scrawled across the expensive stationery.

My dearest Elise,

I can no longer bear to be apart from you, love. If you feel the same way, I'll have a coach waiting after midnight.

Hawksley

A great wave of despair washed over Jillian and she pressed a fist to her mouth to stifle a sob. *Oh, Mama, what have you done?*

She glanced back over her shoulder to find her sister hovering in the doorway. "Maura, wake Iverson! We must fetch a physician at once!"

There was a moment of silence. Then, "Jilly?"

"Maura, we don't have time for this. Father needs a doctor and—"

"But Jilly, look!"

There was an urgency in her sister's voice that Jillian couldn't ignore, and she suddenly became aware of another sound in the room. A sound she hadn't noticed before over the pounding of her own heart.

A muffled whimpering.

She looked up, her eyes following Maura's pointing finger toward the far corner of the room, where the darkest shadows lurked. There, huddled on the floor against their father's massive desk, was their youngest sister, Aimee. She was rocking back and forth, her elfin countenance bleached of color, tears streaming down her cheeks and arms wrapped about her head as if protecting herself from a blow.

With a cry of distress, Jillian pushed herself to her feet and managed a few swift steps toward her little sister. But as she drew near, her gaze fell upon the tableau the bulk of the desk had previously hidden from her view, and she stumbled to a disbelieving halt.

It was the lifeless body of the Marchioness of Albright.

Jillian's stomach lurched, her mouth going dry with horror as the world spun around her.

"Mama . . . ?"

But even as the word escaped her constricted

throat, she knew her mother wouldn't answer. The marchioness's amber eyes were wide open and glazed over, staring blankly up at the ceiling. A growing pool of crimson spread out from her head like a halo, staining the Oriental rug beneath her.

Mama would never answer her again.

Chapter 1

Even the most difficult case can be brought to a close if one employs reason and perseverance.

London, 1817

"They say she was once a stage actress, you know."

Standing in the shadows of the terrace, Connor Monroe looked up from his brooding contemplation of the moonlit landscape beyond the balustrade at the sound of the feminine voice. Cool and disdainful, it drifted through the open French doors from the ballroom, cutting across the pleasant waft of orchestra music with the sharpness of a knife.

"Well, *I* heard she was a gypsy who put a curse on Lord Albright and refused to remove it unless he agreed to wed her."

The round of high-pitched titters that followed that statement had Connor wincing.

Dousing his cheroot and sending it arcing out into the darkness, he unfolded his broad frame from his casual slouch against the railing and turned to face the house just as a group of young ladies swept out onto the veranda.

Just bloody wonderful, he thought, stifling a growl. The last thing he needed was to get caught out here by a gaggle of gossiping chits just barely out of the schoolroom.

Where the hell was Tolliver?

Connor had lost track of how long he'd been waiting here for the Bow Street Runner to return from wherever it was he had disappeared to. It seemed as if it had been hours, and he was fast running out of patience.

From the moment he and Tolliver had arrived at the luxurious mansion on Park Lane in the midst of a ball they obviously hadn't been invited to, Connor had felt as restless and out of place as a virgin at a Bacchanalian revel. At nearly thirty years of age, he might have been part owner of a prosperous shipping company, wealthy and well respected in his own right, but he had never been one to mingle with the titled and aristocratic members of the *ton*. Though the Runner had assured him that the person they'd come here seeking tonight could possibly be of great help to their investigation, Connor had trouble believing that anyone who belonged to such a golden and glittering world could offer any insight whatsoever into Stuart's death.

Or who was responsible for it.

For a fleeting instant, an image of his friend and partner, slumped over his desk at the shipping office, eyes wide and unseeing as blood spilled from the gaping knife wound in his throat, flashed across Connor's inner vision. But he pushed it away and forced himself to focus on the chattering females who had so unexpectedly joined him.

Fans waving wildly and heads bent close together, the little assemblage had come to a halt and formed a loose semicircle just in front of the French doors, unaware of his presence in the gloom on the far side of the terrace.

One of them, a striking blonde with an air of icy superiority, spoke in an imperious tone that could easily be heard over the babble of the others around her. "My mother told me that Lady Albright behaved like a hoyden whenever the pair of them were in the city. Once, Mama even saw her galloping her horse across Hyde Park, riding astride like a man. Can you believe such a thing?"

"Of course." This from a tall, thin stick of a girl with a long, angular face and rather pinched features. She was clad in a hideous shade of pastel pink that clashed with the bright red tresses piled high in an elaborate coiffure. "What else can you expect from a woman of such common origins?

I understand she was quite the accomplished flirt, as well. There were rumors that she'd had affairs with half the men in London. One can only believe that Lord Hawksley did the poor marquis a favor when he . . . well, *you know.*"

There was a general murmur of agreement.

"Such a scandal!" another young lady piped up. "The woman was an absolute disgrace."

The redhead gave a sage nod. "And Lady Jillian has caused her own share of gossip. After that whole debacle with Lord and Lady Ranleigh's heir three Seasons ago, I'm surprised her father even allows her to show her face in town. I know *I* certainly have no wish to associate with her."

Connor frowned and shifted with impatience, longing to escape, yet unwilling to risk drawing their attention by attempting to do so. Damnation, but he had no desire to linger here and listen to these spiteful cats rake some poor soul over the coals, and he couldn't help but feel an uncustomary nudge of sympathy for the unfortunate young lady they were maligning in such a vicious manner. Was it any wonder he avoided society misses like the plague?

The blond-haired girl shuddered. "Who could blame my darling Shipton for changing his mind about offering for her? She cares not at all for her family or reputation. One never knows what sort of outrageous stunt she may pull next. Why, I caught her strolling about Lord and Lady Fitzwater's estate at their house party last year barefoot and wearing *breeches,* of all things!"

"I can't understand why the Dowager Duchess of Maitland seems to have taken Lady Jillian under her wing and insists on inviting her and her family to functions such as this," one of the others interjected with a sniff.

"Well, her father *is* a marquis, and it is my understanding that Her Grace was a good friend of the late Lady Albright." The blonde tossed her artfully arranged curls in a studied manner that had a quietly observing Connor restraining the urge to roll his eyes in disgust. "And we all know that the dowager duchess is considered to be more than a trifle eccentric herself since the death of the duke. I believe that she has agreed to act as a sponsor of sorts for the debut of Lord Albright's middle daughter, Lady Maura." One corner of her mouth curved upward in a condescending smile. "One can only hope that the girl makes a better job of it than her older sister."

"Perhaps Lady Jillian is a gypsy like her mother. Or a witch who can conjure up a spell to reel in some hapless, unsuspecting suitor for the Lady Maura."

The blonde gave a tinkling laugh at her red-haired friend's comment. "Really, Beatrice, Lady Jillian isn't getting any younger, you know. Why, she must be all of one and twenty, at least. I expect she would be much better served to conjure up such a spell for herself."

"Oh, if I were going to cast a spell, Lady Gwyneth, I rather think I could come up with something a bit more original than that."

The calm words came from the direction of the French doors, resonating with the impact of a shout despite the softness with which they were spoken, effectively bringing an abrupt halt to the conversation.

Absolute silence descended.

Something about the unfamiliar voice arrested Connor, its low, throaty cadences sending a tingle up his spine, stroking over his senses like the softest of velvet.

Could this be the infamous Lady Jillian they'd been discussing?

Curious in spite of himself, he moved forward just enough so he could see past the group of females to the figure who had stepped out onto the flagstones. In that instant, a shaft of moonlight spilled over the newcomer, illuminating her in a pale glow.

And Connor's mouth went dry with unmistakable desire.

Tall and statuesque, she wore a bronze satin ballgown that hugged every inch of her lushly endowed form, leaving very little to the imagination. Her raven-black locks were a riot of curls, the ringlets framing a face of dusky-skinned, almost exotic beauty. A pointed, stubborn-looking chin and high, patrician cheekbones were offset by a tip-tilted nose and the fullness of ripe, sensuous lips. Slanted eyes of a color he couldn't quite determine from this distance surveyed the females before her with thinly veiled contempt.

"If I didn't believe it was impossible," she

continued in that unusually husky voice that had so affected Connor, "I might be tempted to try my hand at turning the lot of you into gracious and less shallow human beings. But alas, I'm afraid that's beyond the powers of even this heathen gypsy, so I shall have to think of something else. Toads, perhaps?"

There were several gasps, and Lady Beatrice's face burned as red as her hair.

Lady Gwyneth, however, leveled the Lady Jillian with a chilly stare. "This is a private conversation."

One elegant dark eyebrow arched upward. "I do beg your pardon, but I gathered you were talking about me and my family. I just thought I'd offer you some insight, as you know absolutely nothing about either."

"I'm sure I know more than I need to know. And your rude behavior only illustrates your distinct lack of manners and lends credence to what I was saying. I can only hope for the Lady Maura's sake that she has more skill at exhibiting the social graces than you do."

Connor saw something shift in the Lady Jillian's expression. But though she looked as if she longed to speak, she merely glared at Lady Gwyneth, saying nothing.

Lady Beatrice cleared her throat and plied her fan nervously, looking from one verbal combatant to the other. "Ladies, I do believe I hear the orchestra striking up to begin the next set. We'd best return to the ballroom before we are missed."

She herded the other young women in the direction of the French doors, and Lady Gwyneth followed behind. But at the last second, as the rest of them disappeared inside, the blonde spun back to face Lady Jillian with a calculating look. "I've just realized that you have yet to congratulate me on my engagement. The Viscount Shipton and I are to be wed in the spring."

Connor noticed that the Lady Jillian's countenance didn't alter in the slightest. Yet he could sense the sudden tension that had settled over her, vibrating in the air with palpable intensity. "Yes, I read the announcement in the *Times*. Congratulations."

"You don't sound very sincere. Why, I might almost believe you weren't happy for me, Lady Jillian."

"I assure you, Lady Gwyneth, that I am quite happy for you."

"Are you certain? I know that you and Thomas were once . . . close."

Lady Jillian gave a careless shrug. "That was in the past, and no longer of any importance. I truly wish you and Lord Shipton all the luck in the world. Heaven knows, the viscount shall need it should he marry you."

Lady Gwyneth visibly stiffened, and Connor felt his mouth twitch with suppressed humor. *Bravo, my lady,* he thought in admiration. Obviously, the dark-haired miss well knew how to stand up for herself.

There was a long, drawn-out pause, then Lady

Gwyneth stuck her nose in the air, whirled, and vanished into the house.

As soon as she was out of sight, the Lady Jillian expelled an audible breath, and some of the starch seemed to seep out of her spine. Connor watched as she turned and wandered over to stand next to the balustrade, head bent and white-gloved hands gripping the railing.

Now was his chance. With her facing away from him, he should be able to slip back through the other set of French doors that led into the foyer of the mansion, unnoticed. The faster he could locate Tolliver and attend to their business here, the better.

But something held him in place. A tangible magnetism that drew him to this mysterious beauty against his will. Never mind that she was exactly the sort of female he had long ago made up his mind he wanted nothing to do with. The daughter of a lord, wealthy and more than likely spoiled beyond measure. Her boldness and fiery spirit as she had defended herself against the slings and arrows of the Lady Gwyneth intrigued him, and her exquisite features and velvety voice were potent lures.

You don't have time for this, Monroe, he warned himself. *You must remember you have far more important things to contend with.*

Such as hunting down the criminal who had turned his existence into a living hell.

Pain knifed at his chest and he closed his eyes against another mental picture of Stuart. If only he had taken all of this seriously from the beginning, from the moment he had received that first threatening missive, he might have been able to stop it before things had gone so far. But he hadn't. And now he had his partner's blood on his hands, as well as Peg's and Hiram's.

Just three more names to add to the list of deaths he was responsible for. A list that had begun six years ago.

With Brennan.

Connor's hands tightened into fists at his sides. This murderous bastard had to be caught before any more lives were lost, and he couldn't afford to allow himself to be distracted right now. Even should he be tempted to approach the captivating Lady Jillian, he had no idea what he would say. He had always been a very blunt and straightforward sort of man, and he had never had much of a gift for engaging in idle small talk or polite flirtation.

He should walk away. He knew that.

But she looked so dejected standing there alone . . .

And suddenly, without his volition, he found himself starting across the terrace toward her, pulled forward by some invisible force he couldn't seem to fight or put a name to.

The sharp echo of his footsteps on the flagstones must have alerted her as he neared, for she glanced back over her shoulder and started as she caught sight of him. At her surprised expression, he came to an immediate halt still several paces away. He was well aware that his battered visage could be intimidating at the best of times, and he had no wish to frighten her.

He inclined his head in a slight bow, giving her what he hoped was a reassuring smile. "I'm sorry, my lady. I didn't mean to alarm you, but you appeared so melancholy that I was concerned. I thought I would ask if you were in need of assistance."

"Assistance? No, I—" She blinked, peering past him in the direction from which he'd come before returning her wary gaze to his face. "How long have you been out here?"

"For quite some time, I'm afraid."

Even in the dimness, Connor could make out the becoming tide of color that flooded her cheeks. "Then . . . then you heard . . . ?"

"Your interesting altercation with the Lady Gwyneth? As a matter of fact, I did." One corner of his mouth gave a rueful quirk. This close, he could finally see that her eyes were a stunning shade of amber, shot through with specks of molten gold. Cat's eyes. "And may I say that I have never seen an enemy so thoroughly vanquished with little more than the power of a few well-chosen words?"

For what seemed a small eternity, she just stared at him, seemingly at a loss. Then, her look of bemusement faded away to be replaced by one of quickly growing anger.

Swinging away from the railing, she faced him with hands on her hips. "No, you may not!"

she hissed, those eyes shooting hostile sparks. He doubted she was aware of it, but her rigid stance thrust her generous breasts forward, calling his attention to the firm mounds where they swelled above the low-cut, pearl-studded neckline of her bodice.

God, but she was even more magnificent when she was in a fury. Connor felt his heart skip a beat and a wry chuckle escaped him as he raised his hands, palms outward, in a sign of surrender. "Please, my lady. I am raising the white flag and ask that you not strike without due cause. I am very much afraid I wouldn't survive the lash of your tongue."

"How dare you? How dare you slink about like a common criminal and eavesdrop on people's private conversations?"

Wait just one moment! That accusation rubbed him on the raw and he dropped his hands, frowning at her. "I was hardly slinking about. I was out here minding my own business and enjoying a good cheroot when Lady Gwyneth and her coterie decided to join me. Uninvited, may I add."

"And you could not have made your presence known?"

"I wished to save anyone any embarrassment."

"Well, in that regard, you have failed." She took a step toward him, lifting her chin at a defiant angle. "No true gentleman would ever behave in such a fashion."

That did it. Now Connor's own formidable temper was roused. Lady Jillian was apparently every bit as haughty and difficult as every other society female he'd had the misfortune to meet, and he couldn't deny the keen sense of disappointment that tugged at him.

He had told himself this wasn't a good idea. Why hadn't he listened?

Closing what was left of the distance between them in just a few determined strides, he took a fierce satisfaction at her startled gasp as he scowled down at her. "I never said I was a gentleman, my lady."

"No, you certainly didn't." Despite her obvious disgruntlement at his nearness, she didn't back down, but studied his tall form with suspicion. "And now that I think about it, I don't remember seeing you in the ballroom this evening. For that matter, I don't recall ever meeting you before, and I thought that I was well acquainted with all of Theodosia's close friends. Just who are you?"

Connor felt a muscle ticking in his jaw. Here was the question he'd hoped she wouldn't ask, but he didn't see how he could possibly avoid answering it. "My name is Connor Monroe, of Grayson and Monroe Shipping. And no, I wasn't present in the ballroom. I wasn't exactly invited."

"I see. Then what *exactly* are you doing here?"

Not knowing what to say in reply to that, he remained silent.

At his reticence, Lady Jillian's glowing amber eyes narrowed dangerously. "Very well, Mr. Monroe. If you won't tell me, then you can make your explanations to the dowager duchess. I'm sure she'll be interested to know that there is someone present who isn't on her guest list."

She started to march off toward the house, but Connor reached out in one swift, desperate motion and seized her upper arm, pulling her to him.

And in that moment, he knew he'd made a mistake.

At the feel of her silken smooth skin beneath his fingertips, those delectable curves brushing up against his length, a wave of heat slammed into him with the force of a lightning bolt, bringing his nerve endings to singing attention and seizing his breath in his lungs. Every logical thought was chased right out of his head, leaving him aware of nothing but the perilous need she seemed to be able to stir within him.

And there could be no denying that Lady Jillian was just as affected, for she stilled in his grasp and stared up at him with eyes wide in consternation. She was tall for a woman, the top of her head on a level with his mouth, their faces only inches apart, and her fragrance filled his nostrils, a heady blend of jasmine and spice. Full lips parted on a choked sound, and one of her hands fluttered up to rest against his chest as if to push him away, though she made no move to do so. Connor was certain she must be able to feel the frantic pounding of his heart beneath her palm.

What would she do, he wondered dimly, if he were to lean forward and cover those lips with his own, if he were to taste her the way he suddenly realized he longed to? Never mind that he had only just met her. Never could he remember being so aroused by a female before.

"Ah, there you are!"

The hearty voice rang out in the stillness, breaking the spell that seemed to hold the two of them in its grip, and Connor looked up to see a rotund, gray-haired figure hurrying toward them.

Morton Tolliver.

Immediately, he dropped Lady Jillian's arm and took a step away from her, praying that neither she nor the Bow Street Runner would notice the telltale bulge in his breeches. What the bloody hell was wrong with him? He had no doubt that if it hadn't been for the Runner's timely reappearance, he would have wound up kissing this woman.

A woman he had no business even touching.

Exerting every bit of willpower he possessed, he forced himself to face Tolliver as the man puffed up to join them, his plump face red with exertion. "I've been looking everywhere for you, Monroe. I thought I left you in the foyer."

"You did." When he spoke, Connor was pleased to note that his voice remained steady and even, betraying not a hint of his disquiet. "I felt in need of some fresh air, so I decided to step out here for a short while."

"Of course, of course. I didn't mean to keep you waiting for so long. I still haven't managed to—"

"Mr. Tolliver? What are you doing here?"

Connor swung his head toward Lady Jillian to

find her staring at the Bow Street Runner in stunned recognition.

"Why, Lady Jillian." A pleased smile spread over Tolliver's countenance and he offered her a polite bow. "Fancy that. Here I've had the dowager duchess's footmen combing the ballroom looking for you and you were out here all the time."

"Wait a minute." Connor's gaze went back and forth between the two of them, and even before he asked the question, he was very much afraid he knew the answer. "You two know each other?"

"Indeed we do." The Runner's grin widened. "Mr. Connor Monroe, allow me to introduce you to the very person I brought you here to speak to. Lady Jillian Daventry."

Chapter 2

Rid yourself of any pre-conceived notions. Making assumptions before you have all the facts can prove to be an investigator's downfall.

"I can't tell you how sorry I am for approaching you here, my lady."

Morton Tolliver's words pulled Jillian from the depths of her reverie.

Ensconced on a brocade-covered love seat in the study of the late Duke of Maitland, she forced herself to concentrate on the conversation at hand and looked up to meet the Bow Street Runner's kind brown eyes. As he sat across from her in a matching armchair, his apologetic countenance conveyed the depth of his sincerity.

"I know this isn't precisely the proper venue," he continued, his tone rueful, "but I'd heard you would be attending the dowager duchess's ball tonight, and it seemed preferable to calling round at your family's town house. I didn't think you would want his lordship or your aunt to know you were speaking to me."

No. No, she certainly didn't want that. Not after she had promised Papa just that morning that she would try to behave for Maura's sake.

Aware all the while of the quiet, charismatic figure standing in the shadows on the far side of the room, observing her with a hooded expression, she tried to ignore the weight of that unsettling stare and clasped her hands in her lap. So far, Connor Monroe had contributed little to the discussion, allowing Mr. Tolliver to do most of the talking. But she could feel the heat of his presence as if he were sitting right next to her, even though he had been careful to maintain his distance ever since she had led the two gentlemen to the privacy of the study.

What was it about this man that affected her so strongly? Good lord, she'd almost let him kiss her! If Tolliver hadn't come along when he had . . .

Well, she simply refused to even consider what might have happened.

Shaking off her preoccupation, she offered the Runner a slight smile, praying none of her fascination with his companion showed on her face. "It's quite all right. And you were correct. It is best if my family doesn't know of this meeting."

"Yes, well, I realize it has been a while since I enlisted your aid. I wouldn't have done so now, but I'm afraid we have a rather urgent matter on our hands and the circumstances have become quite desperate."

"What sort of matter?"

"A man's death."

The answer came, not from Tolliver, but from Connor Monroe. She started, a gasp escaping her as he stepped forward into the circle of light cast by the lamp on a nearby side table.

"The matter, my lady," he went on in that deep, gravelly voice that sent a shiver coursing through her, "is murder."

Jillian felt an uncomfortable warmth seep into her cheeks at the intensity of his regard.

Large and brawny of frame with broad shoulders and thick, auburn hair that fell in untamed waves to his collar, Monroe lacked the conventional handsomeness of most males of her acquaintance. But there was something about that harsh-featured face that was arresting, nonetheless. Eyes of a shifting color somewhere between blue and green peered out from a craggy visage of bluntly carved planes and angles, and his sharp blade of a nose looked as if it had been broken at least once in his lifetime. The only hint of softness in that otherwise granite mask was the sensuous curve of his chiseled lips.

Lips that had come far too close to capturing her own.

From the moment Jillian had turned to find him behind her on the terrace, he had enthralled her as much as he had angered her. Though he had attempted to present a charming front, she had sensed the coiled power, the leashed tension he held in check. Despite the obviously expensive and well-tailored clothing that fit his muscular physique to perfection, a wildness lurked behind that deceptively civilized façade.

Never could she remember being so attracted to a man before. Not even Thomas.

Clenching her hands in the folds of her skirt, she leveled him with what she hoped was a cool stare. "I see."

"Do you?" He cocked his brow in a mocking fashion. "Somehow I rather doubt that."

A little flare of temper ignited inside her, but she reined it in. She supposed he had every right to be a bit put out with her. She never should have lashed out at him the way that she had earlier. But after her run-in with Lady Gwyneth, it had been humiliating to learn that he had been privy to the entire conversation regarding her mother and her own ill-fated association with Lord Shipton.

Facing the Bow Street Runner, Monroe crossed his arms over his wide chest, one corner of his mouth turning downward in a frown. "I must say, Tolliver, I have a bit of trouble understanding of what help the Lady Jillian can be to our investigation." He cast her an unreadable glance. "No offense intended, my lady, but this isn't a situation someone of your ilk should have any involvement with."

Jillian bristled at his condescending tone. She had no idea why his attitude irritated her so. She had faced just this sort of reaction more than once, and she had never let it bother her before. But something about his patronizing manner made her see red.

She cut in before Tolliver could reply. "I'll have you know, Mr. Monroe, that I have been of a great deal of help to Bow Street over the years."

There was no denying the doubtfulness in those aqua eyes as he surveyed her. "Really? And how is that?"

"My father, the Marquis of Albright, is a renowned expert in the relatively new field of criminal investigative procedure. He has written numerous books and papers on the subject and has consulted with Bow Street in the past."

"In that case, perhaps we should be approaching *him*?"

Jillian felt her heart give a painful squeeze as the memory of her father's lost and grief-stricken expression on the day of her mother's funeral washed over her, but she firmly pushed it away. The marquis's lack of interest in the life he'd lived before his wife's death was of no one else's concern. "I'm afraid he doesn't do that sort of work anymore."

Monroe shook his head. "Then I fail to see how you could possibly aid us."

Tolliver answered for her. "Lady Jillian has followed in Lord Albright's footsteps, in a manner of speaking. She's studied his research in great detail, and I can tell you about quite a few of my investigations that might have never been solved if it hadn't been for her invaluable advice." He paused for a moment, then looked over at her, his face grave. "However, I must admit that I, myself, hesitated to come to you with this, my lady. It is a rather . . . well, I'm afraid it's every bit as violent and brutal as the Ratcliffe Highway murders."

Jillian remembered when her father had assisted the law with the case the Runner had mentioned several years back. The crimes had been particularly gruesome and seemingly without motivation, and the marquis had never been fully convinced that the right man had been caught. If this was such a case . . .

A chill of premonition crept up her spine. "Who was murdered?"

"Mr. Monroe's partner, Mr. Stuart Grayson. He was found in his office at the shipping company early this morning, and a message of sorts was left behind."

Something shifted in the depths of the Runner's eyes and he held her gaze with a curious sort of intentness. Jillian had been acquainted with Tolliver long enough to know that there was far more afoot here than a typical murder investigation. There *had* to be.

But what?

She looked to Monroe. "And how was Mr. Grayson killed?"

To her surprise, a stark and unflinching grief briefly suffused the man's hard features at her question before he slid his mask of detached composure back into place. When he finally spoke, his words were flat and succinct, with not a hint of the pain that he had just revealed. "His throat was slit. From ear to ear."

If Jillian hadn't been aware that he was deliberately trying to shock her, his brusque manner might have put her off. But she had seen the torment that lurked behind that impassive exterior. He wasn't nearly as unemotional as he pretended to be. It was there in those aqua eyes, in the muscle ticking in his jaw, though he tried to hide it, and it touched her in spite of herself.

Connor Monroe had cared for Stuart Grayson. Cared for him a great deal.

"And the message?" she prompted. "What did it say?"

Tolliver sent an inquiring glance in Monroe's direction. When the younger man gave a sharp inclination of his head in response, the Runner replied. " 'You will pay.' It was . . . written in blood at the scene."

"What leads is Bow Street following?"

"The wrong ones."

The hoarse statement returned Jillian's attention to Monroe. "Excuse me?"

He didn't bother to explain himself, however, but spun on his heel, striding over to stand rigidly next to the fireplace, his back to the room.

After an awkward second, Tolliver cleared his throat and elucidated. "I'm afraid that those in charge at Bow Street have made up their minds as to the identity of the killer and are refusing to look any further. They are conducting a search for the man even as we speak."

"Whom do they suspect?" Jillian asked.

"A former employee of Grayson and Monroe Shipping by the name of Wilbur Forbes."

The name slammed into her with the force of a blow and her eyes flew to meet Tolliver's. The man gave her an almost imperceptible nod in response to her hopeful look.

So, there *had* been another reason he had sought her out!

Wilbur Forbes. The Runner had finally managed to locate the very person she'd spent the last four years desperately searching for. The person who just might be able to give her the answers to all the questions that had haunted her since the night of her mother's murder.

Her heart pounding in her ears, she forced herself to speak through a suddenly constricted throat. "Former?"

This time, Monroe responded, though he didn't turn back around. "Forbes worked for us at our shipyard for a little over a year, and in that time he proved to be more trouble than it was worth in order to keep him on. He consistently showed up late—and drunk—and couldn't seem to get along with his fellow workers. We gave him several chances to redeem himself, but almost two months ago he severely injured another employee in a brawl, and Stuart was forced to make the decision to send him on his way."

As Jillian watched, he bowed his head and

rested one big hand on the mantelpiece before him, his blunt-tipped fingers flexing before doubling into a white-knuckled fist. "Forbes swore he'd make us pay, and Bow Street is certain that this was his way of seeking revenge."

"And you think Bow Street is wrong in its suspicions?"

Monroe whirled to face her, his powerful muscles bunching beneath his coat in a smooth economy of motion that was unusual in a man so large. No longer did he look remote. His eyes blazed with fierce conviction. "I *know* they're wrong. Forbes is a drunkard and a bully, but he's no killer. He's the sort to react in anger, not cold-bloodedly sit down and plot out a murder. If he was going to seek revenge, he would have done so two months ago and not waited until now."

Jillian mulled over what she had been told. That certainly matched what information she'd been able to glean about Forbes's character from the few people who had known him during the time he had served as Lord Hawksley's coachman.

She glanced over her shoulder at Tolliver. "What do you think?"

The portly Runner shrugged, well aware that she was asking for more than his opinion of Connor Monroe's theory. "I think he's right, but so far I'm the only one at Bow Street who will even consider the possibility that the culprit could be someone other than Wilbur Forbes. Of course, I still think it's a good idea if we track the man down as soon as possible." He gave her a knowing look. "If only to eliminate him as a suspect in the eyes of the law, you understand."

Oh, Jillian understood, all right. Dear, sweet Tolliver had just presented her with the opportunity to become involved in an investigation that could put her into contact with someone who might actually have been a witness to events on the evening her mother had been killed. Papa and Bow Street might believe that the case of Lady Albright's death was closed, but she wasn't so certain. Too many pieces of the puzzle didn't fit, and until she could figure out why, until her doubts had been appeased, she would never be able to put the nightmare of what had happened behind her.

Now, after all these years, she finally had a chance to do so. And all she had to do was convince Connor Monroe that he needed her help.

She studied his grim countenance surreptitiously from the corner of one eye. That just might be easier said than done. He didn't look open to the possibility of accepting any assistance from her, regardless of Mr. Tolliver's faith in her capabilities. And she had to admit, if only to herself, that her initial attraction to him made working with him in any capacity dangerous to her peace of mind.

Not to mention her heart.

Jillian bit her lip to quell an unaccustomed rush of uncertainty. There was also her promise to her father to consider. She certainly didn't want to disappoint him again, and she had no desire to ruin her sister's chances of a successful debut. Maura would never forgive her, and Aunt Olivia would be sure to ring a peal about her head if she brought any further scandal to the family name.

But surely it would be worth risking their disapproval in the end? a little voice in the back of her mind insisted. If she could prove to them that her suspicions regarding the night Mama had been killed were correct, they would *have* to understand. They would finally have to take her seriously.

She straightened her shoulders with a renewed sense of determination, then rose from the love seat and crossed the room to stand before Monroe. This close, she could feel the masculine magnetism, the passionate energy he fought so hard to contain, coming off him in tangible waves, affecting her as profoundly as it had out on the terrace, making her pulse race.

Calling on every ounce of willpower she possessed, she met his gaze. "Is there something else? Something that makes you believe Forbes isn't responsible?"

Monroe's changeable eyes narrowed before he acknowledged her query with a stiff nod. "In the past few weeks, I've had several threatening letters delivered to my town house. Letters that warned me in no uncertain terms that the people I care about are in danger. This is a personal vendetta, and Stuart had nothing to do with it. I'm positive these murders are merely a way to strike back at me."

"Murders? There has been more than one?"

A look of disconcertment flashed across his features, as if he were surprised to realize that he had revealed such a thing to her. But after a moment, his visage darkened and he leaned close to her. Too close for comfort. His tone was low and grating when he spoke. "I would suggest, Lady Jillian, that you refrain from asking any further questions. As I have no intention of allowing you to become involved in such a grisly business, there is no need for you to know any more of the details."

Jillian raised her chin, taking a step back from his discomfiting nearness. "And why is that, Mr. Monroe? Because I am a woman?"

"That is certainly one of the reasons."

"I will have you know that the fact that I am a female does not negate my ability to use logic and deductive reasoning. Both of which you will need in order to solve a crime such as this."

One corner of Monroe's harsh mouth canted upward in what might have almost been amusement. "Far be it from me to denigrate whatever skills you might possess, my lady, but I can't say that I ever expected to hear the words 'logic' and 'female' used in the same sentence."

Jillian once again felt her temper sputter to life. Of all the nerve! "Now, see here—"

But Monroe cut her off with a single, sharp

gesture, his smile fading. "Lady Jillian, we are talking about a murder investigation, not an afternoon tea party."

"I am aware of that, sir, but as Mr. Tolliver has said, I've spent a great deal of time studying my father's work. I've had some experience—"

"I am sorry, my lady, but *some* experience does not qualify you to take part in such an affair." He brushed past her, leaving her flesh tingling in his wake, and stalked across the room to Tolliver's side. "This simply won't do, Tolliver. A lady such as she has no business mucking about in a murder investigation. We've wasted our time."

His gaze locked with Jillian's for what seemed to be a small eternity, and something sizzled in the air between them, heated and intense. For a fleeting instant, she was flung back to that moment on the terrace when he had held her so close, his musky male scent scattering her senses and his lips only inches from her own . . .

Then he whipped about and started for the door with long, fluid strides.

Tolliver hastily got to his feet. But before following after Monroe, the Runner stepped to Jillian's side and took her hand in his, speaking urgently under his breath as he bowed over it. "My lady, we shall be at the shipping company offices tomorrow morning should you decide to join us. I will do my best to talk Mr. Monroe around by then. I truly do believe we could use your help. And not just because of Forbes."

As he hurried away, Jillian glanced down at

the scrap of paper he had pressed into her palm.
A scrap of paper bearing a scrawled address.

She closed her fist about it, crumpling it into a
ball as she glared after their departing figures.
She had no intention of giving up on this. The
chance to finally learn the truth about what had
happened to her mother was far too important.

Regardless of what the infuriating Mr. Monroe thought, this was far from over.

Chapter 3

Remember to remain open-minded to new methods of investigation.

"Bloody hell, Tolliver, what were you thinking?"

Once in their hired hackney and on their way back to his town house in Piccadilly, Connor crossed his booted feet and glared over at the Bow Street Runner who sat facing him.

"She's the daughter of a marquis," he continued, his tone gruff and full of annoyance. "A *lady*. Of what possible use could she be to us as far as the investigation into Stuart's death is concerned?"

Tolliver shrugged. "More than you might imagine," he replied enigmatically.

Connor barely stifled an irritated oath. He knew he owed the Runner quite a bit and he shouldn't be unleashing his frustration on him. After all, he was the only officer at Bow Street who had listened to Connor, who had taken his suspicions regarding his partner's murder seriously. But his confrontation with the Lady Jillian had left him disturbed and unsettled, ready to snap at the least provocation. The woman had breached his normally rigid control with very little effort, and he didn't like it one bit.

He exerted some of that control now and managed to keep his voice calm and even when he spoke again. "And what is that supposed to mean?"

There was a pause, then Tolliver gave another careless shrug. "As she said, she has been of great help in some of my past cases."

"And that tells me absolutely nothing," Connor growled, reaching up to rake a hand through the tousled length of his hair in an agitated gesture. "*How* has she been of help? Make me understand why you would waste my time by dragging me to some fancy ball to see her when there is a killer out there ready to strike again."

"I never would have brought you if I hadn't thought she could be of assistance."

At the impatient sound Connor made in response to that, the Runner released a resounding exhalation of air. "Monroe, I can only reiterate what she has already told you. Her father was a well-reputed scholar in the area of scientific investigation and has been writing articles and journals on the topic since his days at Cambridge."

"Yet we sought out the daughter instead of the father."

"I'm afraid his lordship seems to have lost his taste for such things. I haven't consulted him on a case in quite some time. Not since the death of his wife."

Curious about Lady Jillian's family in spite of his determination to put his unsettling encounter with her behind him, Connor studied Tolliver with sharpened interest. "Oh?"

"A nasty business it was." The Runner shook his head. "The late marchioness was once a stage actress of rather . . . er, notorious reputation. The young Lord Albright attended one of her performances and fell head over heels in love. Their marriage caused quite the scandal. As a matter of fact, the former marquis nearly disowned his son over it."

"And?"

"And after a while the relationship began to fall apart. Society wasn't kind, and there were rumors that Lady Albright had started taking lovers. Then, one evening about four years ago, she was apparently murdered in her own home by one of them. The Earl of Hawksley. Lord Albright himself found the man standing over the body and was injured in a scuffle with him. It was in all the newspapers at the time. You might remember hearing about it."

As a matter of fact, Connor did recall the incident. "Hawksley . . . If I remember correctly, didn't the man . . . ?"

"Do away with himself rather violently?" Tolliver grimaced and gave an affirmative nod. "Yes. Shot himself that very same night after fleeing the scene. Of course, no one was surprised at all. His own reputation was far from spotless. He was a drunkard and a wastrel and estranged from his own family. A wife and son, I believe."

Connor was silent for a moment as he contemplated the tale he'd just been told. It seemed Lady Jillian had led far from the typical life of a pampered young lady, and he felt another strong tug of sympathy. Sympathy . . . and something more.

Something he firmly pushed away before speaking again. "You said 'apparently,' Tolliver."

"I beg your pardon?"

"You said Lady Albright was *apparently* murdered by Lord Hawksley. There was some doubt?"

"Not particularly. At least, not on the part of Lord Albright or the officers in charge at Bow Street."

"But on *your* part?"

There was a slight hesitation before the Runner replied. "There were a few aspects of the investigation that I felt weren't looked into as thoroughly as they should have been. But as far as the law is concerned, the case is closed and has been for some time."

Connor's eyes narrowed. There was something more here. But it was obvious in the way Tolliver shifted in his seat and looked away that he didn't want to talk about it. If Connor wanted more information about the death of Lady Albright, it seemed he wasn't going to get it from the Runner.

So he changed the subject. "And just how did you come to know Lady Jillian?"

Tolliver visibly relaxed. "I have been acquainted with her for quite some time due to my association with her father. She's always taken an interest in the marquis's work." The Runner's mouth curved in a fond smile. "A most canny female."

That much had been obvious from the questions she had asked this evening, Connor had to acknowledge with reluctance. Probing and astute queries that he would have never expected from a marquis's daughter. "And you think that alone qualifies her to assist with this investigation?"

Tolliver's brow lowered in a frown as he met Connor's gaze. "If I were you, Monroe, I wouldn't make the mistake of underestimating her. She's a very perceptive and resourceful young woman who is capable of more than you might think."

Connor didn't doubt that. There could be no denying the gleam of shrewd intelligence he'd seen in those amber eyes as she'd faced him so defiantly. As he remembered the firm set of her jaw, the way the lamplight in the study had bathed her dusky skin with a rosy glow, he felt his body stir to life in a most uncomfortable fashion, and he trapped a groan in his throat.

He couldn't understand why she aroused him so. She was lovely, it was true. But he had met women equally as lovely in the past. His current mistress, a widowed dressmaker by the name of Selene Duvall, was stunning by anyone's standards. But though the blond beauty was quite skilled at keeping him physically satisfied, not even she had ever come close to having this effect on him.

Even if he believed that Lady Jillian could help them find Stuart's murderer, he knew spending any length of time in her company would be foolhardy at best. She was much too dangerous to his peace of mind.

He returned his attention to Tolliver. "And does her father condone her activities?"

The Runner's lined face reddened, and the older man's earlier words to Lady Jillian came back to Connor with sudden clarity.

I didn't think you would want his lordship or your aunt to know you were speaking to me.

"Ahhh," he drawled out slowly, folding his arms over his chest. "He doesn't know, does he?"

"You must understand, Monroe. Lord Albright has . . . changed since his wife's unfortunate passing. About three years ago, I approached the marquis regarding a case involving the theft of some jewelry from the Countess of Ranleigh. He turned me away. Said he no longer had any interest in such matters."

"But Lady Jillian *did* have an interest?"

"She was present during my conversation with his lordship that day, and she came to see me at Bow Street. It seemed she'd done some investigating on her own and had developed a theory, but was insistent upon visiting the scene of the crime before pointing any fingers. Though I was reluctant, it seemed a harmless enough request." The Runner reached up to remove his hat, rubbing at the balding spot on his pate with a rueful expression. "To my surprise, after questioning the countess and a few of the servants, Lady Jillian claimed that the thief was none other than Lady Ranleigh's own son."

"And she was right?"

"As a matter of fact, she was. I was intrigued enough to do some digging, and I found out that the countess's son had a predilection for high-stakes wagering that had left him in debt to half the gambling establishments in the city. His father had cut him off without a cent, and I suppose the son decided to make up for the lost funds by robbing his mother and seeing what he could get for the gems on the black market."

Connor recalled the comment he'd overheard one of the silly chits out on the terrace make regarding the "debacle with Ranleigh's heir" and the light dawned. "And word of the part she'd played in the investigation got out?"

Tolliver's brown eyes clouded with visible regret. "Unfortunately, yes. She was the talk of the *ton* for quite some time, I'm afraid.

Rumors abounded, and the late marchioness's rather ... colorful background didn't help her in the gossipmongers' eyes, either. It was a case of 'Like mother, like daughter' as far as they were concerned."

What else can you expect from a woman of such common origins?

The Lady Beatrice's frosty words echoed in Connor's head, and he wrinkled his forehead in thought. Apparently, the late Lady Albright had been something of an original, and he could well see how her mother's scandalous behavior, along with her own embroilment in something as tawdry as a jewel theft, could have proved detrimental to Lady Jillian's reputation.

He raised a brow at the Runner. "And you don't find it odd that a female of her station would choose to spend her time in the pursuit of criminals?"

"Perhaps. But she has aided me in bringing an end to several cases that might otherwise have remained unsolved if not for her intervention. She has excellent instincts and an eye for detail that I would match against the most experienced of Bow Street officers any day, and she has never been wrong in her conclusions. That's all I need to know."

Maybe that was all Tolliver needed to know, but Connor was far from satisfied. He knew he should let it go, try to forget about the exasperating wench. But somehow he found that he couldn't.

"I may be overstepping my bounds in pointing it out," the Runner said in a quiet voice, his censorious gaze resting on Connor's brooding countenance. "But your behavior toward the Lady Jillian was uncalled-for, Monroe. On the verge of rudeness, I would say."

Connor couldn't deny it, and he found himself wincing even now as he thought back on the harsh way he had spoken to her. Though he was far from suave and sophisticated in his usual dealings with females, he had never treated one so brusquely before.

"You're right, Tolliver. However, I'm afraid I have no excuse other than to say that the Lady Jillian and I put each other's backs up from the moment we met."

"Ahhh. I thought the two of you seemed a bit tense when I stumbled across you on the terrace. What happened?"

What had happened? She had enraged him, enthralled him, and driven him to equal heights of passion and temper in the span of a few short moments. Her exotic beauty and brazen spirit had intrigued him, held him spellbound.

A gypsy, indeed. A gypsy witch whose lush lips and delectable curves made him think of satin sheets, silken flesh, and soft, pleasure-filled moans in the darkness . . .

Connor's mouth curved in mocking self-derision. It wasn't like him to be so fanciful. If there was anything his rather violent upbringing in the stews of London and regular beatings from his stepfather had cured him of, it was that. And after what had happened with Brennan . . .

But he refused to allow himself to be caught up in memories of the past. That way lay nothing but madness.

When Connor failed to answer Tolliver's query, the Runner shook his head and gave him a baleful look. "Lady Jillian could have helped us."

"It's possible, I suppose. But I beg leave to doubt it. And to be frank, I can't believe you thought I would be receptive to involving a woman in something as dangerous as this."

A muscle flexed in the older man's jaw. "You were the one who told me that you were desperate, Monroe. That you were willing to do whatever it took to catch this murderer. Have you changed your mind about that?"

Connor's hands tightened into impotent fists resting atop his thighs. No, he hadn't. If he had his way, no one else was going to die merely because they had the misfortune to be associated with him.

No one you care for is safe . . .

The threat was emblazoned across his mind, a scarlet beacon that he never should have ignored. When he had first started receiving the letters, he'd been positive it was all some sort of joke. But there could be no mistaking it as a prank any longer.

Dear God, how would he ever learn to live with the knowledge that he was responsible for the deaths of the only people who had ever truly believed in him?

Connor shoved aside the crushing grief to answer Tolliver's query. "No, I haven't changed my mind."

The Runner narrowed his eyes and leaned back in his seat. "The Lady Jillian has risked much, has aided me time after time without a thought to herself or her reputation should it be discovered. And though we've done what we can to conceal her further work with Bow Street from others, her involvement in that very first investigation has done its damage. At the very least, it has ruined whatever prospects she had for marriage. In fact, I believe she was being courted by some viscount or other at the time of the Ranleigh case, but when the *ton* started talking, he backed off."

Ah, the mysterious Lord Shipton. The man was an utter fool.

No sooner had the thought occurred to him than Connor blinked in surprise. Now, where in sweet Christ had that come from? Had the woman completely undone him?

"What are you trying to say, Tolliver?" he prompted in exasperation.

"I think you should give her a chance. Work with her. I truly do believe she could be of great service to us."

Work with her? Be damned if he would! One meeting with that stubborn, defiant, intoxicating gypsy witch had been enough. Already she was proving far too distracting. Just the mere thought of being forced into remaining within arm's reach of her sultry temptation for any length of time was enough to make him break out in a sweat.

Not a good idea.

"Be that as it may, I'm afraid we'll have to agree to disagree." When the Runner started to protest, Connor held up a halting hand. "Tolliver, this is a murder we are talking about. How could I concentrate on catching this fiend if I'm constantly worrying about what could happen to her?"

The other man subsided, but he wore a rigid expression that let Connor know the subject was far from closed.

Regardless, he couldn't let himself be swayed. He knew that allowing the Lady Jillian into his world, even in the most peripheral way, would be a mistake. Especially now, when he had to focus all of his energy on locating the man who seemed bent on tormenting him.

No, Connor decided firmly, he would find another way to track down this killer. And track him down he would. As far as he was concerned, there could be no other outcome.

Chapter 4

A clear line should be drawn between an investigator's home life and his job. One should never affect the other.

"**O**h, Jillian, how could you?"

Lady Maura Daventry sailed into the foyer of the family's Belgrave Square town house and turned to face her sister with hands on her hips, blue eyes blazing in righteous indignation.

"You promised you would try to behave yourself," she accused in a voice quavering with unshed tears. "That you wouldn't do anything to embarrass me tonight. I should have known I couldn't put any faith in you."

Jillian sighed and came to a halt in the entry hall, reaching up to rub at the ache in her temple. This evening had rapidly degenerated into one of the worst she could remember, and she certainly wasn't in the mood for any sort of dressing-down. "Really, Maura, I wish you would calm yourself and just tell me what you're on about. You've been fuming ever since we left the ball, and I'm sure I haven't the slightest idea why."

The younger girl sniffed and tapped a slippered foot on the parquet floor, her upswept raven-black curls bouncing in agitation. Dainty and delicately built, Maura had to tilt her head all the way back in order to frown up at her older sibling, a fact that made Jillian, with her towering height, feel even more like a giantess than usual. "Please don't pretend not to know what I'm speaking of. Everyone was whispering about it."

Jillian's mouth went dry with dread. Was it possible someone had found out about her meeting with Mr. Tolliver and Connor Monroe? She had tried to be discreet, making sure no one saw her leading the two gentlemen through the house to the study, but she supposed it was possible. Though surely Theodosia would have warned her?

She looked back over her shoulder at her aunt, who was busy handing her cloak to the butler, Iverson.

"Aunt Olivia, what is she talking about?"

Lady Olivia Daventry turned to face her niece, her expression one of familiar disapproval. A slender woman with graying light brown hair she wore pulled back from her narrow face in an elegant chignon, the Marquis of Albright's spinster sister might have been pretty if it hadn't been for the frosty aloofness that lurked in the depths of her piercing blue eyes and the pinched severity of her features.

"As if you didn't know, young lady," she said sternly. "It was all over the ballroom that you and Lady Gwyneth Wadsworth almost came to blows over her engagement to Lord Shipton."

Jillian was aware of a brief spurt of relief before her aunt's words fully registered. "What utter nonsense!"

Suddenly appearing uncertain, Maura gazed at her sister, her expression hopeful. "You mean the two of you didn't have words?"

"Oh, we had words. But I never even came close to hitting her, though I would have liked to."

Maura's cheeks turned bright red with dismay, and Jillian rushed to placate her. "I'm sorry, Maura. If they had only been maligning me, I would have walked away. But they were talking about Mama, and I couldn't ignore that."

There was an instant of silence, then Lady Olivia spoke again, her tone reproving. "Really, Jillian, one would think you could refrain from leaping to your mother's defense, just this once. For your sister's sake, if nothing else."

Jillian shook her head. The marchioness had suffered enough when she'd been alive because of society's slurs. She refused to allow it to continue now that Mama was dead. "I couldn't do that."

Her aunt's lips tightened into a thin line. "Of course not. You are, after all, your mother's daughter. Elise gave little thought to how her behavior affected this family, either."

A surge of anger pulsed through Jillian's veins at the woman's words. "That's not true."

Maura took a step forward to stand next to Olivia, glaring at her sister with unmistakable venom. "It *is* true. You only ever think about yourself. My come-out has already been delayed once because of you."

Jillian felt a flicker of shame. She couldn't refute that. Maura really should have made her debut last Season, when she'd turned seventeen, but then there had been that unfortunate incident at Lord and Lady Fitzwater's house party . . .

She bit her lip. She truly hadn't meant any harm. All she had wanted to do was escape the cold and formal confines of the Fitzwater mansion for a short while. She supposed the breeches might have been a mistake, and perhaps she should have worn shoes instead of giving in to her longing to feel the soft grass beneath her bare feet. But how could she have known that the Lady Gwyneth and her mother, the Countess of Leeds, would choose to go for an early morning stroll at the exact moment she was attempting to sneak back into the house?

Maura was still speaking, her manner chilly and disdainful. "Now that I've finally managed a Season, you are trying to ruin this for me, as well. You won't be happy until I'm as firmly on the shelf as you are."

"That's quite enough, Maura."

The masculine voice came from behind them, low and firm, and the trio of females whirled about to find the tall, lean form of Lord Albright standing a few feet away, watching them with blue eyes that looked even more red-rimmed and exhausted than usual.

"Papa," Jillian tried to explain, "if you would only hear my side of things—"

But Maura interrupted her. "Someone has to make her see reason before it's too late, Papa. If she continues with this behavior, I shall wind up an old and lonely spinster, just as she is destined to be. I—"

"Maura, I said that's enough!"

It was so unlike the marquis to raise his voice that both young women fell silent, staring at him in stunned surprise.

A pin could have been heard dropping.

"Papa, are you angry with Jilly and Maura?"

The soft query came from above, cutting across the abrupt stillness, and Jillian's attention was drawn away from her father to the landing at the top of the stairs, where a figure stood in the shadows.

Aimee! Good Lord, there was no telling how long the youngest Daventry had been observing them, unnoticed. Shy, quiet, and small for her thirteen years, her little sister had a talent for fading into the woodwork when she wanted to.

Clad in a long, white nightgown and ruffled bed cap, the girl started down the steps, and Jillian felt her heart catch at the look of trepidation that marked those fragile features. Aimee had always been timid, but ever since the night Lady Albright had been killed, she had become even more so. Inside, she was still that frightened nine-year-old child who had witnessed the murder of her mother.

And who had completely wiped the incident from her memory.

Well, perhaps not completely. Even now, Jillian could recall the nightmares that had plagued her little sister for the first few months after that terrible evening. Nightmares she could never remember once she had awakened. According to the physician, Aimee's memory loss was her mind's way of dealing with the trauma of what had occurred, and there was no guarantee that she would ever recollect the events that had caused it.

As his youngest daughter reached the bottom of the stairs, the marquis cleared his throat and came forward to capture her hands in his. "Of course I'm not angry," he told her gently.

"Then why are you shouting?"

When Lord Albright looked nonplussed, Jillian leaned down and smoothed a golden-brown lock of hair from the girl's brow. "It's nothing of any importance, darling. What are you doing awake at this hour?"

"I wanted to see you and Maura when you got home from the ball." The amber eyes Aimee had inherited from her mother and shared with Jillian were alight with excitement as she turned to Maura. "Was it wonderful? Did you feel like a true princess?"

The other young woman flushed, but nodded. "Yes and yes." She sent Jillian a veiled glance before reaching out to wrap an arm about their sister's thin shoulders. "A true princess."

"Now." Lord Albright bent over and pressed a kiss to Aimee's cheek. "I believe it's time for all young ladies to be abed. Maura, would you take your sister up?"

"But—"

"Now, please?" Though their father phrased the command in the form of a request, there could be no doubting the firmness of his tone.

For a second, Jillian was certain her sister would continue to object. Instead, Maura finally inclined her head in acquiescence, then lifted the ribbon-trimmed hem of her lilac silk gown and started to lead Aimee back up the stairs. "Come along, sweetheart, and I'll tell you all about the ball."

Jillian couldn't help staring after them, a painful lump swelling in her throat. She and Maura had once been so close, but in the last few years a distance had cropped up between them. A distance that Jillian couldn't seem to cross, no matter how hard she tried, and it hurt far more than she would ever admit.

As soon as they were out of sight, Lady Olivia, who had been quiet all this time, crossed her arms and leveled her brother a displeased frown. "Philip, I must inform you that your eldest daughter's conduct tonight has been disgraceful. Not only did she wind up in some sort of altercation with the Lady Gwyneth Wadsworth, but—"

Lord Albright raised a hand, cutting her off. "Olivia, I appreciate what you are trying to do. But if you please, I would like to speak to Jillian alone."

The older woman didn't look happy at the dismissal, but she was left with little choice except to concede. "Very well, then. But we *shall* talk in the morning, Philip."

With one last censuring look at her niece, she spun and marched off, her spine stiff.

The marquis waited until his sister had disappeared up the stairs before closing his eyes and reaching up to pinch the bridge of his nose. He appeared unutterably weary, and Jillian was immediately concerned.

Dear God, when had Papa begun to look so very worn?

At fifty, Philip Daventry was still trim and fit, with not a touch of gray in the thick waves of his golden-brown hair to attest to his age. But now that she was studying him closely, Jillian could see that the lines in his handsome visage were more pronounced than the last time she had taken note, and his shoulders seemed bowed by the weight of some invisible burden.

As if sensing her examination of him, he glanced up at her, offering her a smile that was a trifle forced. "Jillian, if you would join me in the library?"

"Of course, Papa."

She followed him across the foyer and down the short first-floor hallway, pausing only momentarily just outside the library door before continuing over the threshold into the dimness of the room. How Papa could spend all of his time closed up in here, in the very place where it had all happened, was beyond her. Just gazing about at the heavy, dark furniture and wood-paneled walls was enough to send images of that night replaying in her mind's eye with disturbing vividness.

Seating herself in the straight-backed chair in front of her father's desk, she tried not to stare at the spot on the polished floor where the Oriental rug had once been. It was gone now, disposed of long ago, but she could still picture her mother's motionless body lying there in the flashes of lightning, still see the pool of blood that had stained the material crimson . . .

Suppressing a shiver, Jillian tightened her hands into fists in her lap and watched as the marquis turned up the wick on a nearby lamp, brightening the chamber a bit before coming to lean against the desk before her, arms crossed. His countenance was unreadable.

"Papa," she ventured, "I know I never should have let Lady Gwyneth goad me into reacting in such a fashion, and I'm sorry for that. But Aunt Olivia isn't aware—"

Her words stumbled to a halt when Lord Albright shook his head. "Jillian, your aunt wants only the best for you and Maura. As she has no husband and children of her own, this family is very important to her. She may be a bit overzealous at times, but I honestly don't know what I would have done if she hadn't offered to help look after you girls when Elise . . . well, we owe her a great deal."

Jillian barely restrained the urge to grit her teeth in frustration. She knew she should be grateful to her aunt. Lady Olivia had come to live with them soon after the marchioness's death in order to offer her motherless nieces the benefit of her female guidance. But she was far from an affectionate or maternal person, and it was no secret that the marquis's older sister had never approved of the late Lady Albright. The manner in which the woman constantly belittled Mama pricked at Jillian's temper.

"I realize that," she said. "I do. But if you could have heard what they were saying about Mama—"

"I can imagine, darling. And I can understand your need to defend your mother when you hear others denigrating her. Lord knows I have been put in that position far too often myself over the years."

A faraway look of sadness suffused his features for a moment, as if he were lost in memories of the past. But after a second, he shook it off and laid a hand on her shoulder. "I'm not asking you to change who you are. I would never do that. I simply ask that you attempt to rein in some of your more . . . unorthodox behavior until Maura's Season is over."

A wave of guilt washed over Jillian, and she wondered what her father would think if he knew that she had been occupying her time for the last four years by continuing his work with Bow Street. If he knew that all the books, papers, and research notes he had ordered thrown out the day after the marchioness's funeral had been rescued by Jillian and now resided in a box underneath the bed in her room.

She couldn't imagine his reaction would be good, especially if he were to find out that she was planning on joining the hunt for a killer.

Lord Albright was still talking, completely oblivious to his daughter's musings. "This isn't just about Maura, sweetheart. You've inherited more than a touch of your mother's stubborn independence, and sometimes it worries me. You have no idea how painful it was to watch what you went through with Viscount Shipton."

Jillian looked down at the floor. She had no wish to talk about Thomas. The man had caused her enough heartbreak to last a lifetime. Once she had made the mistake of believing that the viscount was the one person who could truly love and accept her for who she was. She'd been wrong. "I know."

"The man gave us every reason to believe he would ask for your hand, and when he turned his back on you after that unfortunate fiasco with Bow Street and the Ranleigh heir . . ." A muscle flexed in the marquis's jaw. "I wanted to kill him for hurting you."

Jillian gave a low cry at the agonized expression on her father's face, and she leaped from her chair to throw her arms around his neck. "Oh, Papa, you mustn't even think of him. He wasn't the right man for me, that's all."

"Perhaps not. But you're one and twenty, Jillian, and I'd like to believe that someday you might still have a family of your own." Lord Albright returned her hug, then set her from him, holding her at arm's length as he met her eyes. "You do realize that this ball tonight wasn't just for your sister? The dowager duchess and I had both hoped that you would meet someone who might pique your interest."

For some strange reason, the harshly attractive visage of Connor Monroe hovered before her, and her heart skipped a beat in dismay. Why on earth would he come to mind now? He was certainly not the type of man she should ever be drawn to, yet just thinking of him had her body responding in ways that were foreign and disturbing.

Her stomach fluttered, and she prayed her father wouldn't read her disconcertment in her expression. "Well, I'm sorry to disappoint you and Theodosia, Papa, but at this point I can't say that I have any desire to find a husband. And I truly am sorry for the way I behaved at the ball. But Lady Gwyneth was just so *smug* I couldn't stand it."

"I don't doubt it." Lord Albright released her with a sigh. "But this family has suffered enough because of rumor and innuendo. I had hoped that was all behind us now."

"I know, Papa. All I can do is repeat my promise to you that I will do my best to stay out of trouble."

"I suppose that's all I can ask. But please try to remember that promise."

Oh, she would remember all right. But would she be able to keep it?

She went up on tiptoe to kiss her father's cheek and wish him good night before starting to leave the room. But she had barely reached the door before something compelled her to stop and look back at him over her shoulder.

He seemed so lonely standing there . . .

The words escaped her before she could call them back. "Papa, did you ever regret marrying Mama?"

Every tick of the grandfather clock in the far corner could be heard in the absolute silence that descended. The marquis's face had gone alarmingly blank, and his mouth had tightened into a grim line.

After a long, drawn-out moment, he turned

away to look out the French doors at the night beyond the glass, his back stiff and unyielding.

"Good night, Jillian."

Obviously it was another one of those questions she might never have an answer to.

Chapter 5

Determination is the key to becoming a successful investigator.

Early the next morning, Jillian stepped down
from a hired hack in front of the offices of
Grayson and Monroe Shipping.

Located in a large, weathered-looking building just off Fleet Street, it was within walking
distance of both Temple Bar and Blackfriars
Bridge. Even at this time of day, the streets were
already crowded with traffic, and the sidewalks
bustled with costermongers plying their wares
and merchants and tradesmen hurrying to open
their shops and businesses.

Jillian paid the driver and stepped back, nar-
rowly avoiding a group of young urchins as they
came barreling past her, shouting and laughing.
Reaching up to push a tendril of ebony hair back

behind her ear, she surveyed the impressive structure in front of her.

Well, she was here. Now what?

In order to avoid questions from her family, Jillian had departed the house this morning well before anyone else had arisen, informing Iverson that she would be spending the day with the Dowager Duchess of Maitland. She hated to lie, but it was the only excuse she could come up with for her absence that wouldn't raise her father's suspicions, and she knew that Theodosia would back up her story.

She bit her lip and her fingers tightened on her reticule. Once, Lord Albright had encouraged her interest in his work, had spent long hours discussing and debating his theories of investigative procedure with her. But that had all changed on the night her mother had been killed. If he were to find out exactly what she was up to, he wouldn't hesitate to forbid her to become involved.

And she couldn't let that happen.

Straightening her shoulders with renewed purpose, she started up the steps to the big front doors of the building. She had no doubt she would be in for a difficult time persuading Connor Monroe to let her take part in the investigation, but she was determined to do so. She *could* help him. She knew she could. And if in the process she was able to help herself . . . well, that was something he didn't need to know about.

"Lady Jillian!"

The voice came from behind her, sounding just a trifle breathless. Turning, she watched as Morton Tolliver came hurrying down the sidewalk toward her, his pudgy, flushed face wreathed in a relieved smile.

"You came," he exclaimed, sweeping off his hat as he puffed up the steps to join her. "I wasn't certain you would after the way Mr. Monroe reacted last night."

"Come now, Mr. Tolliver," she said with a slight smile as he bowed over her hand. "You must have realized once you uttered Wilbur Forbes's name that I wouldn't give up so easily."

"Yes, well, I rather suspected that. But Mr. Monroe's attitude can be . . . off-putting to some people."

That was certainly an understatement, Jillian thought with an inward grimace, recalling Connor Monroe's less than enthusiastic response to her offer of help. "Perhaps. But this is the first lead we've managed to stumble across regarding Forbes's whereabouts in four years. I can't afford to let Mr. Monroe's rude behavior chase me away."

She paused for a moment, once more glancing up at the brick exterior of the building that loomed over them before turning back to the Runner. "I don't suppose you managed to sway the man's thinking at all."

Looking sheepish, Tolliver returned his hat to his gray head and sighed. "I'm afraid not. And to be fair, my lady, he has reason to be concerned.

This criminal . . . well, to put it quite bluntly, he's a monster. I would never forgive myself if I endangered you in any way, and should your involvement in this matter become common knowledge—"

"It won't." Jillian lifted her chin. "We'll be discreet, as always. But we both know the only way I'll be able to question Forbes is if I'm involved in Mr. Monroe's case."

"Of course, of course. And I promise to keep you updated on the search for the man. It's just—" The Runner shifted uncomfortably, then met her gaze with anxious eyes. "I know we've discussed this, my lady, but you do realize that even if you find Forbes, there's no guarantee he'll be able to shed any light on the marchioness's death. His disappearance that night could have been mere coincidence."

A cold wave of uncertainty washed over Jillian at his words. She knew that, but she had to believe that Forbes would be able to help her. If she let go of that belief for even one second, she would surely go mad.

"I'm aware of that, Mr. Tolliver," she said quietly, forcing the words out through the lump in her throat. "And while I appreciate what you're saying, I can't even consider that right now. You must understand. It's all I have."

The Runner's countenance softened. "I do understand, my lady. And I admire your tenacity. I wouldn't have continued to keep you informed regarding your mother's case if I didn't think there was something to your suspicions. I just want you to be prepared in case things don't turn out as you had hoped."

Touched by the man's concern, Jillian reached out and laid a hand on his arm. He had been so kind to her over the years, she tended to forget sometimes that he was jeopardizing his position at Bow Street by continuing to work with her. "Thank you, Mr. Tolliver. Your confidence in me means a great deal. More than I could ever express."

Tolliver flushed and patted her fingers on his sleeve in an awkward manner. "Yes, well, I suppose we'd best head inside now. Monroe will be wondering where I've gotten to." He offered her a brief grin. "If we're going to convince him to avail himself of your talents, we'll have our work cut out for us."

Jillian laughed, but deep inside she was aware of a fluttering of anticipation. Was it the fact that after all of these years she was finally on the trail of Forbes? Or was it because she was once again getting ready to confront the enigmatic and intriguing Connor Monroe?

There was a large part of her that was very much afraid it was the latter.

Tucking her arm through his, Tolliver drew her with him through the front door.

Where the bloody hell was Tolliver?

Pacing across the confines of his office, Connor tugged impatiently at his cravat and sent the clock in the far corner a sour look, as if blaming it for the Runner's tardiness.

"He should have been here by now," he muttered aloud, raking both hands back through his hair. Damnation, but the longer they stood around, doing nothing, the more chance there was this madman would strike again.

The eerie silence of the empty building seemed to echo around him. Usually, the corridors would be a hive of noise and activity, but today no one was about except for Connor himself. With the discovery of Stuart's body early yesterday morning, the doors of Grayson and Monroe had been closed and the employees sent home until further notice.

Not that there wasn't work to be done. Connor had learned long ago that life didn't stop for death. But the mere thought of attempting to go about a normal workday without his mentor in his office right across the hall was more than he could contemplate right now.

At that moment, there was a soft tap at his door. Crossing the polished wood floor with swift strides, he flung open the panel and scowled down at the portly figure on the threshold.

"It's about time," he began, but the words froze on his lips as he noticed the woman who stood at Tolliver's side.

Lady Jillian Daventry.

But it was a far different Lady Jillian than he had met the previous evening.

Clad in a walking dress of forest-green

muslin with a high, fluted collar and matching pelisse, every inch of her golden skin was covered this morning, and her midnight-black hair was scraped back from her face and tucked underneath a rather plain poke bonnet. She examined him through a veil of dark lashes, as if awaiting his reaction to her presence.

She didn't have long to wait.

"What the hell is *she* doing here?"

At Connor's outburst, Lady Jillian's eyebrows winged upward, and a hint of a smile curved those full lips. "Really, Mr. Monroe. If this is the way you greet all your clients, it's a wonder your business is as successful as it is."

She pushed past him and marched into the room, trailing the now familiar scent of jasmine and spice in her wake. It had Connor's nostrils flaring and his pulse kicking up a notch in response, and just the brief touch of her body brushing by him was enough to have his manhood standing at half-mast. He had to restrain the urge to adjust the sudden tight fit of his breeches.

Damnation, but she was the last person he needed to deal with right now!

Tearing his gaze away from her, he turned back to Tolliver, who lingered in the doorway, appearing distinctly uncomfortable. "I asked you a question, Tolliver."

The Runner lifted one shoulder in a shrug. "I asked her to come."

Connor gritted his teeth and crossed his arms over his chest. "And might I inquire as to why you would do such a thing when I made it clear that we would not need the Lady Jillian's help?"

"Do please stop trying to intimidate Mr. Tolliver, Mr. Monroe," Lady Jillian spoke from behind him, her tone even. "He may have requested that I join you this morning, but I was the one who made the decision to do so."

Connor faced her once again. She stood on the far side of the room, her expression calm, almost serene. Anyone looking at her now might have been fooled into believing that she was as composed as she had sounded. However, there was a spark in those amber eyes, a defiant tilt to that rounded chin that told him she was not as unruffled as she might at first appear.

He affected her just as strongly as she affected him.

The realization didn't help Connor in the slightest. In fact, it was all the more reason to get rid of her as soon as possible. He didn't need the added complication of an attraction to a woman he knew he could never have, even if the attraction was reciprocated. "Then I regret to inform you that you have wasted a trip, my lady. As I said before, there is no place in this investigation for a female. I have better things to do than play nursemaid when I have a murderer to catch."

Her gloved hands flew to her hips, and just that quickly her mask of composure crumbled, the spark in her eyes turning into a full-fledged conflagration. "Would you stop being so blasted stubborn? I can help you catch that murderer, you wretched man, if you would just let me."

She took a step toward him, and the early morning sunlight streaming in through the window fell over her, bathing her in a soft golden glow. Connor's breath caught in his throat, and once again it was a struggle to tame his body's masculine reaction. Lady Jillian might have believed that dressing like a maiden aunt would draw attention away from her femininity, but she had been wrong. The stark simplicity of her gown only accentuated the exotic elegance of her features, and the material lovingly outlined her abundant curves in a way that had his mouth going dry.

Oh, yes, the gypsy witch was still there underneath that façade, and she was still all too capable of casting her enthralling spell over him.

"Surely you must trust Mr. Tolliver's judgment?" she was saying, her voice now trembling with frustrated anger. "Doesn't the fact that he brought you to me tell you anything?"

Connor closed his eyes and shoved his hands deep into his pockets to hide their shaking. He could not handle this now, on top of everything else. It was taking every ounce of energy he possessed just to stay upright and functioning. He hadn't eaten, had hardly slept in the last two days. And when he *had* managed to drift off for a few minutes at a time, he had been tormented by nightmares of blood and death. Of all the people he had lost.

And when he hadn't been dreaming about

them, he had been dreaming of *her*. Spread, naked and writhing beneath him, her lips wet and swollen from his kisses, her dusky skin coated with the dew of their shared passion, wild with desire.

For him.

Christ, but he could still taste her sweetness on his tongue, could still feel the weight of her plump, silky breasts in his palms, still hear her whisper, husky and quivering in his ear.

Come into me, Connor. Fill me. I want to belong to you . . .

"Mr. Monroe? Are you listening?"

Connor started and his eyes snapped open to find the object of his fantasies less than an arm's length away, her fascinating eyes narrowed as she glared up at him mutinously.

God, what was he doing? He didn't have time to stand here lusting after her like some love-starved schoolboy! What kind of person was he that he could allow himself to become so preoccupied with her when the man who had been the closest thing to a father he'd ever had was dead at the hands of a monster?

He drew himself up and swung on Tolliver, who had come into the office and now observed the proceedings from a spot next to Connor's desk.

"Damn it, Tolliver—" he began, but the Runner brought him to a halt by holding up a hand.

"Look, Monroe, I must be honest," the older man said, looking apologetic, yet resigned. "I am at a loss as to where to go from here. Bow Street is convinced that Forbes is their man, and unless we can come up with some sort of evidence to the contrary, I don't see them changing their minds." He paused, then shook his head. "At this point, I'm afraid we are running out of options."

A hand brushed Connor's arm, and he barely restrained a startled jolt at the heat that singed him at the contact, even through the material of his shirt, as Lady Jillian came around to stand in front of him.

Apparently she had managed to rein in the temper he had previously roused, because there wasn't a hint of anger in her beseeching expression. "Please, Mr. Monroe. Mr. Tolliver wouldn't have asked me to come here if he didn't believe I could help you."

He took a calming breath, attempting to ignore the gloved hand that still rested on his sleeve. "My lady, perhaps you don't understand the risk involved. This is no simple robbery."

"Oh, I understand, Mr. Monroe, but I truly don't believe that the risk is as great as you think. I'm not talking about pursuing this fiend through the streets of London and clapping the shackles on him myself."

Connor felt a reluctant grin curve his lips at the mental image that conjured. Why, he could almost picture the intrepid Lady Jillian doing just that.

As if sensing that his resolve was weakening, she moved a step closer, and her scent once again wafted over him, fragrant and intoxicating. "All

I ask is that you give me a chance. Let me look over Mr. Grayson's office. If I don't find anything, I promise I'll leave without further protest and you'll never be bothered by me again. But if I can turn up something that Bow Street missed, something of use to the investigation, you must agree to accept my help."

Connor furrowed his brow in consideration. It was tempting. Surely she wouldn't stumble across anything important. And despite her assurances, it was highly doubtful that Lady Jillian had ever had any sort of experience with the kind of violence that had been wrought here two nights ago. One glimpse at the scene of the crime and she was almost certain to take to her heels. She would be out of his hair for good.

Which was exactly what he wanted, wasn't it?

His hands tightened into fists at his sides. He hated the mere thought of exposing her to such carnage. It went against every protective instinct he possessed, but he couldn't allow her to become involved in all of this, couldn't let her get too close.

He refused to be responsible for another life. Especially hers.

Lady Jillian removed her hand from his arm, only to hold it out toward him in an expectant manner. "Is it a deal, Mr. Monroe?"

He hesitated for only a second before taking her hand.

"Very well, Lady Jillian. You have a deal."

Chapter 6

Examine the scene of the crime thoroughly, taking note of even the smallest details.

He had agreed!

Stunned, Jillian preceded Connor Monroe and Tolliver out into the corridor.

She couldn't believe it. From the way Monroe had been behaving, she'd been certain she would never get him to relent, and she had no idea what on earth she had said to bring about his abrupt capitulation. But she wouldn't waste time questioning her good fortune. She had every intention of taking advantage of the opportunity he had presented her with.

Stuart Grayson's office was just across the hallway, and as they neared the door, Monroe stepped past her and withdrew a key from his vest pocket. He leaned forward to fit it into the lock, and Jillian found herself watching the rippling play of muscle in that broad back and in those wide shoulders with reluctant fascination. He was a confusing man. And disturbing to her on a great many levels.

She forced her eyes away from him and contemplated the toes of her boots with feigned interest. She'd been so certain she was ready to face him, but the moment he had thrown open his office door and towered over her with that daunting glower, every bit of sense had flown right out of her head. And it was even more disconcerting to realize that her agitation had more to do with her distinctly feminine reaction to him than anything else.

At some point before she and Tolliver had arrived, Monroe had discarded his coat and freed the buttons on his gold-trimmed vest, leaving it hanging open over a thin white lawn shirt that molded to every muscle in his sculpted chest. With his reddish-brown hair tousled over his forehead, his sleeves rolled up past thick forearms, and his cravat hanging loose about his throat, baring a slight wedge of golden skin, he presented a picture of raw masculine appeal that was difficult to ignore, though she had tried.

And would continue to do so.

Clearing her throat, she struggled to keep her voice steady when she spoke. "Did Mr. Grayson often work late here at the office?"

Monroe glanced back at her over his shoulder

as the lock clicked open and he returned the key to his pocket, but he made no move to open the door. "As a matter of fact, yes. It was something of a routine with him. Stuart's life was his work, and he was usually the first one here in the morning and the last one to leave at night."

"And what about you?"

He shrugged. "I prefer our offices at the shipyard warehouse, so I'm rarely here. Stuart had a true gift for dealing with people, so he spent more time handling the clients and the administrative end of the business while I dealt with the physical side of things."

Jillian couldn't help studying his large, brawny frame in admiration. Yes, she could see how that might be the case.

She heard Tolliver give a discreet cough from behind her, and when one corner of Monroe's mouth curved upward in amusement, she felt her cheeks flame.

Good lord, she was ogling him as if she were some common Covent Garden doxy!

She licked dry lips and indicated Stuart Grayson's office with a nervous wave of her hand. "Er, perhaps we should go ahead in."

Monroe's smile disappeared as if it had never been, and he sent her one last unreadable look before pushing the door open.

With her nose in the air, she started to sail by him. But before she even got across the threshold, he stopped her with a hand on her arm. The heat of his palm scorched her through the material of her pelisse, sending a tingle through her not unlike the one she'd felt earlier when she'd touched him. She had to fight not to jerk away.

"My lady," he said in a deep, rumbling voice that stroked over her nerve endings with the gravelly sensuality of rough velvet. "I feel I should warn you that this could prove to be most unpleasant."

She lifted her chin, praying that none of her discomfort at his nearness showed on her face. "I can assure you, Mr. Monroe, that I am quite used to a certain amount of unpleasantness."

A muscle flexed in his jaw at her chilly tone, and he released her with an almost mocking bow. "Of course. Far be it from me to worry about your delicate sensibilities when you've made it more than clear you have none. Please, go right ahead."

Stung by the rapier sharpness of his words, she gave him a haughty glare before moving ahead of him into the room.

Where she came to an almost teeth-jarring halt, stifling a horrified gasp at the sight that met her eyes.

The first thing she noticed was the blood. It was everywhere. Trailing over the floor. Spattered across the expensive furnishings. Smeared on the walls. A particularly large, rust-colored puddle stained the top of a desk that sat next to the far window and had seeped into the papers and file folders scattered across its surface.

The second thing she noticed was the smell.

The brassy, overpowering scent of blood and death was heavy in the air, making her stomach do a slow, heaving roll.

The edges of her vision blurred and she felt herself sway, dangerously close to passing out. They had tried to warn her. Both Tolliver and Monroe. They had tried to tell her what she would find in here, but never would she have believed . . . Dear God in heaven, but no crime scene she had ever visited had come close to this.

Whoever had done this had indeed been a monster.

A strong hand at Jillian's elbow steadied her, and she looked up to find Connor Monroe standing at her side. His countenance as he stared down at her was dispassionate, but he couldn't quite hide the concern that lurked behind that detached façade.

Concern for her.

"I say, my lady, are you all right?"

Tolliver's voice echoed hollowly in her ears, and she glanced back to find that the Runner had followed Monroe into the room and was watching her with obvious anxiety.

She had to get hold of herself. If she fainted now, Monroe would never let her take part in this investigation.

Swallowing with difficulty, she closed her eyes, trying to rein in her wildly teetering control. To her surprise, Monroe's grip was gentle and reassuring, giving her an anchor to cling to in the midst of the chaos.

You must put up a wall, her father's words whispered in her head, a soothing mantra. *Disassociate yourself. From the crime. From your surroundings. From the victim.*

In an effort to do just that, Jillian took a deep breath and reached into her reticule to withdraw her spectacles. She perched them on the bridge of her nose, then straightened her shoulders before looking up at the man who stood so close to her.

"I'm fine now, Mr. Monroe." To her relief, her voice was strong, without a trace of a quaver. "You can release me. I was just caught off guard. That's all."

His probing gaze scrutinized every inch of her features, as if attempting to verify for himself the truth of her statement. "Are you certain? If you need to step back out into the hall, perhaps sit down for a moment . . ."

"No, really." Touched by his genuine solicitude, she reached up to place her hand over his where it still rested on her arm. Their eyes locked, and in that instant something passed between them. Something warm and powerful that swept over her with surprising force, leaving her restless and aching in its wake.

Licking suddenly dry lips, she exerted every bit of will power she possessed to quell her body's disquieting response and offered him what she hoped was a placating smile. "I appreciate your consideration, but I truly am all right."

One of Monroe's eyebrows winged upward, and for an instant she was certain he was going to press the issue further. But after a second or two, he finally inclined his head in a brief nod and withdrew his hold.

Barely stifling a grateful sigh, Jillian shrugged off the lingering effects of his touch and took a step farther into the office, this time forcing herself to survey her surroundings in an analytical manner. Though it took every bit of fortitude she possessed, she managed to keep the horror of what she was seeing at bay by concentrating on the details.

Despite the carnage that had been left behind, there were no signs of a struggle, she noted. No footprints or scuff marks on the floor. No furniture overturned or papers knocked off the desk. Yet the blood was everywhere. Such a mess hadn't been made by simply cutting Grayson's throat.

She felt a shiver of foreboding crawl up her spine as she examined the wall closest to her. It was almost as if the killer had coated his hands with the victim's blood and swiped it over the plaster in a bizarre and macabre imitation of a child's attempt at finger painting.

But it was the gilt-edged mirror that hung on the wall directly across from Grayson's desk that captured her attention. Written across the glass in bloody letters was the chilling message Tolliver had mentioned last night.

You will pay.

Jillian's stomach lurched again, and she placed one hand against her abdomen in an attempt to still its roiling.

"And Bow Street thinks *Forbes* did this?" she choked out, incredulous.

Monroe spoke quietly from where he still stood near the door, legs braced wide and arms crossed over his chest. "They're wrong."

Tolliver made a sound of agreement. "Nothing *human* did this," he muttered, and Jillian could have sworn he crossed himself.

She bit her lip. Monroe was right. Forbes apparently had a reputation as an inebriate and a bully, and while she could see him threatening Stuart Grayson, perhaps even using his fists in drunken anger, she couldn't see him being responsible for anything like this.

Whoever had done this couldn't have been sane.

She adjusted her spectacles, then glanced at Tolliver. "Where precisely was the body found?"

As she had expected, the Runner inclined his head toward the desk. "Grayson was sitting there. The amount of blood indicates that's where he was when the killer attacked. No weapon has been found, but we believe some sort of large knife was used, as the killing cut was quite deep."

"There are no signs that he fought anyone off."

"No. Apparently the attack was unexpected. I doubt he even saw it coming."

Lowering her brows in thought, Jillian wandered over to stand next to the large piece of furniture. Anyone sitting at the desk would have their back to the wall with the width of the room between them and the office door. No one could have possibly gotten behind Grayson without him seeing them.

She looked at Monroe. "You said it wasn't unusual for Mr. Grayson to stay late at the office. Was this common knowledge?"

"Yes," he replied, his eyes hooded as he met her questioning gaze. "Stuart was unmarried and had no children, so there was little waiting for him at home. Quite often he wound up sleeping here overnight."

Tolliver drew Jillian's attention back to him. "All of the employees have solid alibis, someone who can speak for their whereabouts at the time of the murder. Mr. Grayson usually locked the outside doors of the building himself at the end of the day, and the last person to depart on the night of his murder was his assistant, a Mr. Lowell Unger. According to Unger, when he departed for home just after six o'clock, Mr. Grayson saw him off and locked the main door behind him."

"Mr. Unger's story has been confirmed?"

"A shopkeeper across the street was closing up at the same time and saw him leave. Another shopkeeper who was passing by at about ten o'clock saw Grayson standing in his office window."

So, the man had still been alive at ten that evening, Jillian mused, eyeing the window. "And who discovered the body the next morning?"

"Unger." It was Monroe who answered her this

time. "He and I both arrived early yesterday, and I was in my office when I heard him call out."

Once again, Jillian caught a glimpse of the anguish that tormented him before Monroe's mask of stoicism fell back into place. It hadn't occurred to her until right this moment what he must be going through. Despite his rough edges, he couldn't hide the close bond he'd had with Grayson. If seeing all of this was difficult for her, how much harder must it be for him?

Her heart squeezed in sympathy, but she made herself continue in spite of a rather abrupt and unexpected urge to console him instead of question him. There could be little doubt that this man had awakened some very unsettling emotions within her. Emotions she had to overcome if she was going to keep working on this case. "Er, nothing was taken? There weren't any signs of forced entry? No broken locks on windows or doors?"

"No, nothing was taken, and everything was still locked up tight when I arrived. I had to use my key to get in."

"And you and Mr. Grayson are the only ones with keys?"

"Yes."

The one word was simple, succinct, but Jillian could tell by the tensing of Monroe's jaw that he was aware of what was coming next. Though she knew nothing about this man, every last one of her instincts screamed at her that he wasn't capable of something like this. Still, she had to be thorough. "You'll have to excuse me for asking, Mr. Monroe, but where were *you* that evening?"

In the background, Tolliver gasped and started to protest. "My lady—"

But Monroe interrupted him. "It's all right, Tolliver. After all, I *am* the one with the most to gain from Stuart's death." His compelling stare never wavered from Jillian. "I assure you, I have nothing to hide, my lady. There was a complication with one of the shipments we were expecting and I stayed late at the warehouse. Several of the dockworkers can vouch for me. It was after midnight before I was able to leave, and I spent the rest of the evening with a . . . female acquaintance of mine. Bow Street has already spoken with her to verify my story."

Jillian's face heated at the mental picture Monroe's words conjured forth. His big, muscular body, naked and entwined with pale, feminine limbs on a well-tumbled bed . . .

"I see." The image bothered her far more than it should have, and in an attempt to distract herself, she looked about the room once more. "So it appears the motive wasn't robbery. There is no evidence of forced entry. Mr. Grayson must have let his killer into the building. Which means it had to be someone he knew." Her gaze fell on the mirror. "Someone he trusted enough to turn his back on."

"That certainly wouldn't be Forbes. Stuart would never have let the man in, much less turned his back on him."

She gave a start at Monroe's voice so close to her ear. Somehow he had managed to come up behind her without her being aware of it. His breath stirred the tendrils of hair at her temple, and for one wild, wayward instant she longed to step backward into his embrace, to press herself against him and let him enfold her in the warmth and comfort of his strong arms.

Not since Thomas had she been so tempted by a man.

She gritted her teeth and moved away from him, removing herself from his dangerous proximity before turning to face him. "You can't think of anyone who would wish Mr. Grayson ill, Mr. Monroe?" There. That sounded good. Very confident and businesslike.

Too bad she didn't feel that way.

Monroe shook his head. If she hadn't known better, she would have sworn he'd guessed what she'd been thinking, for his blue-green eyes turned molten as they probed hers. "Aside from Forbes, no. Stuart was a good man. He had no enemies that I know of."

"And you're still certain that this is about you?"

"The letters I've received would indicate so, yes."

"I should like to see these letters."

He paused, and she braced herself for his refusal. But to her surprise, he gave a stiff nod. "Certainly. They're at my town house."

Jillian inclined her head in return, then wandered over to stand before the mirror, staring up at its warning with assessing eyes. Compared to the rest of the office, the writing was so neat, so precise, the formation of the red block letters so painstaking.

She tilted her head to study the words from another angle, and a wisp of white sticking out from behind the top edge of the mirror's frame caught her attention.

What on earth?

Her heart skipped a beat. It could be nothing, something secreted away by Grayson rather than left by the murderer. But then again . . .

Despite appearances to the contrary, she was certain every move the killer had made once he had entered this office had been quite deliberate. The message had been meant to draw attention to the mirror. Was it possible that it was also meant to draw attention to something else?

Going up on tiptoe, she carefully slid her hand into the space between the wall and the gilt frame, and her fingers closed around what seemed to be cloth of some kind. With bated breath, she withdrew it from its hiding place.

It appeared to be a woman's lace-edged handkerchief, and as she unfolded it, she noted that the white linen was stained with patches of dried blood. In the upper corner, the initials *P.R.* had been embroidered in an elaborate script.

"My God, it's Peg's!"

Once again, Monroe had managed to come up behind her without her knowledge, and his exclamation was enough to have her jumping in reaction. One hand flying to her chest to still her racing heart, she whirled to face him.

His firm, chiseled mouth was set in a harsh line, and the agony that blazed from his eyes and twisted his features struck her like a blow to the midsection as she allowed him to take the handkerchief from her outstretched hand.

"Who is Peg?" she whispered.

"Peg Ridley is—*was*—my housekeeper."

His use of the past tense had Jillian's heart rate picking up speed once more. "She's . . . dead?"

Monroe's long, strong fingers closed around the scrap of cloth in a white-knuckled fist as his tortured gaze finally met hers. "Yes. And if I'm correct, she was another of this monster's victims."

Chapter 7

Pursue all possible leads, leaving no threads dangling.

J illian stared at him in incomprehension. Then, his telling slip from their conversation the evening before came back to her. "Her death was one of the murders you spoke of?"

He nodded as Tolliver joined them.

"How could Bow Street have missed that?" The Runner sounded amazed.

"As you said, they are certain they know who the culprit is." Monroe glanced up at the other man, his visage grim. "As a result, they only gave this office the most cursory inspection. I doubt they would have realized the significance of this, even if they'd seen it."

Jillian studied the handkerchief still held tightly

in his big hand. "You're certain this belonged to your housekeeper?"

"There's no doubt in my mind. I recognize it as one of a set that I gave to her as a gift for her last birthday."

At his statement, Jillian's eyes flew to Monroe's face in mild surprise. Gifts for a servant?

As if sensing her curiosity, he explained. "Peg and I knew each other for many years before she became my housekeeper. We were close. She was like a mother to me."

She nibbled her lower lip in consideration before carefully broaching her next question. "Is there a reason why Mr. Grayson might have held on to this? Were he and this Mrs. Ridley . . . ?"

A brief glint of laughter shone in Monroe's eyes. "There was nothing romantic between them, if that's what you mean. Peg was nearly twenty years older than Stuart, and she treated him like another son." The humor vanished as his eyes narrowed. "No, the killer left this here. He wanted me to find it, to make the connection and realize these deaths are related."

"We mustn't jump to conclusions," Jillian warned. But despite her words, she couldn't help but suspect the same. From its place of safety wedged behind the mirror's frame, the square of material would have been well shielded from the casual observer. And there was no way it could have gotten any blood on it unless it had been touched by the killer.

Or unless he had placed it there himself.

When neither Monroe nor Tolliver said anything in response, she continued her line of questioning. "Where and when was Mrs. Ridley killed?"

Monroe reached up to shove a wave of hair off his forehead before replying. "At my town house in Piccadilly, a fortnight ago. I was out for the evening, and when I came home—"

He stumbled to a halt, and Jillian was struck by the sudden desire to throw her arms around his neck, to soothe his obvious pain by pulling his head down to hers until their lips met. Slowly, sweetly, deeply . . .

Drops of cold perspiration bathed her forehead. What in heaven's name had come over her? It wasn't like her to entertain such notions. After Thomas, she had decided she had no need for a man in her life, and never had that resolve been tested until now. Connor Monroe's effect on her was growing stronger by the second, and she didn't like it. Especially when she had far more important matters to contend with.

She forced herself to concentrate on the discussion.

"How exactly was she killed, Mr. Monroe?" she asked, gesturing around them. "Was the scene of the crime anything like—"

He interrupted her with a shake of his head. "No. Nothing like this. I never would have suspected that the cases were tied together at all if I hadn't received the note."

"What note?"

Instead of answering, Monroe exchanged a look with Tolliver, and an intangible message seemed to pass between them before he turned back to her. "I think you should come back to my town house."

Jillian felt her whole body go still at the intensity in his voice. His eyes held hers with a steady, penetrating regard that made it impossible for her to tear her gaze away.

Naked limbs entwined on a well-tumbled bed . . .

"I—I beg your pardon?" she choked out.

"We did have a deal, did we not? I imagine you'll need to examine the scene of the crime. And you did say you wanted to see the letters I'd been receiving."

Of course that was what he'd meant. Surely she didn't believe he would proposition her at a time like this? And right in front of Mr. Tolliver, no less! Just because her mind was preoccupied with indecent fantasies didn't mean he was thinking the same thing.

And that was *not* disappointment she was feeling!

"Yes. Yes, you're quite correct," she rushed to agree. "Perhaps Mr. Tolliver and I could meet you there in—"

The Runner interrupted her with an apologetic look. "Alas, I have to get back to Bow Street, my lady. I do have other cases to look after. But I trust that Mr. Monroe will be in good hands with you."

Jillian felt her pulse rate immediately increase.

Follow the gruff and disturbing Connor Monroe back to his residence unaccompanied, without Tolliver there to act as a buffer?

Most definitely *not* a good idea.

"I don't know. It might be best if we wait until—"

Monroe brought her objection to a halt by closing the space between them in an unanticipated move that had her gasping in startled dismay.

His mouth curved into a knowing smile and he leaned toward her, bringing his face so close to hers that she could feel the waft of his warm, minty breath against her cheek. "Forgive me for my effrontery, my lady, but you had given me the impression that you were just as capable as any man of handling every aspect of this case." He cocked his head in an inquiring fashion. "Would a *man* hesitate to accompany me back to my town house if it was necessary to the investigation?"

"Of course not, but—"

"Then perhaps it is the fact that you don't trust yourself alone with me." His voice was a silken purr, its smooth cadences stroking over her already sensitive nerve endings like velvet, his hot stare holding hers captive. "Is there some reason, Lady Jillian, for you to feel insecure in my presence? I can assure you that I will behave most decorously. Or perhaps it is your own behavior you are uncertain of. Should I fear for my innocence?"

Jillian's temper flared. How dare he make light of her in such a manner? "Don't be ridiculous!"

Monroe gave an abrupt nod, as if she had passed some sort of test, then took a step back, finally breaking the connection that had held her paralyzed. "Right, then. So there's no reason for you to refuse. If you'll wait just a moment, I'll fetch my coat and we can all go out together. I'll have to lock up behind us."

She was trapped. If she said no now, Monroe would want to know why. And she had no intention of admitting how much he unsettled her.

She refused to give the dratted man that sort of power over her.

The three of them moved out into the hallway, and she watched as the object of her disquieting thoughts crossed the corridor in long, fluid strides and entered his own office.

"Are you certain you are all right, my lady?"

Tolliver's anxious query from beside her jolted Jillian from her reverie and she turned to face him, offering him a smile she hoped didn't look as false as it felt. "Of course, Mr. Tolliver. Right as rain."

The Runner didn't look at all convinced, and he glanced back over his shoulder with a frown at the room they'd just vacated. "I know you've had some experience visiting crime scenes, but this was . . . well, the sort of thing a lady should never have to see. I did try to tell you."

Her smile became more genuine at the man's sincere concern. "I know. And I truly am fine. It was a bit shocking at first, I admit. But I've recovered." She couldn't contain a slight shiver as the gruesome sight in Stuart Grayson's office once more filled her vision. "A good investigator must learn to become inured to such things, though it isn't easy."

"Yes, well, I knew you would find something, my lady, if you were just given the chance." Tolliver paused, and when he continued, his voice was much softer. "I do appreciate what you're doing, Lady Jillian. I admire Mr. Monroe a great deal. He's worked hard to get where he is in life and he's a good man. A bit hardened, it's true, but a good man, nonetheless."

At that moment, Monroe emerged from his office, buttoning his coat of dark blue superfine as he came toward them, and Jillian could tell by the detached look on his face that he had once again retreated behind that wall of control and reserve. It was enough to make her wonder if those few glimpses of pain and vulnerability had been real or if she had only seen what she had wanted to see because of the feelings he ignited in her.

"I'll have to take your word for that, Mr. Tolliver," she murmured.

Monroe stopped next to them, raising his brow at her in that arrogant fashion that so grated on her nerves, then swept an arm toward the stairs. "Shall we? Or do you plan to solve this case by standing here the rest of the morning? Perhaps this is some new investigative technique I haven't been apprised of."

A chuckle from Tolliver had Jillian lifting her chin with a sniff and marching off down the corridor ahead of them. How she could be so attracted to such a boorish knave was a mystery.

But then again, she conceded with a rueful quirk of the lips as she descended the stairs to the lobby, she'd always had a weakness whenever it came to a good mystery.

Connor Monroe's elegant, red-brick town house stood at the busy intersection of Piccadilly and Bond Streets, and as the hack drew to a jarring halt at the curb in front, Jillian found herself staring out the window with speculative eyes at the well-maintained façade of the structure.

The shipping business, she mused, was apparently a highly profitable venture.

The jarvey hopped down from his seat to open the door, and Monroe climbed from the carriage, turning to hold out his hand to assist Jillian in alighting. "My lady?"

She froze for a moment in indecision. It wouldn't do at all for anyone to see her with him. And at this time of day, someone she knew was bound to notice her, especially in this area of town.

As if reading her mind, Monroe leaned toward her and spoke in a low, reassuring tone. "Don't worry, my lady. I doubt anyone would recognize you in what you are wearing." A thread of mockery entered his voice. "Unless you make it a regular practice to disguise yourself as someone's spinster aunt."

Jillian felt a spark of anger. It was true that in an attempt to make Monroe take her seriously, she had deliberately dressed to downplay her appearance today. But surely she didn't look nearly as bad as he implied?

It was only when she caught sight of his wolfish grin that she realized he was once again trying to goad her.

Raising her chin, she wiped her face of all expression and accepted his help, determined not to let him know he had ruffled her feathers.

"Thank you, sir," she said frostily as she stepped down onto the pavement next to him. "It is good to know that I have succeeded in making myself as unattractive to you as possible."

She tugged at her hand, but instead of releasing her, he pulled her closer, his grip on her fingers tightening.

"Now, now, my lady," he rumbled as he raised her hand to his mouth. "I didn't say that."

Before she could manage to form some sort of coherent reply, he kissed her wrist just above the edge of her glove, the barest brush of his sensuous lips that had the air seizing in her lungs. And all the while, those turbulent aqua eyes held hers, a heat and hunger swirling in their depths that left her stunned.

Though part of her knew she should yank back her hand, should demand that he stop what he was doing, somehow she found she could not. So lost in his gaze was she that she wasn't even aware of the hackney pulling away behind them as his thumb inched the material of her glove upward, baring more of her skin.

And to her shock, his tongue flicked out and tasted her, rasping over her sensitive pulse point in a warm, moist caress.

A moan of pleasure quavered in her throat as she struggled to find the breath to speak. "Mr. Monroe, I—I d-don't think—"

Her shaky voice was enough to have him abruptly letting go. He took a step back and a curtain descended over his features, shutting her out.

"Yes, of course. You're quite right. A man like me has no right to touch a lady in such a fashion. My apologies."

She bit her lip against her instinctive protest. That hadn't been what she'd meant, but perhaps it was best if he believed that. If she was going to concentrate on this investigation, find Stuart Grayson's killer *and* Wilbur Forbes, she had to keep Connor Monroe at a distance. His presence was distracting enough without him touching her all the time.

When she said nothing, merely looked up at him with wide eyes, he finally pivoted on his heel and started toward the building. Picking up her skirts, she hurried after him.

Apparently, Monroe didn't possess a butler, for no one greeted them at the door once they had climbed the set of wide, stone steps to the front stoop. Instead, he whipped out a key and unlocked the oaken panel himself, pushing it open and stepping aside to allow Jillian to move past him.

She came to a halt in the entryway, taking things in with interest.

The town house was surprisingly spacious, she noted, with gleaming marble floors, frescoed ceilings, and a steep, curving staircase with an intricately carved banister that wound its way up from the foyer to the second floor. It was quite obvious that this was a single man's home, however, for while the furniture was tasteful and expensive, it was also large and dark and overwhelmingly masculine.

The door clicked shut behind her, and she whirled to find Monroe laying his hat and gloves on a side table.

"I'll take your things if you like," he tossed over his shoulder in an almost casual fashion. "I apologize for the lack of servants. As a bachelor, I am used to doing for myself, and after what happened with Peg and then Stuart, I decided it was best if the few members of my staff were given some extended time off. I'd never forgive myself if any of them were to wind up like—"

He stopped, but he didn't need to finish. The gruffness in his voice spoke volumes. Though he had made no mention of it, it was quite apparent to Jillian that Peg Ridley and Stuart Grayson had been more to him than merely his housekeeper and his business partner.

"That's quite all right, Mr. Monroe." Reaching up to untie the ribbons on her bonnet, she removed it and handed it over before smoothing back the stray wisps of hair that had escaped her chignon. "And though I haven't said so before, I am most sorry for your loss. I know what it feels like to lose someone you love too soon."

Only the most astute observer would have noticed his slight flinch at her words or the muscle that ticked in his taut jaw, and Jillian's heart ached for him. He was so determined not to let any of his hurt show. Obviously, this was a strong and solitary man who rarely let anyone close, and it was a tragedy that he had lost two of the very few people who mattered to him.

She would have to be careful as to how she phrased her questions, she decided. Though she hated to probe at painful wounds, the more she knew about the victims, the better her chances of coming to understand the murderer and his motivations. "How long had you known Mrs. Ridley?"

He shrugged as he placed her hat next to his things on the table. "For several years. She was a widow who used to run a boardinghouse close to the docks where I grew up."

Hmmm. That was interesting. So Monroe had grown up around the docks? Perhaps his father had been in shipping himself.

Before she could ask him anything further, though, he turned and crossed the floor to stand next to the staircase. "I found her here, at the foot of the steps. Her . . . neck was broken."

Moving forward to join him, she resisted the

desire to lay a comforting hand on his shoulder. "She fell?"

"Or was pushed."

Jillian's gaze went to the landing at the top of the stairs. Such a fall would certainly be enough to kill someone, especially a woman of advanced age, such as Mrs. Ridley must have been. Wasn't it likely, however, that the housekeeper had simply lost her balance?

She looked up to find Monroe watching her through narrowed eyes, and as if reading her mind, he shook his head. "It wasn't an accident."

"What makes you say that?" This was nothing at all like what Jillian had expected after the scene at Grayson and Monroe Shipping, and she couldn't help but be confused. "And how could you possibly tie this in with what happened to your partner?"

"I didn't. Not at first. But there were a few things that struck me as odd about that evening the more I thought about it."

"Such as?"

Monroe shrugged and placed a hand on the nearby newel post, his fingers curling around the polished wood. The whiteness of his knuckles was the only indication of the tightness of his grip—or of the troubled direction of his thoughts. "When I came home, I found the front door unlocked. That, in and of itself, was enough to give me pause." One corner of his mouth canted at a wry angle. "Where Peg and I come from, if you went to bed with your doors unlatched you were asking to wake up with your throat slit, and she never lost the habit of making sure everything was closed up tight before she retired. Especially when the rest of the servants had the evening off and she was here by herself, as she was that night."

He paused for a moment, and when he failed to continue, Jillian prompted him gently. "You said 'things.' Plural. Was there something else?"

"Yes. There was a porcelain figurine that sat on a side table in the parlor." He gestured toward an archway on the other side of the foyer. "I found it in pieces next to her."

Jillian pursed her lips in thought. She supposed it was possible that Mrs. Ridley might have been carrying the figurine when she had fallen. Perhaps the housekeeper had been cleaning the piece, or something equally inconsequential. But it was worth looking into. "Do you mind showing me where this figurine used to sit?"

"Of course not. This way."

Monroe led her through the archway into a luxuriously appointed chamber. Here, the floor was decorated with Oriental rugs in varying shades of crimson and gold that matched the watered silk of the wallpaper and the damask fabric that upholstered the many chairs and settees. A large marble fireplace dominated one end of the room, while at the other, windows framed by heavy draperies looked out over Piccadilly.

"It was on the table over there." Monroe jerked

his head toward a mahogany end table against the far wall.

Jillian made her way over to it, studying the various other knickknacks that littered its surface.

There was nothing that seemed of any significance.

She turned to face Monroe, who stood a few feet away with arms crossed. "What did Bow Street have to say about this?"

His features took on a cynical cast. "Peg had a weak heart, and she was getting on in years. They were certain she must have had some sort of attack or tripped and fallen down the stairs."

"In other words, they believe it was an accident."

A muscle leaped in his jaw and she could see him tense, even with the distance between them. "It wasn't an accident."

"So you say, but—"

"Lady Jillian, someone else was here that night. Peg was pushed down those stairs deliberately, and I'm convinced it was the same man who murdered Stuart. If the unlocked door and the broken figurine didn't arouse my suspicions, the note that was delivered to me the next morning would have more than done so."

Her brows lowered as she contemplated him. "You keep mentioning this note. What exactly did it say?"

Monroe's jaw tightened visibly. " 'She went too easy.' The handwriting was the same as on the others I'd received, but when I tried to show it to the Bow Street officers yesterday after discovering Stuart's body, they did little more than glance at it. They won't even consider the possibility that Peg might have been murdered, and the note is phrased much too vaguely to be deemed a genuine admission of guilt."

Jillian tapped her chin in thought, mulling over his words. Yes, she could see how the law might have viewed such a tale as a bit far-fetched. But to her, the scenario seemed all too plausible. Especially when one factored in the appearance of Mrs. Ridley's handkerchief at the Grayson crime scene.

"Is there any way I could see these letters now?" she asked. Perhaps if she read the missives, she might chance upon some sort of clue that would substantiate Monroe's claims.

He murmured his assent and excused himself to fetch them. But she barely noticed when he bowed and departed the room. Her mind was already racing ahead, and she began to pace, her eyes tracing over the walls and furniture, almost unseeingly.

If the same person is responsible for the deaths of both Stuart Grayson and Peg Ridley, she reasoned, *and if Monroe is right and he is the intended target, then somewhere in this room the killer must have left behind more tangible evidence of his presence. The man would have wanted there to be no doubt in Monroe's mind that he'd been here.*

It was at that moment that she noticed the mirror.

Oval in shape and surrounded by a gold frame, it occupied the wall over the table where the broken figurine had once presided, and Jillian felt her stomach give a queer little flutter. Another mirror. Was it possible . . . ?

Whipping her spectacles from her reticule once more, she plopped them on her nose and crossed the chamber to look up at it. Could the figurine have been a clue, meant once again to draw attention to the mirror?

A compulsion stronger than any she could remember having before drove her up onto her toes to feel behind the upper frame. And sure enough, her fingers bumped into a small, hard object wedged against the wall.

She pulled it out. It was a tarnished pocket watch.

"What the bloody hell are you doing?"

She turned to find Monroe hovering in the archway.

"I believe," she drew out slowly, holding the watch out for his inspection, "that the killer has left you another message."

Chapter 8

In order to understand the mind of a criminal, you must first understand what motivates him.

Connor felt his heart give a leap and set off at a mad gallop as he gaped at the object Lady Jillian cradled in her outstretched hands.

Recognition was instantaneous. The watch was the only thing of value Hiram Ledbetter had ever owned in his life.

A life that had ended in a tumbledown cottage in Billingsgate.

Some of what he was thinking must have shown on his face, for Lady Jillian's amber eyes widened behind the lenses of her spectacles. "You recognize it?"

He tried to speak, but his voice wouldn't come, so he merely nodded. Setting aside the packet of letters he had carried into the room, he reached out to take the watch from her. Yes, he knew it well. There was the familiar gouge in the casing, the one Hiram had stroked almost lovingly with his gnarled thumb every time he'd had occasion to take it out.

"It was Hiram's." Connor's voice was little more than a husky whisper as he ran his own thumb over the groove with the very same reverence he'd once watched the elderly man use.

To her credit, Lady Jillian didn't probe further. As if sensing he needed a moment to regroup, she continued to stand patiently before him in silence.

Finally, he took a deep breath and spoke. "Where did you get this?"

"It was behind the frame of the mirror. Just like Peg Ridley's handkerchief at Mr. Grayson's office."

Then he'd been right after all. He'd never really doubted it, but if discovering Peg's handkerchief at Stuart's office hadn't convinced him of the validity of his suspicions, this would have. Hiram had been killed by the very same villain who had been responsible for both Stuart's and Peg's deaths.

And the murderous bastard wanted Connor to know it.

A wave of blinding rage rose up in him and his fist clenched around the timepiece.

"Mr. Monroe?" Lady Jillian's words were soft, questioning. "Was this Hiram a friend?"

Connor bowed his head. "Friendship" was

such a pallid word to describe the warm relationship he'd had with the kindly old street vendor. "A very good one. He was a costermonger—a fruit seller—and this watch was his one prized possession." The memory of Hiram's wizened body lying limp and lifeless on the floor of his cottage brought a lump to his throat, and he had to swallow it back before he could go on. "A little over a month ago, he was found bludgeoned to death in his home."

"Oh, Connor, I'm so sorry."

The sound of his name spilling from the Lady Jillian's lips for the first time was enough to startle him into meeting her sympathetic gaze. He was certain she hadn't used it deliberately, that it had been nothing more than a slip of the tongue, but its effect on him was undeniable. Hearing her say it in that throaty voice as she looked at him with such gentle understanding made him want to wrap his arms around her and pull her close, to lay his head on her ample breast and let her heal his wounded spirit with the sweet balm of her comforting touch.

But no. If nothing else, the incident between them earlier, out on the sidewalk, had shown him the danger of letting his guard down with her. He had meant only to unsettle her, to shake that infuriating air of implacable confidence. But instead the tables had been turned on him. The tantalizing flavor of her skin, the flutter of her pulse beneath his lips, haunted him still.

Ever since the woman had arrived at his office he had been trying everything he could think of to unnerve her, to chase her away. But it seemed the harder he tried, the more determined she became in her resolve to see things through. And while he couldn't help but admire that determination, it made it all the more difficult to deal with his damnable attraction to her.

An attraction that he knew could ultimately go nowhere.

Glancing down at the watch in his hand, he forced his thoughts back to the conversation. "The law was certain Hiram was the victim of some sort of robbery gone awry. That sort of thing happens often in Billingsgate. Not that he had much to steal, but this watch turned up missing, so I never even questioned their judgment. Until yesterday morning. Then I started to put everything together."

"The letters?"

"Indeed. It was then that I realized they were serious threats. Hiram, Peg, Stuart . . . Their deaths so close together are just too much of a coincidence, but Bow Street won't hear of it. They've decided Forbes is their man and no amount of talking will persuade them otherwise."

Raking his free hand through his hair, Connor pivoted and stalked to the window, staring out at the traffic passing by on the street below with unseeing eyes. Sweet Christ, all of this was his fault.

But that should be no surprise, he thought cynically. His inability to protect those he cared for had been a lifelong affliction.

"I tried to help him, you know." He hadn't meant to speak, but the words escaped him before he could call them back, and once they started tumbling forth he couldn't seem to stop them. "Hiram. When I finally made good I tried to offer him the money to find a residence in a better part of town, but he refused. The old man was stubborn. I did as much for him as he would allow, but . . ." He trailed off into nothingness, embarrassed by his lack of restraint.

"That was kind of you."

Lady Jillian's hesitant observation from behind him had him stifling a bitter, self-deprecatory laugh before he faced her once more. She had no idea how wrong she was. "Kindness had nothing to do with it. At least, not on my part."

At her look of confusion, he exhaled a sharp gust of air and reached up to scrub at the nape of his neck in a weary gesture. He had never liked talking about his past, but he supposed he owed her at least a brief explanation. "When I was a boy, my stepfather ran a tavern on Thames Street, next to the river. He wasn't what you would call the fatherly sort, and my home life . . . well, let's just say my brother and I avoided being there as much as possible."

When Lady Jillian's face lit with avid interest, Connor swiftly realized he had made a tactical error. He had mentioned Brennan, and with her inquisitive nature she was bound to be curious. But he had no intention of telling her about his brother. The subject was far too painful.

He went on with his tale, hoping to distract her. "I spent a great deal of time roaming the streets and hanging about down at the wharf, watching the ships come in, talking to the sailors and dockworkers. And when I was thirteen, I finally ran away from home for good."

His ploy must have worked, for when he paused, she didn't question him about Brennan. Instead, she prompted him to continue. "And?"

"And I lived on the streets for quite some time. That's how I came to know Hiram. Most other people paid little attention to just another dirty-faced urchin, but he always stopped to speak to me, to make sure I was all right. I must have made quite the pathetic picture, because he used to offer me fruit off his cart, even when he had very little himself." One corner of Connor's mouth gave a rueful quirk. "I owed him far more than I could ever repay."

Lady Jillian tilted her head, surveying him from under lowered lashes. "Something tells me he's not the only one you've tried to help. Mrs. Ridley?"

He acknowledged her astute conjecture with a shrug. There was no use denying it. "I met Peg the year I turned sixteen. I was always a bit large for my age, and I was working as a navvy down at the docks to try and make a little money when she offered me a room in her boardinghouse.

She discovered I had always had a fascination with ships, you see, so she introduced me to Stuart, who took me on as his apprentice and taught me the shipping business."

"You said she had a weak heart. You offered her employment when she became ill?"

"I knew it was the only way she would accept my help. She was just as intractable as Hiram, but at least with Peg in the position of housekeeper I could make sure she was taken care of, that she had a roof over her head and the proper medical attention."

"You know, Mr. Monroe, you're not nearly as hard as you'd like people to think. I do believe you are quite the philanthropist."

Something about Lady Jillian's pleased and knowing tone rubbed Connor on the raw. She had no idea what she was talking about, and he had no desire for her to come to the conclusion that he was some sort of bloody do-gooder. She would only wind up full of expectations he could never hope to fulfill.

A muscle flexing in his jaw, he closed the distance between them in one long stride.

"Don't," he warned her quietly, staring down into her startled eyes. "Don't idealize me. I repay my debts. That's all."

Though she seemed more than a bit disconcerted by his nearness, she didn't back away. Instead, she lifted her chin in open defiance. "Really, Mr. Monroe, I fail to see how what I think of you matters—"

He halted her by seizing her arm, then immediately berated himself for forgetting that it wasn't a good idea to touch her. The heat that surged through him made it difficult to go on, but he managed to do so. "I mean it, Lady Jillian. If you insist on seeing me as some sort of hero, I can assure you you'll only be disappointed. Do you understand?"

There was a long, drawn-out moment while their gazes clashed in silent battle, but it was Lady Jillian who finally glanced away, conceding the victory.

"Of course." She pulled her arm free from his grasp, a mask of chilly hauteur descending over her features. "Do you think I could see the letters now?"

The sudden change of topic threw Connor a bit off balance, but he managed to respond with suitable alacrity and equal coolness. "Certainly." He waved at the side table where he had left them earlier. "They're over there."

She whirled and marched across the room to retrieve them, her skirts rustling with each angry step, her spine stiff. Tucking Hiram's watch into his pocket, Connor followed, unable to quell a sense of regret that his actions had caused the return of her animosity. It was for the best. He knew that.

But that didn't reduce his feeling of disappointment—or make him miss her soft look of approval any less.

He watched as she swept the letters off the table

and seated herself on a love seat close to the fireplace. Removing her gloves, she laid them on the cushion next to her along with her reticule and pushed her spectacles farther up her nose before regarding him with frosty inquiry. "Is this the lot?"

He nodded. Then, for some reason he couldn't fathom, an imp of deviltry prodded him into settling himself at the other end of the love seat, less than a foot away from her. He was aware it was an idiotic move, for it placed his left thigh in close proximity to her right and in constant jeopardy of brushing up against her. The position was far from conducive to his peace of mind, but he couldn't seem to resist the opportunity to needle her once again.

Lady Jillian frowned at him, but apparently decided it wasn't worth it to express her displeasure aloud, for she gave a haughty sniff and then bent over the missives.

The minutes ticked by as she perused them. The majority of the messages were little more than a sentence or two, written on torn, dirty scraps of paper in a penmanship that was close to illegible, ranging from matter-of-fact statements—"I'm back!"—to taunts—"I'll bet you don't remember me!"

Connor leaned forward and propped his elbows on his knees, trying to interpret Lady Jillian's expression as she read.

"As I said before, I received the first one about a month ago," he offered, "a week or two after

Hiram was killed. I didn't think much of them. They seemed harmless. Perplexing, vaguely irritating, but I brushed them off. I was sure they would stop after a while."

One of Lady Jillian's eyebrows rose as she scrutinized him. "But they didn't?"

"No. In fact, after Peg's death they started arriving with even more frequency, and the tone became . . . a bit less than friendly."

Your sins are catching up with you. I won't rest until you pay for what you did. No one you care for is safe . . .

The words from the bastard's most recent letter, the one he'd found yesterday morning before departing for the office and discovering what had happened to Stuart, were emblazoned across Connor's inner vision. His jaw set as he recalled the helpless rage he'd felt upon realizing that his tormentor was behind far more than a vicious letter-writing campaign.

If only he'd taken action sooner!

Lady Jillian set the notes aside and folded her hands in her lap. "You say Bow Street showed no interest in these?"

He shook his head. "None. Except for Tolliver. But apparently he doesn't hold much sway there."

"Well, you must admit that at first glance there seems to be nothing there to connect them to what has happened. As you said, except for the last one, they are worded in such a manner that they can't be considered overt threats. There are no specific references to the victims, none of whom were, er . . . dispatched in the same manner. Usually there are some similarities. But a robbery, the apparent victim of an accidental fall, a violent murder?" She ticked them off on her fingers, then shook her head. "They seemingly have nothing in common."

Connor felt his temper begin to seethe beneath the surface of his carefully cultivated façade of control. He had spent hours yesterday trying to convince the officers from Bow Street that his fears had some foundation. He would be damned if he would waste time today trying to convince Lady Jillian of the same thing. "If you don't believe me—"

Her sigh of exasperation interrupted his potential tirade. "I'm not saying that I don't believe you, Mr. Monroe. Simply that this man is very good at cloaking his involvement in all of this. There is no obvious pattern, which is unusual in crimes that are committed by the same person. In the eyes of the law, these cases aren't even related, much less have the same perpetrator. And he was very careful to leave clues that only you would understand the significance of."

His anger mollified, Connor found he couldn't help but be impressed with her assessment of the situation. Of course, Lady Jillian had been impressing him ever since he'd allowed her to see Stuart's office. He had expected her to bolt, but though she had seemed a bit squeamish at first, she hadn't run. Instead, she had plopped those spectacles on her nose and proceeded to go over the scene with an aplomb that the most seasoned law officer would have envied. Not only that, but she had managed to locate a piece of key evidence. Evidence that both he and Bow Street had missed.

So, despite everything inside him that shouted it was a mistake, he had allowed her to take the investigation a step further. Tolliver had been right about her so far. She was proving to be a very intelligent and knowledgeable woman.

"How exactly were these delivered?" she asked suddenly, drawing his attention back to the present.

"Most were shoved under my door in the early hours of the morning," he told her, "so I would find them before I left for the office. A few were brought by street urchins who seemed to have convenient lapses of memory when asked to describe the person who paid them to do so."

"And you can think of no one who would have a reason to hold a grudge against you?"

Actually, he could. At least two of them off the top of his head, both with ties to his distant past. But of those two, one was dead and one had been rotting in Newgate for years, so neither was a likely prospect. "I can't say that I've ever done anything to anyone that would warrant this sort of reaction."

Getting to her feet, Lady Jillian began to pace, her hands clasped behind her back as she stared thoughtfully up at the ceiling. "It is obvious whoever wrote these holds you accountable for something that's happened to him. 'I won't rest until you pay for what you did.' That's quite specific. He has committed these crimes as a way to punish you. But if you are the one he feels is at fault for whatever it is he has suffered, why not attempt to harm you directly in some way?"

The answer came to Connor with a sudden, utter certainty, like a bolt out of the blue. "Because he knew it would hurt me more if he went after the people I feel responsible for."

"So his goal is not just to seek justice for some alleged sin, to make you pay, but to cause you pain. You do realize that this man has more than likely been following you all along? That he probably still is? He would have wanted to see your face when you realized what he'd done. To watch you suffer."

Connor froze. Of course! He didn't know why such a thing hadn't occurred to him before. It was only to be expected. And if that were the case, it meant this bastard had observed him as he went about his daily activities, knew whom he interacted with on a regular basis.

And had more than likely seen everything that had passed between him and Jillian from the moment they had stepped out of the carriage in front of his town house.

At the mere possibility, a cold chill crawled up his spine. There could be no doubt that the killer would have drawn the same conclusion from witnessing that little scene that any other casual onlooker would have.

That this woman meant something to him.

His mouth tightened into a grim line. Damnation, he had known it was a mistake to let her get involved in this, but it was a mistake he was going to rectify right now. He couldn't let anything happen to her because of him. He wouldn't.

Lady Jillian was still talking. "I should like to see your friend Hiram's cottage. Since he was the first victim, it's possible—"

"No." The single word was sharp and unequivocal, and it echoed in the abrupt stillness with the impact of a whip crack.

Her face revealing her surprise, Jillian blinked and peered at Connor over the top of her spectacles as if she were studying something of particular repugnance. "I beg your pardon?"

"I believe I was quite clear. I said no."

"And may I ask why not?"

"Of course." He got to his feet and bent over to retrieve the letters she had set aside, speaking without looking at her. He couldn't. For he was well aware that if he did, she would have him second-guessing the wisdom of his decision, even though he knew it was for the best. "From this point on, your services are no longer required."

"Mr. Monroe, you promised you would let me help you."

"And I have. You have confirmed exactly what I suspected all along, and with the evidence you've found I'm certain I can convince Bow Street—"

"Of nothing." She moved around to stand in front of him, her amber eyes blazing with a militant light. "You know very well that what I've found doesn't mean anything to anyone but you, and I'm sure Bow Street could come up with some perfectly acceptable reasons for why the items were at the crime scenes."

He couldn't deny the truth of her words, so he didn't even try, and his refusal to reply had her hands flying to her hips in righteous indignation. "Apparently you don't care that more people could die simply because you've taken it into your head to be stubborn."

Her allegation once again roused his temper. By damn, she was the one who was stubborn! Couldn't she see he was doing this for her own good?

He spun to face her, the letters he had just finished gathering falling from his hands to flutter to the floor unnoticed. "That is exactly what I'm trying to prevent!"

"What?"

"Your death!"

She sniffed. "You needn't worry about me. I am a woman full-grown who is perfectly capable of taking care of herself."

She was a thorn in his side was what she was. Obstinate and infuriating. And with her cheeks flooded with high color and her ebony curls coming loose from their chignon to frame her face becomingly, she was a temptation he could no longer resist. Her lush mouth beckoned like an oasis in the desert, and he was a man who had denied his thirst for far too long.

"For God's sake, Jillian," he growled. "Do you never stop talking?"

And with that, goaded beyond bearing, he reached out with one hand, cupped the nape of her neck, and jerked her to him as he seized her lips in a ruthless kiss.

Chapter 9

ↂ

Never let emotion get in the way of your judgment. The consequences could prove fatal.

Jillian felt the kiss clear down to her toes. A tidal wave of sensation that washed over her entire body and sent the blood singing through her veins.

This was no tender melding of lips, she thought dimly. No tentative first exploration. She had shared such kisses with Thomas in the early days of their courtship, and while she had liked them well enough, they had never affected her like this.

No, this was a bold claiming, a conquering that thrilled her even as it frightened her. Like a starving man, his mouth plundered hers as if he had every right. But then, she had known from the beginning that Connor Monroe would be the sort of person to take what he wanted, regardless of the consequences and without asking permission.

And once it was his, he would fight to keep it.

In some far corner of her mind, Jillian knew that this was wrong, that she should push him away and slap his face for his effrontery. But instead, she found herself sliding her arms around his neck, returning the kiss with equal ardor as she lost herself in the passion of the moment.

In him.

As if sensing her capitulation, Monroe gentled his grip on her nape, and his hand slid upward into her hair, freeing the pins that held her chignon in place and sending them pinging to the floor. The loosened curls tumbled down around her shoulders in an ebony waterfall, and he sifted his fingers through the mass over and over, seeming to savor the softness of the strands.

His other arm stole about her waist, pulling her closer.

Suddenly, Jillian was aware of every inch of his large, brawny frame. The sculpted muscles of his wide chest, the solid bulk of his thighs. But she was especially cognizant of the hard ridge of his arousal as it nudged her lower abdomen in a most insistent manner, leaving her in no doubt that this man wanted her.

A little thrill went through her at the knowledge, and she gave in to the silent plea, shifting her hips the slightest bit in order to allow the swollen length of his manhood to press up against the soft, secret place between her legs.

He gave a deep, rumbling groan in response and rocked himself against her. The feeling had her gasping, and he took immediate advantage of the opportunity to plunge his tongue between her lips. He tasted strongly of mint, and the feel of his velvety tongue stroking over the inside of her mouth was indescribable. It sent her senses reeling and weakened her knees in a way that had her nails digging into his broad shoulders for support.

Finally, after what seemed like an eternity, yet at the same time like the blink of an eye, Monroe tore his lips away from hers and rested them against her temple with a harsh breath.

"God, make me stop, Jillian," he rasped. She couldn't see his face, but she could hear the gruff need in his voice. "If you don't, I can't guarantee that this won't go any further."

She tried to speak, but the words wouldn't come, and she wasn't certain quite what she would have said. Yes, she should call a halt. There was no question of that. But *could* she? She didn't know if she was capable of it, of bringing such delicious pleasure to an end.

When she said nothing, he gave a broken laugh that sounded oddly pained. "Damn it, I can't do this alone. You have to help me here. Unless . . . this is what you want?"

One of his hands was still indulging in a rhythmic massage of her scalp. Now, it fisted in her hair, tilting her head back so his mouth could skim over the curve of her throat. He nipped at the flesh just above her collar, then soothed the small sting with a flick of his tongue.

"Stop me, Jillian," he murmured against her skin, wringing a shiver from her. "Say no now or it's going to be too late."

As if to emphasize the truth of his warning, the hand that had been at her waist lifted—and unexpectedly cupped her breast.

She released a trembling moan. Even through the material of her pelisse, she could feel the heat of his touch, scorching her, and her nipple reacted to it by tightening almost painfully. The impudent bud nestled into his callused palm, tingling at the contact and setting off a corresponding dampness in her feminine core.

She swallowed convulsively and made a restless movement, rubbing herself against him in an attempt to quell the ache. Against that throbbing part of him that seemed to grow hotter and more rigid with every second that passed.

"Connor . . ." Her voice was a whisper. "Connor, please . . ."

She had no idea what she was begging him for, but her plea seemed to finally give him the strength to act. With a raw expletive, he thrust her from him and stepped away, turning his back to her.

Feeling strangely bereft, Jillian raised a shaking hand to straighten her spectacles, which had been knocked askew by the force of his kiss. She could tell by the stiff way he held himself that

Connor was trying to get himself back under control, so she didn't interfere. She simply wrapped her arms about herself and concentrated on reining in her own teetering emotions.

Just when the silence had gone on for longer than she thought she could bear, he swung back to face her, and she noticed with a slight jab of disappointment that his mask of reserve was back in place, despite the telltale flush that stained his high cheekbones.

"I must apologize, my lady," he said, inclining his head in an incisive fashion. "I don't know what came over me."

My lady. Jillian couldn't help grimacing at the cold formality of it. Just minutes ago it had been *Jillian.* And though she tried to tell herself it was for the best, she couldn't quite make herself believe it. For she was quite certain that she would never be able to go back to thinking of him as merely *Mr. Monroe.*

She licked her sensitive, kiss-bruised lips and struggled to come up with something to say that would put things back on a more comfortable footing between them. "Please don't apologize. It was just as much my fault as—"

"No." He refused to let her finish, his jaw setting at a stubborn angle. "I instigated it. I had no right to put my hands on you, much less . . . Well, you must see this is all the more reason for you to bow out of this investigation. We would both be much better off if we forget we ever met each other."

Jillian's temper sparked. So that was his plan! He was going to use this incident to talk her into giving up her pursuit of Stuart Grayson's murderer, which she had no intention of doing. She couldn't. No matter how awkward this unwanted attraction might make things. Too much depended upon her involvement.

Besides, after what she had seen and heard today, she had to admit this case intrigued her. She knew she could help find this madman, and she wasn't about to just walk away.

Not when it was all too obvious that Connor needed her, no matter what he said to the contrary.

She eyed him from over the rims of her spectacles. "You agreed to accept my help, Con—Mr. Monroe, and I will not let you go back on your word. You cannot deny that I have already been of assistance, can you?"

An exasperated expression crossed his face and he reached up to push a hank of reddish hair back off his forehead, his aqua eyes narrowing in a glare. "No, I can't deny it, but after what happened here—"

This time it was Jillian who interrupted. "I see no reason why this should alter our arrangement. It's not as if I've never been kissed before, Mr. Monroe. I was practically engaged at one time, after all. We're both adults and surely we can behave as such." She tossed her head, then added in a deliberately goading tone, "Unless there is some reason to think you are unable to control yourself."

"Damnation, that has nothing to do with it!" His big body vibrated with a palpable tension and he turned away once again to stride over to the window, bracing his forearm against the frame and bowing his head as if fighting for patience. When he spoke again, his voice was so soft it was barely audible. "Can't you see that I'm worried about you? If you're right, and the killer is following me, what if he should see you with me? It may already be too late."

He was worried about her. Jillian's heart gave a little leap as she let her gaze trail over his rugged profile. It was getting harder and harder to remember that she had once viewed him as being far from handsome. The bold, slightly off-center nose, that strong, square jaw, and those piercing, blue-green eyes were becoming more appealing to her the more time she spent with him. He possessed a charismatic power that went far beyond his looks.

She hoped none of the effect he had on her was revealed in her voice when she replied.

"Come now, Mr. Monroe. I find it hard to believe that I could be in danger merely because I've been seen in your company a time or two. If that were so, you'd have to put every employee at Grayson and Monroe Shipping under guard."

He shrugged, the muscles rippling and flexing in his shoulders with the movement. "Don't think I haven't been considering it. Perhaps I'm being overly cautious, but I would hate for anyone in my employ to be harmed simply because they have the misfortune to work for me."

His easily expressed concern for the people under his care didn't surprise Jillian, any more than anything else he'd told her today. She had suspected there was more to Connor than the hard man he let everyone see, and she had been right. Underneath that tough façade was a wounded yet caring heart, and she couldn't deny a desire to find out more about his past, to heal the hurts that still tormented him.

But no matter how drawn to him she was, she couldn't allow herself to give in to the pull. Even if they weren't from completely different worlds, her relationship with Thomas had taught her that no man, no matter how much he claimed to love or want her, would ever be able to accept her or what she felt compelled to do in order to get to the bottom of her mother's murder.

She doubted Connor Monroe would be any exception.

She took a step toward him, determined to persuade him to see reason. "Mr. Monroe, I appreciate that you are trying to protect me. But you must know I can help you or you wouldn't have allowed me to pursue the investigation this far."

When he didn't answer, just continued to gaze out the window in silence, she recognized that stronger tactics were called for. Clearing her throat, she took a deep breath and screwed up her courage before plunging ahead. "And if you will not take me to Mr. Ledbetter's cottage, I promise you that I will go on my own."

That did it. Rage and incredulity evident in his expression, Connor swung about to face her. "Why, you little fool! Do you have no notion of what you're playing at? You—"

But she raised her hand to halt his flow of angry words. "Please, Mr. Monroe. Like it or not, I am involved now, and I will continue my pursuit of this criminal, with or without your permission."

He glared at her, his resentment at being cornered in such a fashion blazing from his eyes. But her resolve not to be dissuaded must have shown on her face, for after a moment he gave an abrupt nod. "Very well. Have it your way. I'll take you to Hiram's cottage, but it will have to wait until tomorrow morning. I have things that I need to attend to back at the office this afternoon." His brow lowered and his visage darkened. "Before this goes any further, however, I want to make something understood. I am the one in charge in our little partnership, and if at any time I give you a direct order, I expect you to follow it to the letter or our association is at an end. Is that perfectly clear, my lady?"

"Perfectly clear."

"And you can rest assured that I will make certain that nothing like what happened today will ever happen again."

Jillian lifted her chin. "We'll *both* make certain

of it. And you needn't worry about me. I have every confidence that you can protect me should something occur."

She couldn't help but wonder at the bleak look that entered Connor's eyes. "I wouldn't be so sure of that, my lady. I wouldn't be sure of that at all."

Chapter 10

Seeking the advice of a knowledgeable individual can sometimes prove useful.

"It sounds like a ghastly business, dear! Simply ghastly!"

At the exclamation, Jillian set aside the rapidly cooling cup of tea she had been nursing for the past half hour and looked up to meet the apprehensive brown eyes of the Dowager Duchess of Maitland.

The two of them were seated in Maitland House's luxurious parlor, and Jillian had just finished relating the events of the day before. The duchess had grown more and more alarmed as the tale had unfolded, but now her lined face looked positively pale as she leaned forward in her chair, her beringed fingers tightening visibly on the handle of her cane.

"Are you certain you wish to continue with this, my child?" she asked.

Jillian lifted one shoulder in a slight shrug. "I don't see that I have a choice, Theodosia."

"Of course you have a choice. Elise was like a daughter to me, and I am just as anxious as you to have our doubts about that night finally laid to rest. But I certainly don't wish to see you put your life in danger in order to do so, and I don't believe your mother would want you to, either."

"Perhaps not. But if I don't do something, no one else will. And I can't spend the rest of my life not knowing . . ."

Jillian's words stumbled to a halt, and tears blurred her vision. The rest of society might have seen her mother as nothing more than a frivolous flirt, but she had known the caring woman behind that façade. A woman who had always been quick with a laugh and a hug and who had loved her daughters unconditionally.

No, it hadn't been until after her husband had inherited the role of marquis and the *ton* had made their disapproval of her clear that the marchioness had withdrawn, her hurt and disillusionment causing her to hide behind a mask of gay abandon.

After an instant of silence, the duchess sighed and put a comforting hand on Jillian's arm. "I'm sorry I can't be of more help. Elise knew I didn't approve of the way she was handling her estrangement from your father, so she never spoke of any of her gentlemen friends to me." She paused, then continued softly, "I know you miss her, my dear. I miss her, as well."

There was no doubting her sincerity. If anyone could truly empathize with the sense of pain and loss Jillian still felt at her mother's absence, it was Theodosia.

A plump, kindhearted woman, the widowed Duchess of Maitland had been one of the few people in London who had welcomed the late Lady Albright with genuine warmth all those years ago, who had continued to be loyal despite the whispers and rumors that had seemed to follow the marchioness everywhere she went. That connection had, in turn, resulted in her current close friendship with Jillian herself. A friendship that they both had been grateful for many times over the years.

"You must at least promise me you'll be careful," the elderly lady was saying, her expression full of concern. "I don't want you to think that I lack faith in your abilities, but if this criminal is capable of all that you say . . . well, I can't help but be frightened for you."

Jillian offered the duchess what she hoped was a reassuring smile. "I promise I shall employ the utmost caution. I *am* capable of looking after myself, you know."

"Be that as it may, I have to wonder at Mr. Tolliver's intelligence in coming to you with this. I can't see why the man couldn't question this Mr. Forbes himself once Bow Street catches up with him and then simply bring whatever information he is able to glean back to you. Surely you didn't need to be dragged into this reprehensible matter?"

"He needed me, Theodosia. Tolliver has had no help from Bow Street at all, and in the meantime a killer is running around free."

"And that is precisely what worries me." At the look Jillian sent her, the duchess thumped her cane on the floor with such force that her snow-white curls bounced. "Oh, you needn't frown at me so. I am well aware you are as stubborn as your mother, and you will do what you must, regardless of what I think. But you do realize that if word of this should get out, that she-beast of an aunt of yours will be the first one to blame me for encouraging you?"

It was true. Theodosia and Lady Olivia had always nursed an obvious disdain for each other. Perhaps their mutual antipathy had been fostered by the friendship the rather eccentric elderly woman had shared with the late marchioness, but there was little doubt that it was only the dowager duchess's lofty title and patronage of the Daventry family that kept the marquis's sister from objecting to their further association with her.

"Papa is quite fond of you, and he would never let her treat you with less than the proper respect," Jillian insisted. "Besides, I'm certain she realizes how much we have to be grateful to you for. If it weren't for your support, we never would have been accepted back into polite society after what happened with Mama."

Despite her words, however, a shard of guilt pierced her. She shouldn't have told Connor Monroe to pick her up here this morning, but when he had insisted upon escorting her to Hiram Ledbetter's cottage in Billingsgate rather than allowing her to meet him there, she had seen no recourse other than to give him the duchess's address. It certainly wouldn't have done to have him call for her at the Albright town house.

"I'm sorry for involving you in all of this, Theodosia," she ventured. "I needed to tell Papa *something*, otherwise he would have grown suspicious, and you were the only one I could trust to . . . well . . ."

"Tell a clanker for you?"

"Theodosia—"

"Come now. No need to wrap it all up in pretty paper. That's exactly what I'm doing. Lying to your father by allowing him to believe you are spending your days with me."

"If it bothers you, I'll try to think up another excuse for my absences from home, but—"

The dowager interrupted her by waving a hand dismissively. "Nonsense. Taking part in your little misadventures is the only excitement that I can count on in my dotage. But just you stay on your guard." Her gaze grew troubled. "Your father would never forgive me if anything were to happen to you, and I would never forgive myself."

Touched beyond measure, Jillian got to her feet and leaned over to press a kiss to the duchess's forehead. "I'll be fine. You'll see. And you'll never know how much it means to me to have you to confide in."

Theodosia reached up to pat her cheek. "I'll always be here for you, my child. If that scapegrace of a stepson of mine and his stick of a wife have anything to do with it, you and your sisters are more than likely the closest thing to granddaughters I shall ever have. It would make me quite happy to see all of you safely settled before my time on this earth is through. And notice," she added with meaningful emphasis, "that I said *all* of you."

Jillian stiffened. Not this again. Her friend was getting as bad as Papa when it came to wanting to marry her off. And after a night spent tossing and turning, unable to sleep for all the thoughts running through her head, she lacked the energy and fortitude needed to defend her position.

"Now you are starting to sound like Papa. He can't seem to understand that a woman can be happy without a man in her life."

A pair of piercing aqua eyes flashed across Jillian's inner vision, and though she tried valiantly to erase them, she found she could not. Connor Monroe had been a large part of the reason she had suffered from insomnia the evening before, and it maddened her that she couldn't seem to get him out of her mind.

Moving to stand before the windows that over-looked Park Lane, she stared out at the carriages jockeying for position on the street and the pedestrians strolling along the sidewalks under the late morning sun. Ever since she had made the decision to continue with her father's work, she had been trying to convince herself that she was content with her life as it was. But yesterday's kiss had disabused her of that notion with swift efficiency. It had awakened all of the old girlish hopes and dreams she had once thought were gone for good. Dreams of a man who would truly love her, who could accept her for who she was and who would stand beside her, no matter what.

But with Thomas's abandonment, she had learned to her detriment that such dreams could be dangerous to the very heart that nurtured them, and she refused to be drawn back into the trap of believing they could ever come true.

"You know that after what happened with Thomas I have no interest in marriage," she finally said over her shoulder. "I've gotten too independent, too used to going my own way. No man would be happy with those qualities in a wife."

There was a sound from behind her, and the duchess joined her at the window. "Shipton was a fool, and no mistake. I've informed his aunt of that sad fact often enough. But that doesn't mean that the rest of the eligible males in London are fools, as well."

When Jillian turned to face her, eyeing her

askance, Theodosia gave a gruff *hmmphh*. "Oh, very well. Perhaps the majority of them are, but that doesn't mean there aren't a few out there who wouldn't appreciate the lovely, intelligent young woman you are. My own Randall was one who liked a challenge, God rest his soul, and I didn't make things easy for him. But to give him his due, he never gave up on me until he had his ring on my finger." A reminiscent smile curved her mouth.

Tucking her arm through Theodosia's, Jillian drew the older woman with her back toward the sitting area. "Yes, but your Randall was a rare find, indeed. There aren't many like him out there anymore."

"Well, that's true enough. It's too bad that boy of his is already wed. If anyone could have made a man out of him . . ." The dowager gave a bark of laughter when Jillian glared at her. "Very well. I can see this conversation is getting me nowhere, so we shall move on for now. Why don't you tell me a bit more about this Connor Monroe of yours?"

Jillian froze in the act of helping the elderly lady back into her chair. "He's not mine."

At the sharp response, a shrewd gleam entered the duchess's eyes. "I see. Is he handsome, then?"

"Yes. No." Flustered, Jillian tried to compose herself. It wouldn't do at all for Theodosia to catch wind of how the infuriating Mr. Monroe affected her. "I mean . . . well, I suppose he looks well enough. Certainly not handsome in the way Thomas is. But some women might find him attractive."

"*Some* women, eh?"

"If you happen to like the big and brawny sort."

"Ah. Big and brawny. Now, there's a good combination. Especially if he happens to be big and brawny in the right places."

Jillian felt her face heat. Even if she hadn't felt the bold evidence of his masculinity pressed against her in such an intimate fashion, she would have been forced to acknowledge that Connor Monroe had been far from lacking in that respect. "Theodosia! I really don't think it's proper to speculate about such things!"

"Nonsense. Every female of age to be wed speculates about such things, even if she won't admit it." The duchess tapped her chin in thought. "Now, you say he's wealthy, so that's in his favor. I'm assuming that his background is a bit less than desirable, but that doesn't have to be a stumbling block, as we both well know. He could be worth considering, my dear. Unless you find him completely objectionable, that is?"

Before Jillian could even begin to formulate some sort of reply that wouldn't incriminate her, there was a sharp rap at the parlor door, and she could only thank the saints for the interruption.

At Theodosia's summons, the stoop-shouldered

butler poked his balding head into the room. "Your Grace, a Mr. Connor Monroe is here to see Lady Jillian. Should I show him in?"

"Ah, speak of the devil. Yes, please do, Fielding." The dowager glanced at the clock on the far wall before sending Jillian a sly wink. "At least the man is prompt. That's more than can be said for most."

A moment later, the butler bowed Connor into the room.

Jillian felt her heart speed up at the sight of him, so tall and imposing as he loomed on the threshold. Clad in a coat of bottle-green superfine that hugged his wide shoulders and dark breeches that did the same for his muscled thighs, the picture he presented was in stark contrast to his rumpled appearance the day before. His snowy white cravat looked as if it had been tied by an expert hand, and he had even managed to tame his unruly auburn locks into some semblance of order, the reddish-brown waves a perfect frame for his rugged, slightly off-center features.

Theodosia faced the newcomer with a charming smile, one hand extended in welcome. "Mr. Monroe. What a pleasure it is to finally meet you."

Crossing the chamber in a few long, powerful strides, Connor took her wrinkled hand in his and bent over it, raising it to his lips with a refined elegance that startled Jillian.

"Your Grace," he murmured in that raspy voice that sent shivers up her spine. "The pleasure is mine, I assure you."

"Well, aren't you the charmer?" Theodosia blinked and examined him as he released her hand and straightened. "I've heard a great deal about you, young man. A great deal. And so far, I like what I've heard."

Connor's mesmerizing eyes shot to Jillian where she hovered behind the elderly woman's chair, subjecting her to an intense scrutiny that had her wishing she could sink into the floor. "Really?"

"Oh, yes." The dowager's aged countenance grew serious. "But I must give you fair warning. This dear gel is very important to me, and if anything should happen to her, I would take it quite personally. I do hope we understand one another?"

Jillian watched, unable to tear her gaze away, as one corner of that harsh mouth tilted upward in a wry slant. "I can assure you that I have no desire to see Lady Jillian come to any harm. And if she has told you about me, Your Grace, then she must have mentioned that I was most reluctant to allow her to take part in this investigation. In fact, I must admit that I was hoping you could talk some sense into her."

"Oh, I've tried. But she's hardheaded, I'm afraid."

Beginning to resent the way the two of them were discussing her as if she weren't even there,

Jillian opened her mouth to offer a stinging rejoinder, but Fielding's announcement from the direction of the parlor door cut across her words.

"The Viscount Shipton."

It was so startling that at first she was certain she couldn't have heard the butler correctly. But when a familiar figure appeared in the doorway, she realized to her horror that she hadn't misunderstood after all.

Dear God, Thomas was here!

Every bit of blood in her veins seemed to drain into her toes, pooling there in an icy puddle and leaving the rest of her body feeling numb all over. She was lost, floundering, with no clear idea of what to do or say.

For the past three years, through a mixture of pure luck and some skillful maneuvering on her part, she had managed to avoid any unanticipated meetings with her former love. No easy feat, considering that his aunt was a very close friend of Theodosia's. But now it seemed her luck had run out. They were about to come face-to-face for the first time since he'd broken things off with her. And to compound the nightmare, it was going to happen right in front of Connor Monroe, who was bound to take all sorts of pleasure in witnessing her discomfort.

She couldn't imagine a way things could get any worse.

"Your Grace." Seeming oblivious to anyone else's presence, Thomas swept off his hat with an easy grin, combing his hand through his close-cropped, dark brown curls as he came toward the duchess. Halfway across the chamber, however, his gaze fell on Jillian and his step faltered, his mouth dropping open in an almost comical expression of astonishment.

The silence stretched out for what seemed like an eternity. Then Jillian took her courage in both hands and ventured a greeting, stiff and uncertain though it sounded. "Good morning, Lord Shipton."

He snapped his mouth closed, a veil of polite reserve descending over his features. "Lady Jillian. I didn't know you were here. Your carriage isn't out front."

It was obvious from the note of tension in his voice that her presence was far from a pleasant surprise. "Yes, well, it was such a lovely day I decided to walk."

He offered her a stilted nod in acknowledgment of her explanation, then turned to the duchess. "I apologize for calling on you so unexpectedly, Your Grace. I had hoped to speak with Maitland, but when Fielding said he wasn't in, I decided I should at least pay my respects."

"How kind of you, dear boy." Always the consummate hostess, Theodosia welcomed Thomas with perfect civility. Only the most discerning observer would have noticed the hint of frost in her demeanor, or the anxious glance she cast Jillian over his shoulder before continuing. "And how is your aunt?"

"Quite well. She sends her fondest regards."

As the two of them continued to exchange pleasantries, Jillian took the opportunity to draw in a deep breath and gather together the frayed threads of her control. Now that the initial shock of their encounter had started to wear off, it was much easier to do than she had expected.

Foolish chit, she scolded herself sternly. *You should be past all of this. You certainly can't go around behaving like such a ninny every time you happen to run into him.*

At that moment, she became aware of a sudden tingling at the nape of her neck, and she looked up to find Connor Monroe hovering at her elbow. To her surprise, instead of appearing as if he were taking any sort of delight in her predicament, there was a definite touch of concern in those aqua eyes as he peered down at her.

For some reason, the feel of his solid bulk at her side steadied rather than unnerved her, so that when Thomas spoke her name again, she was able to face him without any sign of her earlier distress.

"It has been a while since we last saw each other, Lady Jillian," the viscount was saying, his expression amiable, yet guarded. "You are looking well."

"Thank you, Lord Shipton. As are you." It was true. Thomas had changed little with the passage of time. He was still lean and handsome, his angular face and patrician features possessing that same combination of urbane sophistication and boyish charm that had so appealed to her as a girl of eighteen.

But as she stared into his gray eyes, she realized that somewhere along the way, he had lost some of the power he had once held over her. She felt nothing. No stirrings of attraction. No betraying flutters of the heart. Nothing.

Instead, it was the big man standing next to her who was getting under her skin. To her consternation, she was conscious of every move he made, even though she wasn't even looking at him. She could feel the heat from his muscled body radiating off him in waves, surrounding her like a warm blanket, and his musky male aroma reminded her rather inopportunely of the last time she'd been so powerfully aware of his intoxicating masculine scent.

Yesterday afternoon. In his arms.

"How is your father?" Thomas asked her, drawing Jillian's attention back to him. "And your sisters?"

"Fine, thank you. I shall be sure to mention that you asked after them."

There was a slight hesitation, and a shadow of what might have been regret flitted across the viscount's features. "I suppose you've heard about my engagement to Lord Leeds's daughter?"

Beside her, Connor shifted, the movement abrupt, almost angry. She glanced up at him to find that his eyes had narrowed to dangerous slits, and he was glowering at Thomas as if the man had committed some grievous error.

What on earth was the matter with him?

Seeking to divert the confrontation she feared was coming, Jillian hurried to reply. "Yes. Yes, I have, and I wish you every happiness."

But it was too late. As if noticing Connor for the first time, the viscount's eyebrows arched upward and he surveyed the other man in an almost imperious manner. "I'm sorry. I don't believe we've been introduced."

Connor visibly stiffened, and Jillian could have sworn a soft growl vibrated in the air between them.

Thankfully, Theodosia chose that moment to intervene. "Lord Shipton, allow me to make known to you Mr. Connor Monroe of Grayson and Monroe Shipping." Heaving herself to her feet with the use of her cane, the duchess made her way forward to join them. "Mr. Monroe is a business associate of my stepson's who, like you, stopped by to pay his respects. But as I informed him that Warren is not in town at present, I believe he was just getting ready to leave. Isn't that right, Mr. Monroe?"

Connor tore his fierce gaze away from the viscount's face, a muscle leaping in his tautened jaw, though he managed to respond with admirable courtesy. "You're quite right, Your Grace. I thank you for your hospitality."

The dowager nodded, then turned to Jillian.

"And darling, didn't you mention that you needed to drop some books off at the lending library for your dear aunt Olivia?"

Jillian seized upon the excuse with gratitude. "Thank you for reminding me, Theodosia. I had forgotten all about it, and I certainly wouldn't want to incur my aunt's wrath."

"Then I shall see you both out. And Thomas, when I return we'll have a nice, long chat over a cup of tea."

Without giving anyone time for a more formal farewell, the duchess shepherded Jillian and Connor out into the hallway, leaving behind a very perplexed-looking viscount.

Once the parlor door had closed behind the three of them, Jillian felt a wave of relief wash over her. The last thing she needed was Thomas finding out what she was up to. That had been much too close for her peace of mind, and Connor's behavior hadn't helped, either.

She whirled to face him with her hands on her hips.

"What were you thinking?" she hissed. "All we need is for Thomas to end up wondering about you and asking questions. Whatever possessed you to start bristling like some stray mongrel protecting a bone?"

Connor stared down at her with an inscrutable expression for a long moment. When he finally spoke, his voice was compelling and utterly serious.

"Shipton never deserved you, you know."

Without another word, he pivoted on his boot heel and stalked off down the hallway toward the foyer.

Rooted to the spot, Jillian gaped after him in stunned amazement, until a soft chuckle drew her attention to Theodosia.

The duchess's eyes were sparkling with knowing delight. "I like your Mr. Monroe, my dear," she informed Jillian, her voice tinged with amusement. "And if you won't consider marriage, may I suggest a torrid affair?"

Chapter 11

Never rule out the possibility that the culprit may return to the scene of the crime.

Connor leaned against a cracked and peeling wall in Hiram Ledbetter's one-room cottage, booted feet crossed and hands shoved deep in the pockets of his breeches as he watched Jillian examine her surroundings with the same single-minded focus that she had displayed at both crime scenes the day before.

Dressed in a modest, high-necked gown of plum-colored muslin with her hair once again pulled back in a tidy chignon and her spectacles perched on the end of her nose, the picture she presented was one of businesslike reserve. She was seated on the edge of Hiram's sagging mattress, sifting through the items scattered across the top of the bedside table and doing a quite thorough job of ignoring his presence in the process. She hadn't once met his eyes since they'd departed Maitland House.

But who could blame her? He'd behaved like an utter fool.

With a stifled oath, he reached up to tug at his cravat, hardly noticing when the intricate folds he'd worked so hard to produce in front of the mirror this morning came undone, the limp ends of the material straggling down the front of his shirt. He supposed it didn't matter now. It certainly wasn't as if he had a hope in hell of impressing her. Not that he'd dressed like some bleeding dandy with that sole purpose in mind.

He glanced down at the black armband that encircled his bicep. Stuart's memorial service had taken place that morning, a melancholy affair with few in attendance aside from Connor, Lowell Unger, and one or two clients with whom Stuart had maintained a good rapport. And as it had turned out, they had been far more concerned with the state of the company now that the driving force behind it was gone rather than paying their respects. It seemed to Connor a sad statement that a man as good as Stuart hadn't had more people left behind to mourn him.

"It doesn't make any sense."

At the sound of Jillian's voice, Connor tore himself from his dispirited musings and looked over at her expectantly. "What?"

But instead of replying, she shook her head

and took up a position before the moldering fireplace, gazing down at the ashes on the hearth as if deep in thought.

And that was fine with him, he decided, subsiding back against the wall. The truth was, he had no idea what he was going to say to her when they finally *did* get around to speaking to each other.

The journey to Billingsgate in their hired hackney had been made in subdued silence. Jillian had spent the entire time staring out the window at the passing scenery, her fingers knotted together in her lap, and when they had pulled up in front of the cottage, she hadn't even waited for assistance in alighting. She'd vacated the carriage as if the hounds of hell themselves were at her heels.

Connor bowed his head and reached up to scrub at the back of his neck. He knew he couldn't leave things like this, with the tension between them so thick and tangible that he could feel it settling over him like an invisible shroud. The least he could do was try and alleviate some of the strain.

Clearing his throat, he ventured into the breach. "I suppose I owe you an apology for my earlier behavior."

Jillian glanced at him over her shoulder. "You only *suppose*?"

"Very well. I *definitely* owe you an apology." Connor couldn't stifle a chuckle at her haughty tone and the superior arch of her brow. She wasn't going to make this easy. "I'm afraid I'm not quite sure what came over me."

Perhaps it had been pent-up emotion left over from saying his final good-byes to Stuart that had made him react in such an unaccustomed manner. But something feral and dangerous had seized him in the moment he had realized that he was in the same room with the infamous Lord Shipton, and he had been filled with the undeniable urge to plant his fist in that aristocratic face.

This was the man Jillian had once believed she would marry, a taunting voice in his mind had whispered. The man she had once loved. That it was possible she still loved.

At the thought, Connor felt his anger rise up again, choking him, but he managed to tamp it back down with a supreme effort of will. If he didn't know any better, he might actually believe he was . . . jealous.

But he shook off the possibility before it could even begin to take hold. Connor Monroe had never been possessive of a female in his life, and he wasn't about to start now.

Turning away from the fireplace, Jillian came to stand before him, scrutinizing his features with narrowed eyes, as if assuring herself of his sincere contrition. And after several long seconds, she finally inclined her head in a nod.

"I accept your apology, though it is Lord Shipton you should be offering it to."

Connor made a sound of disgust deep in his throat. "Lord Shipton is an ass."

"Mr. Monroe, it does little good to apologize if you are simply going to turn around and be insulting again."

Her lush mouth was pursed in displeasure, and as he stared down at her, he was momentarily swept back in time to the day before and the kiss they had shared. The memory of sweet, honeyed lips moving under his own, of her ripe curves nestled in his arms, had tortured him throughout the night, leaving him tossing and turning in bed, his body painfully aroused from the mere recollection of it.

Never could he remember a mere kiss affecting him so powerfully before.

He leaned in close to her, taking delight in the softly indrawn breath he heard hiss through her teeth. "Oh, come now, Lady Jillian. Surely you must agree that the man is a bloody fool? It may not have been up to me to point out the fact, but insulting or not, it was the truth. He didn't deserve you. You are far too spirited, too intelligent for him, and he never would have been capable of appreciating all the unique traits that make you such a compelling woman."

Color washed into her cheeks and she took a jerky step back, separating herself from the sensual haze that suddenly seemed to hover around them. "I must thank you for the compliment. But if you don't mind, I'd rather forget about Lord

Shipton for now and concentrate on the matter at hand."

Connor stiffened at the coolness of her words, pulling back himself, both mentally and physically. Damn it, she was right. He had to stop this. Regardless of how attracted he was to her, of how much he admired her strength and determination, a relationship with her was out of the question. Even if he would allow himself to get that close to her in the current circumstances, she was the daughter of a marquis. It was doubtful her father would ever approve of a man of Connor's background as a suitable match for his daughter.

No, she wasn't for him. And maybe if he repeated that mantra often enough, he would finally come to believe it.

"Mr. Monroe? Where was Mr. Ledbetter's body when he was discovered?" Jillian asked, all business as she called his attention back to her.

Grateful for the chance to give himself something else to focus on, Connor moved to stand at the foot of Hiram's bed, nodding toward the floor. "He was there, crumpled in a heap." His stomach twisted at the mental image that filled his vision, but he forced himself past the pain and continued. "He'd been beaten in the head several times with some sort of blunt object. A walking stick or a cudgel."

"And his watch was missing." Jillian wandered over to join him and surveyed the area on the floor that Connor had indicated. There was a faint, rust-colored stain on the planks, but other than that, nothing betrayed that a body had once lain there. "Nothing else was gone?"

"No. But this time there *were* clues that someone had forced his way into the cottage." Connor jerked his head in the direction of the back door. "The latch was broken and the room looked as if it had been ransacked."

Jillian glanced about. "It doesn't make any sense," she repeated her earlier words, her voice rife with frustration. "Three people dead at the hands of the same killer, yet each of the scenarios are so different. It doesn't fit. Unless . . ."

"Unless?" Connor prompted with impatience when her words dwindled away to nothing.

"Unless he is deliberately varying his methods."

"Why would he do that?"

"I'm only guessing, but I would assume it's because he doesn't want Bow Street to draw any link at all between these cases. He leaves just enough evidence behind so *you* will be aware that the same man is committing these crimes, but not enough that the law will take you seriously should you decide to try and go to them with it."

Connor's jaw tightened in impotent fury. "It's another way of getting at me."

"I'm afraid so." Hands going to her hips, Jillian moved away a few paces, her mouth turned downward in a frown. "However, if the same man is responsible for Mr. Ledbetter's death— and I am just as certain as you that he is—then he would want you to know that he did this. He would have left something behind as he did before. Yet I've been over every inch of this cottage, and unless I'm overlooking it somehow, there's nothing here. No messages behind the mirror this time. Nothing."

She paused for a moment, then turned to face Connor. "There is nothing here that looks out of place to you? That just seems wrong somehow? Like the unlocked door of your town house the night of Mrs. Ridley's death?"

"No. Nothing obvious, at any rate."

"Then I don't understand. I— What's that?"

Surprised by Jillian's rather abrupt question, right in the middle of a sentence, Connor eyed her curiously. But after a second, he too became aware of the same faint noise she had apparently already heard.

It came from outside. A muffled rustling, as if someone were moving stealthily up the back steps from the alleyway that ran along behind the row of dilapidated cottages.

Connor felt a sudden burst of adrenaline rush through his veins. Ever since Jillian had pointed out yesterday that the killer could be following him, he had tried to remain on his guard, keeping a sharp eye out and staying alert to his surroundings at all times. He had noticed nothing out of the ordinary so far, but that didn't mean it wasn't possible that someone had managed to escape his detection and trail them here.

Dear God, but he would never forgive himself if something were to happen to this woman while she was in his care. He knew he should never have given in to her blackmail yesterday, but he hadn't doubted that she would do exactly as she had threatened and continue investigating without him. He had convinced himself that it was better if she were with him, where he could keep an eye on her, rather than having to worry that she was haring about the city on her own at all hours of the day and night.

But it just might turn out that at his side was the most dangerous place she could be.

Determined to steal a march on whoever it was before they could strike, Connor pressed a finger to his lips to indicate to Jillian that she should remain quiet and stay where she was. Then he started to move toward the back door with slow, cautious steps, taking great care to keep his boots from making any sound on the planked floor.

His hand closed around the knob, and he was grateful that no telltale squeak or groan gave him away as he turned it and eased the wooden panel open the slightest bit. Through the crack, he could peer out into the debris-scattered alley, but it was much too shadowed and dim to see anything clearly. The day that had started out so brightly had become quite overcast, the sun having long ago disappeared behind a bank of threatening gray clouds, lending the already dismal landscape an almost menacing atmosphere.

All was still, and Connor was just beginning

to think what they'd heard had been nothing more than a rat nosing through the refuse that littered the ground around the cottage, when he caught a vague flash of movement out of the corner of his eye.

There was definitely someone out there.

Hoping for the element of surprise, he threw the door wide and stepped out onto the stoop.

And nearly tripped over the form that huddled there.

"What the—" The figure lurched unsteadily to its feet with a startled yelp, and Connor instantly recognized the tall, spare frame, the bulbous nose, and reddened eyes that glared up at him in disgruntlement.

"Patchett? What the bloody hell are you doing?"

Wincing at Connor's less than dulcet tone, Elmer Patchett reached up to rub at his ear with a shaky hand as he collapsed back onto the steps. "You don't 'ave to yell, guv'na. I ain't 'urtin' nothin'. I just felt a mite peaked, and seeing as 'ow the old codger kicked the bucket and all, I didn't think anyone would mind if I rested 'ere for a while."

"You mean if you *hid* here for a while." The strong scent of liquor and the stench of the alley mixed with the odor of fish that drifted from the nearby river, making for a practically overpowering aroma that had Connor stifling the urge to gag. "You just didn't want to go home and face Bessie in your current condition. Sweet Christ,

Patchett, I'd give you a few sovereigns, but you'd probably waste it on more drink when you're already too soused to stand up."

"There's nothing wrong with a man enjoying a drink or two to 'elp settle 'is nerves."

"I'll wager it was more than a drink or two. And there *is* something wrong when it's only just gone past noon and you already smell like a bloody distillery."

"What's going on out here?"

Jillian's voice coming from so close behind him caused Connor to start, and he looked back over his shoulder to find her standing in the open doorway of the cottage.

"I thought I told you to wait inside."

"Don't be ridiculous." She brushed past him out onto the stoop. "You obviously know this man, and if he posed any danger you'd already be on the way to Bow Street with him." Her gaze bounced back and forth between him and Patchett, her eyes alight with inquisitiveness behind the lenses of her spectacles. "Aren't you going to introduce me?"

Connor exhaled a weary gust of air and managed to refrain from pointing out to her that just the day before she had promised to follow his orders to the letter. He was certainly in no mood to argue with her right now. "Lady Jillian Daventry, this is Mr. Elmer Patchett. He and his wife live a few cottages down and looked in on Hiram for me from time to time." He sent the older man a meaningful glower. "And he was just leaving."

Patchett pushed himself to his feet, as if he were going to do exactly that. But instead of turning and walking away, he stood there, swaying a little as he stared at Jillian, and an expression of wonderment settled over his flushed features. "Cor! 'E said a real lady would be coming 'ere, but I thought I was just dreaming."

Connor frowned. Someone had told the man that Jillian would be at Hiram's cottage? For some reason, he didn't like the sound of that. He hadn't mentioned he would be bringing her here today to anyone except Tolliver. "What did you say?"

"You 'eard me."

"Damn it, man, this is no time for your drunken gibberish!"

Connor started to reach out and seize Patchett by the arm, planning on shaking it out of him if necessary. But Jillian intervened, stepping in front of him and giving him a beseeching look through a veil of lashes. "Connor, wait. Let me try."

She didn't wait for his assent, but turned to the other man and spoke in a low, soothing tone. "Please, Mr. Patchett. You'll have to forgive Mr. Monroe if he seems a bit impatient, but you must understand this is very important. You said someone told you I'd be here. Who?"

Patchett shrugged in reply. "Don't know. Couldn't see 'is face. It was too dark. I was takin' a little nap 'ere on the old codger's stoop last night, when some bloke suddenly looms up and shoves 'is boot in me side. I was ready to tear 'is bleedin' foot off, I was, until 'e said 'e had a job for me to do."

"A job?" Jillian prompted.

"Yes. 'E said 'e wanted me to deliver a message." Patchett scratched the bridge of his nose with one filthy finger, then glanced over at Connor. "Said you and some hoity-toity dark-'aired lady would show up 'ere today, asking questions, and I was to wait for you and tell you . . . tell you . . ."

When the man's voice trailed away and he stared off into space, blinking as if he'd lost track of the conversation, Connor took a threatening step forward.

"Damn it, Patchett!" he roared. "Tell me what?"

"Give me a bloody minute, Monroe. It's a bit blurry, and 'e said as 'ow I 'ad to say it exactly the way 'e told me." Patchett scrunched his florid features into a mask of concentration. " 'E said, 'Tell Connor me boyo and 'is little doxy that it's only just begun.' Yep, that was it."

Connor felt as if someone had punched him as hard as they could in his chest, for all of the air seemed to seize in his lungs and he suddenly found that drawing a breath was a near Herculean task.

Could it be . . . ?

Oblivious to the shock that held him paralyzed, Jillian faced him with a satisfied air. "Well, it seems I was right. It looks like the killer left you a message after all."

Yes, and it revealed far more than she could even guess.

Connor me boyo.

Only one man had ever called him that, and it was a man who had every reason in his sick, twisted mind to hate Connor and hold him responsible for all of his misfortune. A man Connor had been certain was living out his years in a darkened cell in Newgate prison, never to see the light of day again.

His stepfather. Ian Trask.

Chapter 12

Sometimes in order to solve a mystery, one must go back to the very beginning.

Once they had managed to send a less-than-steady-on-his-feet Elmer Patchett on his way and had returned to their original task of searching Hiram Ledbetter's home, it didn't take Jillian long to notice that Connor had become strangely silent.

With a mixture of puzzlement and anxiety, she watched him as he paced back and forth within the confines of the cottage, his countenance closed off and brooding, before finally coming to a stop in front of the only window. His thoughts were clearly far from pleasant.

How she wished he would confide in her. Never mind her resolve to maintain her distance from him. She couldn't possibly keep such a resolution when he looked so very alone. But Connor Monroe wasn't the sort to reveal any deep, dark secrets about himself, no matter how much he was hurting. And she knew he *had* to be hurting. He had just received proof that what he had suspected all along was true.

The taunting letters. The murders. The messages left behind at the crime scenes. It was all part of some sadistic and deadly revenge plot aimed at *him*.

Feeling a need to see if she could draw him out, Jillian took an uncertain step toward him and cleared her throat before breaking the silence. "Well, now that we've definitely established that these cases are linked, at least in our own minds, perhaps we can put our heads together and come up with some idea as to where this man plans to strike next."

Connor didn't answer, merely continued to stare out the dirt-smeared glass at the alleyway beyond.

Refusing to give in so easily, she tried again. "Mr. Monroe? Are you listening?"

One corner of his mouth slanted upward at a wry angle and he glanced over at her. "Yes, of course. I was just . . . thinking."

"Is there anyone else you've helped over the years? Anyone you've aided in the same way you did Mrs. Ridley and Mr. Ledbetter?"

"A few, but no one I've maintained contact with or that I was as close to as Peg and Hiram."

"Then it's not beyond the realm of possibility

that the killer could decide to come after you next."

A chilling intent settled over Connor's features, and his eyes glittered with a menacing light that had the nape of Jillian's neck prickling with foreboding. "Let him come. I look forward to it."

That was exactly what she was afraid of.

"With Tolliver's help," she ventured, "we might be able to set up some sort of trap. We could—"

"We?" He cut her off, contemplating her with cool detachment. "My lady, as far as I'm concerned, your part in this investigation is finished."

Jillian froze. What was this? Surely she couldn't have heard him correctly? "Finished? What do you mean?"

"Precisely what I said."

"But you agreed—"

"I agreed to bring you with me to Hiram's cottage and I have done that. I fulfilled my side of the bargain, and now it's time for you to follow through with your side of it."

"My side?"

"To obey my orders without question."

Frantic now, Jillian sifted through her options, trying to come up with some way to make Connor change his mind. She'd been so certain they had settled this, but apparently he had thought better of it.

Why?

She couldn't allow him to cut her off, to shut

her out like this. This case was her only connection to Forbes. And if she were honest with herself, she would admit that she was coming to care about what happened to this proud, stubborn man. She couldn't stand the thought of walking away from him when it was within her power to help him.

Crossing her arms, she glared at Connor. "I won't let you do this, you know. I meant what I said yesterday. I *will* keep investigating. On my own if I have to."

He lifted a broad shoulder in a negligent motion. "And in that case, I shall feel compelled to report your activities to your father."

Jillian's breath escaped her on an outraged gust of air. "You wouldn't dare!"

Something shifted in Connor's expression. Something that might have been remorse. But not a hint of it betrayed itself in his curt manner when he replied. "I assure you, I would."

Dear Lord, if he did that, Papa would never permit her to continue with her work. She would have to give up any hope of ever discovering what had really happened to her mother.

"I thought that you had come to believe in me and my abilities, that I had proved myself to you." Despite her determination not to let him see how much his edict had wounded her, her voice shook. "Obviously nothing I've done for you in the past couple of days makes any difference at all."

Her accusation seemed to finally succeed in

cracking Connor's shield of icy reserve, for his mouth tightened into a thin line and he spun away from the window to stalk toward her, closing the space between them until he was right on top of her. He seized her by the shoulders with an unexpectedness that was startling. "Of course it makes a difference! But did you hear what Patchett said? The killer deliberately made mention of you. What do you think that means?" He gave her a little shake, causing several strands of her hair to come loose from her chignon. "Use that quick brain of yours and put two and two together. It means he's added another name to his list of potential victims."

Warmth flooded over Jillian. Though his tactics might be a bit high-handed, there could be no denying that he was truly worried. His concern was there to see, lurking in his eyes, and it touched her in ways she didn't want to examine too closely. "Is that what this is about? Mr. Monroe, I told you before that I have every faith that you can protect me should anything happen. I—"

"And I told you not to be so certain of that. Anytime anyone has counted on me to protect them in the past, I've let them down."

"I don't believe that."

"You should. It's the truth."

Unable to ignore a tug of sympathy at the bitterness in his voice, Jillian touched his forearm, a fleeting caress meant to soothe. Instead, it sent a jolt of awareness zinging through her.

Shoving aside the reaction, she plunged onward. "Please. I wish you would tell me why you feel that way."

Connor gave the slender fingers resting on his coat sleeve an unreadable look before releasing her. "It's not a pretty tale, my lady. I doubt you'd want to hear it."

"I wouldn't have asked if I didn't." Obviously, this was something that had been weighing on him for quite some time, and she had learned from experience that sometimes sharing a burden could make it that much lighter to carry. "You can tell me."

He studied her with particular intensity for what seemed like a small eternity. And just when she was certain he wasn't going to answer her, he expelled a soft gust of air and tore his gaze away to stare down at the floor.

"When I said that I didn't precisely have the best of childhoods, that was a bit of an understatement," he told her. His tone was low and grating, almost as if the words were being dragged from him against his will. "My father died when my brother and I were both infants, and by the time I was nine years old my mother had married a tavernkeeper by the name of Ian Trask. He turned out to be a cruel and vicious man who thought nothing of beating his new wife to the point of unconsciousness simply because she had the effrontery to let his dinner get cold. Or of lashing his stepsons until they bled if they were too slow in doing their chores to suit him."

Jillian had to stifle a soft gasp of dismay. Now that Connor was being so forthcoming, she didn't want to interrupt and perhaps remind him that he had no desire to share this with her.

But to her relief, he didn't appear to hear her. The expression on his face was far away, as if he were focused on something in the distance. Something that only he could see. "He made our lives a living hell, and it didn't take long for him to completely cow my mother into a state of utter submission. I can't tell you how many times I pleaded with her to take me and my brother and run, but she was too terrified of him to ever attempt it. Sometimes I think he even had her believing that she didn't deserve any better."

A lump clogged Jillian's throat as she pictured the little boy Connor must have once been, so young and defenseless in the face of his stepfather's tyranny, and she had to swallow several times before she managed to speak past the obstruction.

"I'm so sorry, Connor." His name escaped her on a whisper before she could call it back, but she didn't let herself dwell overlong on the slip. Somehow, the intimacy of it seemed appropriate in the circumstances. "So very sorry."

"That was just the beginning. A year after they wed, I discovered quite by accident that Trask was a criminal as well as an abusive bastard. I walked in on him one afternoon while he was meeting with a few of his compatriots in the back room of the tavern and overheard them discussing a recent robbery they had committed."

"What did you do?"

"What *could* I do? I tried to warn my mother, but it did little good. And when Trask found out, he was livid. I think I got the worst thrashing I'd ever had in my life that day. And after that, things only got worse. He deliberately looked for reasons to tear a strip off me. In fact, he took particular enjoyment in it."

"My God, he must have been a monster!"

Connor shrugged at Jillian's exclamation, but the muscle that flexed in his jaw let her know that he wasn't as unaffected by the tale he was relating as he might appear. "It wasn't as if I hadn't suffered through beatings before. But he soon came to the realization that it hurt me far more whenever he tormented my brother, and he used that as a weapon against me. Brennan had always been the quieter of the two of us, the weaker one, the one less capable of standing up for himself, and more often than not I wound up having to do it for him."

A sudden tension seemed to grip his already rigid frame, and his big hands tightened into white-knuckled fists at his sides. "One evening, when I was about thirteen, I came home from wandering the docks to find Brennan cowering in a corner of our room. He was cut and bruised and babbling incoherently. It took forever to finally get him to tell me what had happened, and when he did—God, I don't think I had ever wanted to kill someone so much in my life!"

He met Jillian's eyes, and the anguish in those aqua depths nearly undid her. "That was the day I found out that Trask was into a bit of flesh peddling, as well. He sold my brother to a bloody catamite for some afternoon sport!"

One hand flying to her mouth to hold back a horrified cry, Jillian felt her stomach lurch at the pure evil of the man who had been Connor's stepfather. Dear God, but how had he survived living with such a person?

"I tried to tell my mother what happened," he went on, a muscle working in his jaw, "but she just turned a deaf ear. Something in me died after that, I think. It was the moment I realized we truly meant nothing to her anymore. So that night I packed up our things, and Brennan and I left."

He fell silent, and Jillian hesitated, longing to comfort him in some way, but not quite sure how. She licked her dry lips and spoke carefully, mindful of the sensitive territory she was treading in. "Connor, what happened to you and your brother was awful. But it wasn't your fault. Your mother was the adult in that situation, and it was *her* job to protect *you*. Not the other way around. You couldn't—"

He interrupted her, his tone sharp, abrupt. "You don't understand. That's not the end of the story. My failure in that regard was bad enough. But what came later—"

When he choked to a halt, seemingly unable

to finish the sentence, Jillian couldn't keep from touching him for another second. Reaching out, she caught one of his fisted hands between both of her own. After removing her gloves earlier, she had never bothered to put them back on, and the feel of his warm skin beneath her palms was vaguely disconcerting, but she once again ignored her tingling nerve endings and prodded him to go on. "Tell me."

Connor raked his free hand back through his hair in a rough gesture. "Like I told you before, we lived on the streets for quite a few years. And after what happened to him that day, Brennan changed. He became hard, sullen, and he put up a wall between us that I couldn't seem to penetrate, no matter how hard I tried." His visage darkened. "I thought after Peg took us in and Stuart took us under his wing that things would get better. But they didn't. Brennan wouldn't let down his guard. He wanted nothing to do with the shipping business, and he seemed to resent my relationship with Stuart."

"And?"

"And I couldn't understand it. Stuart treated us both like sons, but Brennan resisted every effort he made to reach out to him. While I was eager to learn everything I could about Grayson Shipping and spent most of my time at the offices and the shipyard, my brother was hanging about on the streets, drifting further and further away from me with every day that passed."

Connor tugged free from Jillian's grip and

moved a short distance away, standing with his back to her, his spine poker straight and unyielding. "As we got older, Brennan started disappearing for weeks, sometimes months, at a time. I never knew where he was or what he was doing. Until one day, he just . . . never came home."

There was a long pause, and Jillian prompted him gently. "What happened?"

"I suppose I should have let him go. At that point he was well over one and twenty and free to live his own life as he saw fit. But I went looking for him. And when I found him, I couldn't believe it." Connor looked back at her over his shoulder, his firm mouth twisted into a grim caricature of a smile. "He had actually gone back to my mother and stepfather, had become a part of Trask's gang of robbers and cutthroats. And when I caught up to him and confronted him with it, he told me in no uncertain terms to mind my own business. He even bragged about some of the crimes he had committed. It was as if I didn't even know him anymore."

He shook his head. "By the time I left him, I was stunned, desperate to come up with some way to get through to him. And in my disillusionment and anger, I made a decision I later regretted."

Jillian could guess what was coming. The look of torment and guilt that suffused Connor's features told her more than words could. Yet she still held her breath as the rest of the story spilled out of him.

"I paid a visit to Bow Street. I don't know what I was thinking. Maybe that if I got Trask thrown into Newgate, it would somehow loosen his grip on my brother. I thought that Stuart and I could swoop in and warn Brennan, get him out of the way before the law showed up."

He faced away from her again, shutting her out, and when he showed no signs of continuing, Jillian hurried forward. Moving around to stand in front of him, she looked up at him, holding his gaze with hers. She wouldn't let him retreat from her. Not now. "Tell me, Connor. Get it out in the open and maybe it will finally stop torturing you."

"I doubt that." Pain and self-recrimination marked his battered features. "I betrayed my brother, Jillian, and by the time I got smart enough to question the wisdom of my actions, it was too late. Stuart and I arrived at the tavern just as Bow Street descended on them, and the fools didn't go quietly. They fought back, and Brennan was in the thick of things."

His voice became gruff, hoarse with suppressed emotion. "He had a pistol, and when he grappled with one of the Runners, it went off and shot him in the chest. The force of it knocked him off the edge of the dock and his body wound up in the Thames. Unrecoverable. I don't even have a grave to mourn over."

Jillian's own eyes filled with tears, her heart aching for him. "What about Trask and your mother?"

"The last I heard, Trask was living out the rest of his misbegotten life in Newgate. My mother died soon after, and I never shed a tear. Why should I care? She certainly never cared about us."

Despite the coldness of his words, Jillian suspected that Connor had been far more affected by his mother's passing than he would ever let on. She might have turned her back on him, but this man was far too good to ever truly turn his back completely on the woman who had borne him.

"After that, I threw myself into Grayson Shipping. I had to focus on something in order to make it through the days. And a year later, when I turned five and twenty, I accepted a full partnership in the business from Stuart. But I knew I didn't deserve it. My brother was dead and it was all my fault."

Incensed that he would shoulder the blame for all that had happened to Brennan, Jillian grabbed his arm, her nails digging into the material of his shirt. "No, Connor."

"Yes! I fail the people I care about, Jillian. Don't you see? Hiram, Peg, Stuart. And I failed Brennan most of all. The one person in this world I loved without reservation. I let him down not once, but twice. Is that really the sort of man you want to be around?"

Once again, he tried to yank away from her,

but she clung, determined to make him see how wrong he was. "You listen to me, Connor Monroe! You did the best you could, and I admire you more than anyone else I have ever met. Tolliver told me you were a good man, and I realize now that he was right. And there is no one—*no one*—I would trust more with my life."

He scowled down at her, his eyes blazing with a fierceness that filled her with sudden trepidation, even as it fanned the flames of the fiery emotions that she had been struggling to hold at bay for most of the day. "You stubborn little fool!"

And the next thing she knew, she was in his arms, and he was kissing her with a wild and irresistible passion.

Chapter 13

An effective investigator is one who knows how to separate his heart from his mind.

Connor realized the instant his arms closed around Jillian that he had made a mistake. *Damnation!* was all he had time to think as his mouth seized hers. He had promised himself—and Jillian—that he wouldn't let this happen again. But the feel of her sumptuous curves pressed against him was enough to rob him of every last one of his senses, not to mention all of his good intentions.

So much for promises.

Smoothing his hands up the slope of her back, he pulled her even closer, aware of a fierce sense of satisfaction when she melted into his embrace with nary a protest, her own arms lifting to wind around his neck. Her soft, sensuous lips parted under his, as delectable as he remembered, and he conducted a thorough and leisurely exploration of their silken surfaces before nipping them gently with his teeth, urging her to open them even wider.

She did so without hesitation, inviting him into the warm cavern of her mouth with a low moan, and he took the opportunity to deepen the kiss, plunging his tongue inside to meet and entwine with hers over and over in a sinuous dance.

By the time he finally managed to tear himself away from her long enough to suck in a lungful of air, they were both flushed and panting. Jillian's spectacles had been knocked askew, and her eyes were wide and unfocused behind their lenses. Tendrils of her ebony hair had come loose from their pins to cling damply to her forehead and the sides of her face.

Despite the desire that was coursing through him, Connor couldn't contain an amused grin at her rumpled appearance and dazed expression. He lifted a hand to snag her spectacles by an earpiece, plucking them off the end of her nose and tossing them onto a nearby table with a swift economy of motion that had her blinking in bemusement.

"I don't think we need those, do you?" he whispered next to her ear, sliding that same hand into her hair to remove the remaining pins, letting them drop to the wooden planks of the floor one by one. The mass of midnight curls tumbled about her shoulders, and he buried his nose in them, inhaling the intoxicating scent of jasmine that permeated the shining strands close to her temple.

"Somewhere underneath all that prim starch," he murmured, "is the gypsy witch I met that first night. I've been wondering what it would take to strip you out of this bloody old-maid disguise and bring her out of hiding. And before I'm through, I plan on doing exactly that."

It was a statement of unequivocal intent, but he didn't give Jillian long to contemplate it. Instead, he leaned over to nuzzle the delicate shell of her ear, then skimmed his lips down the side of her throat, leaving a moist trail in his wake. She obediently tilted her head back to give him better access, and he rewarded her by taking a tiny nibble of the pulse that beat just above her high collar, wringing a shiver from her.

Forcing his mouth from the perfection of her flesh, Connor straightened and surveyed her slumberous features. Her lids had fallen to half-mast, and her amber eyes glowed up at him like molten gold from underneath the veil of her lashes. Her lips were bruised and kiss-swollen, their glistening contours practically begging him to capture them once more. The erotic sight had his manhood stirring to throbbing life, reacting with wholehearted approval.

"I want to see all of you." His voice was raw with need as he wrapped his arm more tightly about her waist, and his other hand slid from her hair, going to the buttons at the front of her gown. "I want to see the woman you are underneath all of this. Every luscious inch."

A hesitant look crossed Jillian's face, but before she had time for more than a fleeting second of doubt, he had slipped the first few buttons free from their holes, halting any objection she might have made. The plum-colored muslin parted, revealing the white linen of her chemise and the stiff fabric of her corset.

Connor took in the wanton picture she made. With her cheeks stained a becoming shade of pink, her blue-black curls spilling around her, and the mounds of her full breasts rising and falling with each of her ragged breaths, pressed upward by whalebone stays, she possessed an exotic beauty that made his mouth water. She looked like a seductive goddess sent to earth to tempt him.

Or the gypsy witch he had likened her to before. A gypsy witch who had long ago cast her spell on him, dooming him to never again be the same man he once was.

Cupping one plump breast in his hand, he reveled in its satiny texture, in the lush, firm weight filling his palm as he ran his tongue over the high, rounded curve where it swelled above the lace edge of her chemise. The succulent flavor of her skin was a potent and addictive aphrodisiac. One he was far from immune to.

"God, you taste so bloody sweet," he rasped. "Like warm honey drizzled over my tongue. I could feast on these beauties for weeks and never get my fill."

His harsh growl drew a muffled gasp from her, and she arched her back, thrusting her breast even farther into his grasp. The mauve shadow of her nipple was just visible through the sheerness of the linen that covered it, and it tightened under his lustful gaze and the teasing stroke of his thumb until it stood at rigid attention against the material, diamond-hard and quivering.

A film of sweat coated his brow. Sweet Christ, but he wanted to take that taut little nub into his mouth, to lick and lave it with his tongue, to suckle it until it was ripe and rosy and tender from his ministrations and she was sobbing out her pleasure in his arms.

It was an enticement he couldn't resist.

He bent his head, fastened his lips around the distended peak, and sucked it into the scalding heat of his mouth, chemise and all.

At his unexpected action, Jillian let out a keening cry, her fingernails digging into his broad shoulders, and Connor couldn't help wondering if that was the sound she would make when he was moving deep inside her, pumping in and out of her slick feminine channel. When he increased the suction on her nipple in response to the carnal image, her hips bucked, then rocked against him, bringing his already aroused maleness to nestle within the juncture of her thighs.

Exactly where he belonged.

Connor groaned low in his throat, releasing

her breast as she moved against the hard, aching length of him in a restless rhythm. His hand at her waist glided downward to cup the twin spheres of her bottom, holding her against him in just the right spot so that the delicious friction would continue.

"That's right, Gypsy," he encouraged her, guiding her movements with deft hands. "Rub your sweet little honey pot right there. That feels so good."

God, if he weren't careful, he would be coming in his breeches before he ever had her beneath him. And that wouldn't do at all.

"Connor."

The sound of his name was barely audible, and he turned his attention back to Jillian's face to find her staring up at him with a longing that had his heart giving a strange little leap in his chest.

It struck him most profoundly in that moment that this woman wasn't at all like any of the other females he'd met or bedded over the years. She affected him in ways no one else ever had, and his ardor for her was above and beyond anything he had ever felt in his life. He yearned to see her under him, naked and wanting, as desperate for him as he was for her.

But most of all, he wanted to sink himself into her creamy velvet depths, wanted to hear her scream out his name in ecstasy at the culmination of their loving.

A violent craving washed over him. One of

such strength and intensity that it was almost painful.

"I want you, Gypsy, and if I don't get inside you right now I'm going to go bloody mad."

The words escaped him before he could call them back, rough and grating, and he felt Jillian go ominously still in his arms. Tension seeped into his large frame, and he waited with bated breath for her reaction.

Just when he was certain she was going to push him away from her, she moved her hands from his shoulders to cup his face, her eyes meeting his with utter assuredness.

"I want you, too."

Thank God! Connor didn't think his tortured libido could have withstood a refusal.

With fingers that were amazingly dexterous, despite the fact that he quaked on the inside, he undid the rest of her buttons and pushed her gown and petticoats down past her ample hips until they pooled around her ankles. He also somehow managed to work loose the lacings on her corset, and it joined her other garments on the floor. Then, with one easy motion, he swept her into his arms and carried her toward the bed.

Jillian felt her world tilt off balance as Connor lifted her off her feet and bore her toward the bed in the far corner of the cottage.

He truly wanted her. The mere thought set her already sensitized nerve endings tingling. The fierce pressure of his mouth on hers, the bold jut of his maleness against her abdomen, had left her in little doubt of his desire for her. And there could be no question that she wanted him. Never could she recall ever feeling passion this strong. It mattered not that there was little chance that the two of them could ever be together, that their worlds were so far apart that she didn't dare even hope for such a thing.

All she knew was that she wanted this man to be the one to show her what making love was all about.

And it seemed that she was about to get her wish.

Laying her on the sagging mattress, Connor followed her down, slanting his lips across hers in another long, drugging, tongue-thrusting kiss that left her head reeling. Then, propping himself on an elbow, he trailed his smoldering gaze over her trembling form as he reached out to graze a finger over the slope of the breast he had just recently lavished with such loving attention.

"I want you naked," he murmured, his voice a silky purr. "I want to run my hands and mouth over every inch of you. To find out if your skin is this same lovely dusky shade of gold all over."

Though she struggled to contain the shiver his heated words evoked, Connor sent her a knowing half-smile, as if he knew exactly how he affected her. Then, pursing his firmly chiseled lips, he blew a humid puff of air across the moisture his mouth had left behind on the material of her chemise, molding it to the stiff peak of her all too sensitive nipple.

It sent goose bumps rippling across the surface of her flesh, but when he hooked his thumb under the lacy strap of the undergarment and started to peel it slowly down her arm, she reached up and caught his wrist, bringing him to a halt.

He looked down at her questioningly.

She wasn't sure how she managed to speak with any sort of coherency when her brain was so muddled that her thoughts barely made sense, but somehow she got the words out in spite of the clumsy thickness of her tongue.

"I want to see you, too, Connor. Please?"

One of his eyebrows arched upward as he regarded her for several ticks of the clock on the other side of the room. Then, taking her hand in his, he sat up and brought it to his chest in a blatant invitation. "Then take my clothes off, Gypsy. I dare you."

Jillian's heart fluttered. His big body had fascinated her from their very first meeting, and she needed no further urging to look upon what she had been furtively admiring for days. Connor had undone the buttons of his coat when they had first arrived at the cottage, and all she had to do was shove it off his shoulders. He helped her by shrugging out of it and throwing it over the back of a nearby chair. Then came his waistcoat.

She was shaking with eager anticipation by the time she got to the fastenings on his shirt.

Yet she still managed to free them and push the edges of the white lawn back, exposing a wide, heavily muscled torso with taut skin toasted to the color of burnished bronze.

She swallowed convulsively. That broad expanse of satiny flesh tempted her with the urge to stroke, to caress.

Seeming to read her mind, Connor peered down at her through eyes that had narrowed to slits, the irises appearing more green than blue in the dim light of the cottage. "Go ahead, Gypsy. Touch me. You have no idea how much I want to feel your hands on me."

She complied, taking an unspoken delight in the way his breath hissed through his teeth as she traced the powerful muscles in his sculpted chest, savoring the way they rippled and flexed under her tentative fingertips. Hair a shade darker than that on his head dusted his steel-hard pectorals, and she could feel the beat of his heart, steady and reassuring, beneath her palms.

He was so strong . . .

So absorbed was she in her examination of him, that she didn't notice that Connor had finished easing down the strap of her chemise until his hand once again closed over her breast.

Her bare breast.

This time there was no cloth barrier between them to blunt the effects of his touch. When he rolled her puckered nipple between his callused thumb and forefinger, she felt the jolt of it all the way to her toes.

And when he lowered himself over her and seized that eager, pouting crest in his mouth, suckling voraciously, a mewling cry escaped her. It was almost more than she could bear. Each sharp, hungry tug of his lips, each swirl and flicker of his tongue, set off a corresponding ache in the soft, secret place between her thighs that had her lower body surging upward in an attempt to appease it.

"Easy, sweetheart." Connor's hand glided downward from her breast to smooth across the quivering muscles of her belly in a gentle massaging motion that should have been soothing, but instead only seemed to increase the restlessness that wracked her. "I know you want it, and I'm going to give it to you. I promise. I'm going to make you feel so good, but I have to know you're wet for me."

He positioned himself between her legs so that the thick, rounded head of his phallus nudged the inside of her thigh in a tantalizing fashion, then moved his palm even lower to locate the slit in her drawers. Sifting through the nest of curls that guarded her feminine mound, he separated her damp folds with expert precision and inserted his finger little by little into that tight, pulsating channel that had never before known a man's touch. The sensation of fullness, the brush of his thumb against the swollen nub of her clitoris, had Jillian biting her lip and tossing her head on the pillow. And when her hips jerked against him, her inner juices rushing forth to coat his finger and the walls of her passage clenching as if to draw him deeper, he shot her a look of pure male arrogance.

"Sweet Christ, but you're hot and dripping and creamy, Gypsy. All for me." He leaned in closer to her, as if wanting to impart something of utmost importance. "Do you know how badly I want to put my tongue in you? I want to taste your spice and make you come over and over until you beg me to stop."

Jillian shuddered, his deliciously wicked confession inspiring her to share one, as well. "I'll never want you to stop, Connor. I want to feel you inside me. All of you. As deep inside me as you can possibly get."

Her admission tore a ragged groan from him, and he rested his forehead against hers for a brief moment. "I don't deserve this, you know. Or you."

She could tell by the suddenly pained and uncertain look on his face and the husky note in his voice that he sincerely believed what he was saying, and she knew that she couldn't let things go any further without convincing him how wrong he was.

Reaching up, she cupped his face in her hands. "Yes you do. You're a good man, Connor." She paused as his bitter self-recriminations from their conversation earlier echoed in her ears, then lifted her head to press a kiss to his beard-stubbled chin. "And no matter what you believe, you do not deserve the torment this depraved monster has delivered upon you. I promise we'll catch him and he won't have a chance to harm anyone else."

She'd meant to offer him a bit of comfort, but it seemed her reassurances did exactly the opposite, for Connor froze, and there was an instant of chilling silence. Then, his visage darkening, he jerked his hand from between her legs and sat up, levering himself off the bed with a stifled curse.

Stunned by the abruptness of his withdrawal, Jillian was left floundering, cold and bereft without the warmth of his body covering her. Tugging up the strap of her chemise to conceal her naked breast, she wrapped her arms about herself and stared after him in bewilderment. "Connor, what is it? What's wrong?"

His back rigid, he barely spared her a glance over his shoulder as he quickly fastened the buttons of his shirt and reached for his waistcoat draped across the foot of the bed. "I owe you an apology, my lady. Please forgive me."

"For?"

"Putting my hands on you in such a way. I never should have let things go so far."

Jillian pushed herself to a sitting position, raking her tumbled curls back off her face. She didn't understand. Here she was, still tingling and breathless from their encounter, and he was behaving as if it hadn't affected him in the slightest. How could he go from kissing and touching her as if he couldn't get enough to being so blasted remote? "But I wanted your hands on me, Connor. Why—"

He interrupted her by finally whipping about to face her, his eyes blazing from under lowered brows. "Damn it, Gypsy, can't you see it was a mistake?"

A mistake? A welter of emotions overwhelmed her at his words: hurt, anger, shame, confusion. But there was no time to sort them all out, because he was still speaking, his tone clipped and reserved. "God, I touch you and all I can think about is . . . well, I suppose that's obvious. And this only shows me how right I was about the two of us working together on this case."

Jillian went cold all over. No. Surely he wouldn't. Not after everything that had happened.

But his next sentence proved that he would. "Our association is now officially at an end, Lady Jillian."

She opened her mouth to protest, but he held up a hand before she could even find her voice. "And you can save your breath. I never should have let you blackmail me into changing my mind yesterday. It would have saved us both some embarrassment."

"Embarrassment" didn't even begin to sum up the pain and humiliation Jillian was feeling. But she could tell by the determination that suffused his features that it would be useless to argue. He would not relent.

Not this time.

He retrieved his coat from the chair next to

the bed, looking more distant and unapproach-able than he had since the first night they'd met. "I'm sorry, but you must see this is for the best. I refuse to jeopardize your life any further."

When he met her gaze again, something shifted in his eyes, but it was gone before she could be certain of what it was. "You should get dressed. I'll wait for you in the hackney."

With that, he departed the cottage, shutting the door softly behind him.

Chapter 14

～◦◦◦～

The first conclusion is not always the correct
one.

Connor dragged his weary body up the wide
stone steps of his town house and let him
self into the darkened foyer. It was just before
dawn, though its light hadn't yet touched the
horizon, and the silence echoed almost oppres-
sively around him.

It had been almost forty-eight hours since he
had let Lady Jillian Daventry out of their hired
hackney and left her standing on the steps in
front of the Dowager Duchess of Maitland's residence, looking lost and forlorn. In that time, he
had done his best to try and wipe what had
passed between them at Hiram's cottage from
his memory. But he was finding that doing so
was damn near impossible.

He could still hear her soft moans of pleasure in his ears, feel the silk of her skin under his fingertips, taste the honey of her lips and the berry sweetness of her nipples.

And picture the look on her face when he had insisted that kissing her, touching her, had been a mistake.

With a gusty exhalation of air, he tossed his hat and gloves on the hallway table and reached up to comb an errant wave of hair back off his forehead. He knew he had hurt her with his pretended indifference, and he hated that fact. But there could be no denying that he'd done the right thing in pushing her away. Making love to her, especially with the situation as it was, would have only complicated things for both of them.

Not to mention that if he was right about the identity of the murderer he was seeking, then it would be for the best if Jillian stayed as far away from him as possible.

As Connor started down the corridor toward his study, Elmer Patchett's words replayed themselves in his mind.

Tell Connor me boyo and 'is little doxy that it's only just begun.

My God, but it was Ian Trask. It had to be. He hadn't wanted to even consider the prospect, but the killer's message sounded all too much like something his stepfather would have said. And as far as he knew, Trask was the only man of his acquaintance, past or present, who would be mad enough to set out on such an insane campaign of revenge.

Entering the study, he lit a lamp and moved to the sideboard to dash a finger of brandy into a cut-crystal snifter, tossing it back without hesitation before pouring another. He usually wasn't one to overly imbibe, especially at this time of the day, but he felt the distinct need for the sort of numbing sustenance that only strong spirits could provide.

It seemed the past had come back to haunt him with a vengeance.

Directly upon parting from Jillian two days ago, Connor had stopped by Bow Street to speak with Tolliver. Though disappointed that they would no longer be availing themselves of Lady Jillian's services, the Runner had understood once Connor had explained his suspicions and had agreed to look into the possibility that Ian Trask had somehow managed to escape his confinement at Newgate prison.

In the meantime, Connor's hands were tied. There was little more he could do with regard to the investigation except stay on his guard and wait for the other shoe to drop, and the enforced inactivity and accompanying sense of helplessness weighed heavily on him.

How long would it be before Trask—if he *was* the culprit—struck again?

Lowering himself into the padded chair behind

his massive mahogany desk, Connor leaned back and crossed his booted feet, staring moodily out through the mullioned windows as the slowly rising sun painted the sky with a rosy glow. Around him, Piccadilly and its environs were starting to awaken, the occasional horse cart clopping by in the street or household servant hurrying past on an early morning errand. But he noticed none of it. He was too engrossed in contemplating the nightmarish tangle his life had become.

And in thinking about the woman who was beginning to occupy his thoughts far more often than she should—or than he would ever admit.

Jillian.

The Grayson and Monroe Shipping employees had finally returned to work yesterday morning, and Connor had spent most of the afternoon and evening at the office, attempting to catch up with the mounds of paperwork, correspondence, and other business affairs that awaited his attention. But even there he found that the image of Jillian served as a constant distraction. Every time he closed his eyes, he could still see her splayed across the bed at the cottage, one plump, perfect breast exposed to his gaze, her thighs willingly spread for his tender exploration, her expression dazed and blissful.

His manhood stirred even now at the recollection.

By the time he had finally made his way home

just after midnight, his body had been hard and aching, restless with unspent passion, and he had tossed and turned in his bed for hours before he had come to a last-minute decision to rise, dress, and pay a call on Selene. But while his mistress had welcomed him with the same enthusiasm she always displayed, he had realized the instant she had pressed her lips against his in greeting that he never should have come.

This isn't the woman you want! his mind had protested. The figure in his arms had been slender and willowy rather than lushly curved, and the cloying fragrance of roses had filled his nostrils, instead of the more subtle, exotic blend of jasmine and spice that he had come to prefer.

It was enough to have his flesh wilting before he had even begun to remove his clothes.

He wanted no other woman but Jillian. His gypsy.

To give her credit, Selene had taken his sudden disinterest with good grace. Connor supposed she was used to such things. But as she had shown him out of the tastefully decorated flat above her dress shop, she had given him a sad little smile, fully aware that this was the last time he would visit.

"Whoever she is," she'd told him softly, "she's a very lucky woman."

Thinking back on it now, Connor shook his head, idly twirling his brandy snifter between callused fingers. Though her words were flattering, the truth was that even Selene had been too good for the likes of him. And Jillian . . . God, she was so far beyond his reach that his obsession with her was almost laughable. He *knew* that.

But then why did the fact that he could never allow himself to have her cause such a twisting, tearing feeling deep in his gut?

Draining the last of the amber liquid from his glass, he set it aside and laid his head against the cushioned back of the chair, closing his eyes in exhaustion. But Jillian continued to torment him, visions of her dancing across his mind until he released a growl of frustration.

Why would she not leave him in peace? And how had she become so important to him in such a short amount of time? Never before had he felt such a connection with a female on so many different levels. Her strength, intelligence, and stubbornness alternately intrigued and challenged him. And her understanding nature as well as her willingness to listen had tempted him to confide in her, to share things with her he had never shared with another living soul.

He had told her about Brennan, and she hadn't turned from him in disgust. Hadn't cast blame. Instead, she had reached out to him, had assured him that it wasn't his fault.

But he knew better. He *was* at fault for what had happened to his brother. Just as he was at fault for what had happened to Stuart, Peg, and Hiram. He had failed to protect them, just as he had failed to protect Brennan. And if he wasn't careful, he would soon have another name to add to the list of casualties that could be laid at his doorstep.

Jillian's.

Connor felt a muscle leap in his jaw and his hands tightened into fists on the arms of his chair. He would not let that happen. And the only way to ensure her safety was to keep her from getting any more involved with him than she already was. Trask wouldn't hesitate to strike back at him by harming Jillian if he believed for one minute that she meant something to Connor. And if anything ever happened to her because of him . . .

Sweet Christ, but he didn't think he would be able to survive it.

At that moment, the bell on the front door sounded, bringing Connor out of his musings, and he glanced at the grandfather clock in the corner to discover that it was half past six. He had been sitting here for well over an hour.

Stumped as to who could be calling on him this early, he rose to his feet and left the study, traversing the short hallway to the foyer and swinging open the door just as the bell rang again.

Two Bow Street Runners stood on his front stoop. Immediately, he recognized the taller, skinnier of the pair as Albertson, the officer in charge of the investigation into Stuart's death and the one he had been unable to convince of Wilbur Forbes's innocence before.

And it was obvious from the look on the man's pinched, rather weaselish-looking face that something had happened.

"Monroe." Albertson inclined his head in a stilted nod as he swept off his hat. "I apologize for disturbing you this early, but we've had a new development in the case that we wanted to discuss with you."

Despite the politeness of his words, there was something stiff, almost guarded about the man's demeanor. But Connor was far too focused on the officer's revelation to let himself be bothered by the manner in which it was delivered.

He stood aside, allowing the two Runners to step past him into the foyer.

"You say you've had a development?" he asked, his pulse speeding up as he mentally debated the possibilities. "What sort of development?"

It was the other Runner—a younger, obviously less seasoned officer than Albertson—who replied. "We've managed to locate Wilbur Forbes."

Connor felt a flare of hope spark to life within him. If they had Forbes in custody, surely it would only be a matter of time before the man cleared himself with the law. Once that happened, they would be forced to acknowledge that it was time to pursue other angles in the case. If Connor showed them the letters again and explained about his stepfather, he just might be able to convince them that it was worth looking into.

In spite of his growing sense of anticipation, he kept his tone calm and steady when he spoke again. "Have you questioned him yet? Did he have some sort of alibi for the night of my partner's death?"

The two Runners exchanged a pointed glance that had a sudden tingle of foreboding racing up Connor's spine and his hackles rising. Something more was going on here. But what?

Albertson turned back to face him, his gaze hooded, his expression revealing nothing. "He won't be providing us with any alibi, Monroe. He's dead."

The shock of the Runner's disclosure was like a dash of icy water over Connor's renewed confidence, chilling in its unexpectedness. "Dead?"

"That's right. Murdered. His throat slit, same as Mr. Grayson." A piercing gleam entered Albertson's narrowed eyes as he surveyed Connor. "And I'm afraid, Monroe, that I shall have to inquire as to your whereabouts last night."

"Jillian? Jillian, are you listening?"

At the sound of her aunt Olivia's strident voice, Jillian looked up from the food she'd been toying with on her plate to find her entire family studying her with varying degrees of worry and annoyance from around the breakfast table.

Oh, dear. She bit her lip as she laid down her fork and clasped her hands together in her lap, praying the linen of the tablecloth hid their white-knuckled grip. She hadn't meant to do it, but it seemed she had drifted off into her own thoughts once again and had lost all track of the conversation going on about her.

It was something that had been happening far too often since her final parting from Connor Monroe.

On the way back to Maitland House in the hired hack after what had happened between them at Hiram Ledbetter's cottage, Jillian had made every attempt to change Connor's mind about allowing her to continue her investigation, but he would not be swayed. He had refused to even consider her pleas, and by the time he had bid her farewell, she'd been both angry at his continued obstinacy and hurt by his ability to push her away, even after all they had shared.

Drat the man! His intractable nature would be the death of him, no doubt. She was well aware that he only believed he was protecting her, but that didn't alleviate any of her fury at being shut out. And though she had to admit that part of her frustration stemmed from losing her only access to Forbes, it was more than that. Somewhere along the way, aiding Connor had become just as important to her as discovering the truth about the night her mother was killed.

It would do little good to keep brooding over it, however. He had decided that he didn't want her help, and it was obvious that he would not alter his decision. She had done all that could be done at this point. After leaving Maitland House, she had returned home and penned a message to Tolliver to apprise him of the situation, and he had written back with apologies and reassurances that he would keep her informed as to any developments regarding Forbes or Connor's case.

She could only hope that the Runner would keep that promise. In the meantime, she would have to try to focus her attention on other things.

A task she was finding far from simple.

Shrugging off her melancholy mood, she turned to her aunt. "I'm sorry, Aunt Olivia. You were speaking to me? I'm afraid I was woolgathering."

The woman sniffed and raised her chin. "Obviously." Gesturing to a servant to pour her another cup of coffee from the carafe on the sideboard, she examined her eldest niece with cool severity. "You've seemed a bit preoccupied all morning. Is something troubling you?"

Jillian barely restrained a grimace. She should have known that Lady Olivia would notice her distracted mien. But just as she opened her mouth to deny there was anything wrong, she felt a slight brush against her sleeve that drew her attention to the person sitting next to her.

"Are you all right, Jilly?"

Aimee's question was soft, so tentative it was barely audible. Her amber eyes were wide with obvious alarm as she stared at her older sister, twirling the tip of one of her long, golden-brown braids around her slender finger over and over in nervous agitation.

Jillian felt her heart catch. Ever since the death of their mother, Aimee had become so very fragile, easily upset at the least sign of unrest. Taking her younger sister's hand in hers, she gave it a gentle squeeze before facing her aunt again. "I'm fine. I just have a slight headache. That's all."

"I'm sorry, dear." Her father spoke from his place at the head of the table, peering at her over the section of the London *Times* he had been perusing, his own countenance full of concern. "Perhaps I should ring for Mrs. Bellows to bring some headache powder for you."

"No, please. Don't bother Mrs. Bellows, Papa. It's only a small one, and I'm sure it will go away on its own."

"Are you quite sure? After all, the Hayworth ball is tonight and I wouldn't want you to—"

Lady Olivia interrupted her brother with a wave of her hand. "Really, Philip, you needn't coddle the girl. If she says she is fine, then I'm certain she is." She took a sip of her steaming coffee, eyeing Jillian with inscrutable reserve before going on. "I was just saying that I hoped your visit with the dowager duchess the other day was productive. Although I can't imagine what you found to talk to her about for so long. You were rather late coming home, weren't you?"

"She didn't return until well into the afternoon, Aunt Olivia."

This came from Maura, who was seated on the other side of their aunt and who had been strangely quiet up until now. Dressed in a modest frock of apricot silk with her midnight hair a tumble of artfully arranged ringlets at her temples, she looked as fresh and innocent as a fairy queen. But the smile that curved her Cupid's bow lips was far from innocent. In fact, it was rather smug, and there was a flash of bitter hostility in the depths of her blue eyes that Jillian couldn't fail to notice.

She frowned. As much as she loved her sister and longed for a return to their former closeness, there was a little devil on her shoulder urging her to catch a handful of those dusky curls and wipe the smile off that piquant face by yanking as hard as she could.

"Hmmm." The sound Lady Olivia made in response to Maura's revelation was speculative, but she didn't comment. Instead, she asked another question. "Are things well with Her Grace? I'm afraid I didn't have much chance to converse with her at the ball the other night."

"She is doing splendidly." That devil perched on Jillian's shoulder prodded at her, and this time she couldn't resist the temptation. "And Theodosia inquired after you also, Aunt Olivia. She so hopes that you are well, as she knows how age can affect one's health."

There was an instant of silence, punctuated only by a strangled giggle coming from Aimee's direction that was abruptly cut off.

Lady Olivia's face seemed to freeze into an impenetrable mask. Only the most astute observer would have noticed the slight twitch of her left eyelid, a clear indication that she was well aware that her niece was being facetious and that she was less than pleased at the impudence. "How . . . thoughtful of her."

Seemingly oblivious to the tense undercurrents sizzling through the air, the marquis finally folded his paper and laid it aside. "I do hope you expressed our appreciation to the dowager duchess for her championship of Maura this Season, Jillian. After all, she has done quite a bit for this family, and we should be suitably grateful."

He raised a brow at his sister, and Jillian stifled a laugh. Perhaps Papa wasn't quite as oblivious as he appeared.

Lady Olivia's lips thinned. "Yes, we do have much to be thankful to her for."

"You know, Jilly, I forgot to mention it, but Aunt Olivia and I went visiting the day before yesterday, as well."

Maura's sudden change in topic caught Jillian off guard, and her eyes flew to the younger girl's face. Her sister was busying herself slathering marmalade on the slice of toast she held in her hand, but there was something just beneath the surface of the deliberately casual tone with which she spoke. Something that hinted there was more behind her nonchalant statement than her manner suggested.

"Lady Elliot and her daughter, Lady Ramona, invited us over to take tea with them."

Jillian went numb all over. Oh, dear heavens! Lord and Lady Elliot lived only a few doors down from Theodosia on Park Lane. Was it possible . . . ? Could Maura have seen her leaving the house with Connor?

She waited with bated breath to be exposed.

By the time Maura lowered the knife and glanced up, Jillian's heart was beating fit to burst from her chest. But though a touch of suspicion imprinted those delicate features, there was nothing overtly threatening or accusatory in her sibling's expression. "As we were passing by in the carriage, I noticed a man climbing the front steps of Maitland House. A man I didn't recognize."

"Oh?" Lord Albright seemed more than mildly interested as he sent his eldest daughter an inquiring look. "Did the duchess have a visitor while you were there? You didn't mention that."

Jillian struggled to think of an answer that wouldn't incriminate her. Surely if Maura had witnessed something more than what she had already revealed, she would have said so. Wouldn't she? "I believe he was a business acquaintance of Theodosia's stepson. Once he found out that the duke wasn't in residence, he didn't stay long and I'm afraid I don't even recall his name."

"I see. I had hoped—" The marquis paused for a moment, then shook his head. "Well, I suppose it doesn't matter."

Jillian held back a weary sigh. She knew very well what her father had hoped for. That Theodosia had taken it upon herself to introduce her to some eligible gentleman who would suit her fancy. As if any other man could capture her interest after—

She tried to halt the thought before it could fully form, but there was no stopping it.

After Connor.

She felt her cheeks heat as she remembered the way he had touched her in Mr. Ledbetter's cottage. The way he had kissed her. The feel of his hungry mouth suckling at her nipple, of his fingers moving in the wet heat of her feminine channel, was like a burning brand in her memory, and not something she would be able to easily forget.

Her pulse pounded in her ears. God, she had to stop this before someone in her family noticed her blushes and her heightened breathing and demanded to know what was causing it. The last thing she needed was to open herself up to their conjectures.

Strangely enough, it was Lady Olivia who came to her rescue—though not at all in a way Jillian would have preferred.

Laying her napkin next to her plate, the woman craned her neck to scrutinize the grandfather clock on the far side of the room before turning her penetrating gaze on her youngest niece. "Aimee, isn't it about time for you to join your governess for your morning lessons?"

Aimee paled as those glittering blue eyes settled on her and shrank back in her seat, as if she were trying to make herself as small as possible. "Yes, Aunt Olivia," came her hesitant reply.

"Then perhaps you should do so. Now."

The sharpness of the words set Jillian's blood boiling. She had never been able to understand why she seemed to be the only one who noticed the underlying coldness in her aunt's attitude toward Aimee. While the woman was disapproving of Jillian and tolerant of Maura, she could be exceedingly harsh in her dealings with Aimee, and she had very little patience when it came to the girl's shyness and timidity.

Jillian smothered the initial impulse to take Lady Olivia to task with difficulty. Stirring up strife at the breakfast table wouldn't help her sister. Besides, she had discovered over time that the best thing to do was to remove Aimee from the situation as quickly as possible. And as she was eager to escape the dining room herself, she seized upon the opportunity with alacrity. "If you all would excuse me, I believe I shall escort Aimee upstairs to Miss Hinkle and then lie down for a bit. My headache, you know."

She barely waited for the murmured chorus of assent from the others. Hooking her arm through Aimee's, she rose and drew her sister along with her as she departed the room.

Once out in the hallway, she paused and leaned against the wall, letting her eyes fall shut as she savored the release of tension. Precisely when, she wondered, had sitting through a family meal become such an arduous chore?

"Are you really all right, Jilly?"

At Aimee's query, she blinked and looked

down at the girl standing next to her. The uncertainty in those amber eyes so like her own, so like their mother's, broke her heart, and she had to swallow the lump that filled her throat before she could offer what she hoped was a reassuring smile. "I really am."

Wrapping her arm around her sister's shoulders, she started toward the stairs. But before she had gone more than a few feet, a voice from behind her had her halting in her tracks and glancing back over her shoulder.

The butler, Iverson, was hurrying after her. "My lady?"

"Yes, Iverson?"

"A messenger just arrived at the door and asked that I make sure you receive this."

The servant held out a rather crumpled envelope, and Jillian felt a wave of trepidation wash over her as she reached out to take it. Only Tolliver would have reason to write to her. But was it good news? Or bad? "Thank you, Iverson. That will be all."

The butler nodded and continued on his way.

Tearing open the envelope, Jillian extracted the single sheet of paper and read the hastily scrawled words with slowly dawning horror. It *was* from Tolliver, and the information he had to impart left her suddenly paralyzed, trapped in a nightmare from which there was no escape.

I regret to inform you of Wilbur Forbes's death. It seems he has been murdered in much the same manner as Stuart Grayson, and Connor Monroe has become Bow Street's chief suspect. I must see you at once. Though he has not yet been taken into custody, I'm certain it is only a matter of time . . .

Some of what she was feeling must have shown on her face, for Aimee moved a step closer, her convulsive grip tightening on Jillian's arm. "What is it? What does the note say?"

Fighting to regain control of her wildly teetering emotions, Jillian folded the note and tucked it into her skirt pocket. She had to calm herself, or she risked panicking her sister. But she knew it was imperative that she get to Connor at once.

He would have to listen to her now. He just had to.

"It's nothing for you to worry about, lamb," she told Aimee, giving the girl a nudge in the direction of the stairs. "Why don't you go ahead up to Miss Hinkle? And if anyone should inquire as to my whereabouts, I shall be at Theodosia's."

"Please, Jilly, tell me what's wrong."

But Aimee's entreaty fell upon deaf ears. Her mind racing ahead, Jillian was already rushing off down the corridor, leaving her sister staring worriedly after her.

Chapter 15

Even in the face of adversity, a good investigator never gives up.

One hour later, after making a hasty visit to Bow Street, Jillian found herself in a hackney, one gloved hand holding tight to the strap above the carriage door as it barreled its way along Piccadilly at a breakneck pace.

Though he has not yet been taken into custody, I'm certain it is only a matter of time . . .

The words Tolliver had written in his note to her echoed in her head in a menacing refrain, and she glanced over at him where he sat slouched in the opposite seat. With his mouth fixed in a grim line and a frown wrinkling his forehead, the Runner looked as anxious as Jillian felt.

Her teeth sank into her lower lip and she mentally urged the coach to go faster. Dear

God, but she had feared something like this might happen. Without Forbes to pin the blame on, it was only natural that Connor would be considered a suspect. After all, he had wound up with complete control of the shipping company after the death of his partner. And because of his background, the law was more likely to arrest him without making any effort at all to find the true culprit.

A wave of despair washed over Jillian. The murder of Wilbur Forbes had robbed her of the chance to speak to the one person who might have possessed some insight into what had happened the night of her mother's death, and if she would let herself, she could all too easily sink into the miasma of desolation and helplessness that waited to overwhelm her and drag her under. But the knowledge that Connor needed her gave her something to focus on, kept her going. She refused to give up.

Not on finding the truth about her mother. And not on Connor.

At that moment, the hack drew up to the curb in front of Connor's town house.

There was a moment of silence, then Tolliver looked over at her with a wry expression. "You do realize that he may not be happy about this. He is quite determined to keep you from involving yourself in this case any further, and I never told him that I planned on apprising you of the circumstances."

Jillian raised her chin in determination. "Then

he shall just have to be *un*happy, for I will not let him drive me away, no matter how surly he gets. That stubborn man is innocent, and I intend to prove that fact to Bow Street, whether Mr. Monroe likes it or not."

With that, she swept from the coach without waiting for assistance in alighting, the Runner's amused chuckle ringing in her ears.

Unlike the last time she had paid a visit to Connor's residence, Jillian was far too preoccupied with her concern for him to worry about the possibility that someone she knew might see her entering his abode. It wasn't until she was halfway up the wide steps to the front door that it occurred to her that she had been a trifle less than cautious in her approach. And by then it was too late, for the panel suddenly swung open and two men emerged from the house, stepping out onto the front stoop.

She came to an abrupt halt. While the younger one of the pair didn't look familiar, she recognized the older man as a Bow Street Runner she had encountered more than once in the years since she had taken over her father's work. Of course, she had never met the officer face-to-face, had only passed him on occasion in the hallways at Bow Street, so there was always the chance he might be unaware of her identity, that he might not realize who she was.

It was a very small chance, but a chance nonetheless.

Her breath caught in her throat as the two Runners looked up and noticed her standing there.

The officer she didn't know smiled and offered her a polite inclination of the head. There would be no trouble from that quarter. But the other man's probing stare narrowed on her face for a long, pulse-pounding moment . . .

Then skimmed past her to her companion, who was puffing up the steps behind her.

"Tolliver." The greeting was cold, clipped, and far from welcoming.

Tolliver responded with an equal lack of warmth. "Albertson."

"Still wasting your time trying to find a more likely suspect in these murders than Monroe?"

"It's only a waste of time if there *isn't* a more likely suspect, and I believe that there is."

"So Monroe claims." One corner of Albertson's mouth curved in a patronizing smirk. "You're that certain the man is innocent?"

"I'm that certain."

"For the sake of your reputation as a Runner, Tolliver, you'd better pray you're right. But I find it highly doubtful."

Albertson cast one last, unreadable glance in Jillian's direction before sketching her a brief bow and continuing down the steps, his partner hurrying in his wake.

Tolliver glowered after them as the twosome disappeared around the corner. "Condescending bore," he muttered. "Once Albertson makes up his mind to something, he can be impossible to sway, and it won't be easy to convince him that he's wrong about Monroe. We'll have to be careful of him, my lady."

Jillian couldn't help but agree. Albertson came across to her as a rather superior sort who wouldn't take kindly to being proven wrong in his assertions. Especially if a woman such as herself played a part in doing so.

"I thought I told you our association was at an end, Lady Jillian."

The gruffly sardonic voice coming from above them jerked Jillian from her musings, and she whirled about to find Connor standing in the open doorway of the town house, arms crossed and his countenance inscrutable as he stared down at her. "I suppose I should be surprised at your temerity in showing up here. But somehow, I'm not. After all, you do have a rather bad habit of sticking your nose into situations where you're not wanted."

Jillian gasped, her hands flying to her hips. But before she could think of a suitably stinging rejoinder, Tolliver intervened.

"Don't blame her, Monroe," the Runner said softly, stepping forward. "It's my fault she's here. But surely you must see by now that we need her help? At this point, we can't afford to turn anyone away. Not when Bow Street appears to be so convinced of your guilt."

Connor reached up to pinch the bridge of his

nose in a weary manner, and some of Jillian's self-righteous anger seeped away as she noticed the dark circles under those blue-green eyes, the tousled disarray of his chestnut hair. He looked as if he had spent the night pacing and raking his fingers through the disheveled strands, and her heart squeezed in sympathy at his obvious exhaustion.

Finally, he gave a careless lift of one broad shoulder and shifted aside to allow them to enter. "As you're already here, you may as well come in. But that doesn't mean I've changed my mind." His brows lowering, he placed special emphasis on his next words. "About anything."

Jillian's spine stiffened, but she refrained from commenting on the man's obstinate nature and brushed by him into the house.

Once Tolliver had joined her in the foyer, she waited as Connor closed and bolted the door, studying him surreptitiously from under lowered lashes. In the muted light of the entryway, his craggy profile was cast in shadow, giving him a vaguely saturnine appearance. And for a brief instant, she was thrown back to the moment when he had loomed over her on the bed in Hiram Ledbetter's cottage, that strong, muscular body pressed the length of hers, his cheekbones flushed with color and his eyes glittering with heated desire. His rugged features had been suffused with a fierce possessiveness, and the memory of it was enough to send a shiver through her even now.

It made her long for him to look at her that way again.

Shaking off the disconcerting recollection, she cleared her throat and looked up at him. "Albertson has questioned you?" she ventured.

Connor's firm lips quirked, but there was no humor in his expression. "Thoroughly. That was the second time the man has been here since early this morning."

"The second time?"

"The first time, he asked me to give him a full accounting as to my whereabouts last night. I assume this visit was to let me know that he has been checking up on my alibi."

"You had an alibi?"

Connor stalked a few short paces across the foyer to stand with his back to them, his spine rigid. "Yes. Apparently Forbes was seen entering the boardinghouse in St. Giles where he was staying under an assumed name sometime after midnight. A short while later, sounds of a struggle were heard coming from his room, and his body was discovered at around two o'clock this morning. If it weren't for the fact that I had paid a call on a lady friend of mine at about that time, I would probably be in Newgate awaiting hanging right now."

Jillian felt her stomach lurch. She was very much afraid she knew what he meant, but that little devil that seemed to have become her constant companion of late pushed her to prompt him further. "A lady friend? Is this the 'lady friend' you were with the night of Stuart Grayson's murder?"

It was an obviously abashed Tolliver who answered, his usually ruddy complexion reddening even more as he explained. "Yes. A . . . er, dressmaker by the name of Selene Duvall. She has been acquainted with Monroe for quite some time and—"

"Come now, Tolliver, let's not beat about the bush," Connor interrupted, turning back to face them. "Lady Jillian claims to be capable of handling all manner of things in her guise as an investigator, so let's just come right out and say it."

He stared into Jillian's eyes with a detached indifference that constricted her throat, that filled her with the instinctive need to cry out in protest at the emotional distance he had placed between them. "Selene is my mistress."

Though she had been expecting it, the wound his words dealt her was crippling, and her hands fisted at her sides as she fought to wade through the waves of pain that bombarded her. She was certain she must have swayed under the force of it. He had gone to another woman last night, had solicited his mistress for something Jillian herself had been only all too willing to give him. She had practically begged him to take her, yet he had turned her away as if what she had to offer him wasn't good enough and had gone to this Selene instead. Why?

Hanging on to her control by a thread, she examined him closely, taking in the harsh white lines that bracketed his mouth, the tic of a muscle in his taut jaw. The harsh planes of his face were drawn into a taciturn mask, but she detected a tension about him, a curious sort of watchfulness as he contemplated her, almost as if he were awaiting her reaction.

And suddenly she knew. She knew with an utter conviction that there was a reason behind Connor's behavior toward her. His cutting comments, his deliberate coldness, his acknowledgment of his relationship with Selene. It was all part of a calculated strategy on his part, designed to chase her away, to hurt her enough so that she would refuse to have anything more to do with either him or this case.

And she would not allow him to get away with it.

In spite of the blow her emotions had taken, her pride came to her rescue. Taking a deep breath, she managed to hold his gaze unwaveringly. "And Albertson questioned her? She will corroborate your story?"

For a fleeting instant, Connor seemed surprised by the calmness she displayed in the face of his confession, though he recovered quickly. "Of course. But then, you have little need to concern yourself with that, as you won't be taking part in the investigation."

"I beg to differ, Mr. Monroe," she informed him haughtily. "It is Mr. Tolliver who approached me to ask for my help, so it is Mr. Tolliver I answer to.

Not you. If he needs my help to look into this case, I shall give it to him and you have nothing to say about it."

Connor's jaw tightened even more and he took an intimidating step forward. "By damn, I do have something to say about it," he gritted out through clenched teeth. "If he insists upon continuing to involve you in this, I shall dismiss him from my employ at once."

From behind her, Jillian heard the Runner gasp and start to object, but she was so outraged on his behalf that she spoke over him, her voice rising with indignation. "You can't do that!"

"Oh, I assure you, I can. I am the one who engaged his services and I can dispatch them as I see fit."

Jillian shook her head, aware of a sinking feeling deep in the pit of her stomach. He was going to fight her on this, drat him. "I don't understand why you're acting this way. I know you expressed some concern for my welfare, but you must realize now that you are the one in danger, not I. Tolliver and I might be the only hope you have at getting to the bottom of who is responsible for all of this."

"Damn it, I already know who is responsible!"

"What?" The matter-of-fact announcement caught Jillian off guard, stunning her. "But I—I thought . . ."

When she stumbled to a stop, at a complete

loss, Connor scowled at Tolliver. "You didn't tell her?"

The Runner moved forward to stand at her side, offering her an apologetic look before shrugging. "I didn't think it was my place to do so."

"You never let that stop you before," Connor muttered, then returned his attention to Jillian. "I suspected who it was the moment Patchett relayed his message the other day. And now that Tolliver has done some further checking for me, I'm left in little doubt. I didn't mention it because it was irrelevant to your further participation in this investigation, but as you're being so bloody stubborn I see no reason to leave you in the dark any longer. It's my stepfather, Ian Trask."

She blinked. Dear God! The monster who had made his childhood such a nightmare? "But you told me he was—"

"Incarcerated? I believed that he was. But it seems he managed to make a cunning jail break about a year after he was arrested that no one ever bothered to inform me of." Connor's visage darkened. "Trask is dangerous and not someone to be toyed with, so you can see now why I can't allow you to have anything further to do with this. He won't hesitate to harm anyone he thinks matters to me, and it's bad enough that I've had to let Tolliver take the risk. I won't risk you, as well."

For a fleeting instant, the shadow of something bleak and haunted flickered in the depths of his eyes. "God, it may already be too late, but the least I can do is try to minimize the damage. If he thinks we've parted ways, it's possible he may forget about you."

She opened her mouth to object, but he raised a hand, halting her before she could say a word. "No more. I've said this before, Lady Jillian, but this time I expect you to actually listen and hear what I say. You *will* stay out of this. And that is my final word."

They eyed each other with mutual antagonism for several long minutes, the angry sparks leaping between them almost tangible.

Then Connor gave a stilted bow. "Now, if you'll excuse me, I need to change and head into the office so I can try and get at least *some* work done today. After all, the company can't run itself, and I've piled far too much on poor Lowell Unger's shoulders lately as it is. I'm sure you both know the way out."

With that, he spun on his heel, strode across the foyer, and disappeared up the curving staircase.

Tolliver started after him with a frustrated growl, but Jillian placed a staying hand on his arm. "No, Tolliver. It's no use."

There was no point in debating the subject with Connor any further, she decided, peering after him with a frown. If the truth were known, she was tired of the arguing, of the endless back and forth between them. And thus far, it had done her very little good.

No. It was time to take matters into their own hands.

"It's all right, Mr. Tolliver," she told the Runner, a militant light entering her eyes. "Mr. Monroe may think he has had the final word. But I'm afraid he has another think coming."

Chapter 16

❧❧

An investigator must know when to employ stealth and ingenuity.

Dancers whirled across the marble floor of the ballroom to the lilting strains of the orchestra, a kaleidoscopic swirl of color and laughter as ladies attired in a rainbow array of fashionable gowns waltzed in the arms of gentlemen in impeccably cut evening clothes. The glittering crystal chandeliers high above cast prisms of light across the gay assemblage, giving the surroundings an almost fairy-tale aura.

From her place of semiconcealment behind a plaster column festooned with decorative garlands of ribbon and assorted greenery, Jillian tapped her fan impatiently against her gloved palm, completely oblivious to the music and animated chatter going on around her. Mixing and mingling with the social elite of London was the last thing on her mind. She was far too busy counting down the minutes until she could put her most recent plan into action.

Smoothing down the satin skirt of her rose-colored ball gown, she glanced over to where her aunt was busy chatting with an elderly dowager a few feet away. Lady Olivia appeared to be absorbed in whatever it was the woman was saying, and had yet to notice that her eldest niece had been slowly inching her way from her side over the course of the last hour.

That suited Jillian just fine. The less her aunt knew about her activities this evening, the better. And with Maura being kept occupied on the dance floor by one of her many dashing and eligible suitors, there would be no better time for her to sneak away.

Tonight, she had every intention of paying a visit to the St. Giles boardinghouse where Wilbur Forbes had been murdered.

The idea had first come to her earlier that afternoon, after she had returned to the Albright town house. If she was to help Connor, it was of utmost importance that she examine the scene of the crime as soon as possible. And while Tolliver had agreed to escort her there himself as soon as he was able to get away from Bow Street, he hadn't been able to tell her exactly when that would be.

Jillian knew that venturing into such a squalid part of town, alone and after dark, wouldn't be the smartest thing she had ever done, but she couldn't just continue to stand around doing nothing when Connor's freedom—and perhaps his very life—hung in the balance. Besides, the Hayworth ball provided her with the perfect opportunity to go about her business without having to worry about any of the members of her family wondering where she was.

It seemed that the headache she had pretended to that morning would prove itself useful in more ways than one. She would simply claim to still be suffering from the megrims, return home early, send the coach back for Aunt Olivia and Maura, and then continue on her way to St. Giles. All she had to do was locate one of Lord and Lady Hayworth's servants to deliver the message to her aunt and call for the carriage and she could be off with no one the wiser.

At that moment, the final notes of the waltz sounded, and the dancers came to a halt. Amid a general shifting of partners and the noisy exodus of those leaving the floor, the orchestra immediately struck up a lively reel, and Jillian decided that now was as good a time as any to make her escape. Casting one last look at her aunt to make sure that Lady Olivia's attention was still focused elsewhere, she edged out of her niche and began to make her way around the periphery of the ballroom toward the exit.

It took her a bit longer than she would have liked to navigate her way through the milling throngs of people, and she was stopped more than once by acquaintances wishing to engage her in conversation. When she finally managed to slip out through the wide double doors into the quiet foyer of the house, she breathed an immense sigh of relief. Now, if she could only find the Hayworths' butler or perhaps a footman.

She had started forward to do so when a slight sound from behind her had her stopping and peering back over her shoulder down the dimly lit hallway that ran alongside the ballroom. At first, though she strained her ears, she could hear nothing except for the drifting chords of orchestra music, and she was just beginning to think she had been imagining it when she heard it again.

A deep, rumbling mutter, followed by a faint, feminine cry laced with traces of pain and fear.

"No! Stop!"

Jillian's heart flew into her throat. There was something unsettlingly familiar about that voice, and before she could think twice, she was already marching with purposeful strides along the corridor, her footsteps muffled on the thick runner.

She didn't have to go far before she came across the source of the disturbance. In a dark alcove, almost hidden from view behind the trailing fronds of a well-placed potted palm, a young woman was struggling against the hold of a large male form who had pressed her back against the cushioned seat of a padded bench and showed no signs of letting her go.

"Come, love," Jillian heard the man rasp as she drew closer, the words coming between harshly grated breaths. "All I want is a little kiss. You know you want it."

In response, the woman gave another vehement protest and shoved at his shoulders, straining away from him, and the faint glow from one of the few wall sconces in the hallway fell over her pale face.

Maura.

Jillian let out a horrified gasp and hurried forward. But before she'd gone more than a few steps, a smooth, velvety baritone wafted out of the darkness at the other end of the corridor, arresting both her and the couple on the bench in mid-motion.

"I do believe the young lady has expressed her desire for you to release her."

A tall figure glided forward out of the gloom to stand before them with indolent ease, and the same light that had illuminated Maura's countenance spilled over thick golden curls and the sort of elegantly carved features that would have put an angel to shame.

Jillian's mouth fell open in astonishment. She couldn't have been more startled if the devil himself had come to their aid. For if anyone had been the subject of more cruel gossip, speculation, and innuendo among the *ton* during the last four years than the members of the Daventry family, it was Gabriel Sutcliffe, the current Earl of Hawksley.

And the son of the man who had been accused of their mother's murder.

Attired in dark, well-tailored evening clothes that fit his lean, broad-shouldered frame to perfection, the earl folded his arms across his wide chest and tilted his head, surveying the man who had leaped from the bench at his approach with hooded green eyes that glittered like emeralds. Firm, sensuous lips quirked, but there was nothing humorous in his remote expression. In fact, though he had a reputation for lazy indulgence that more than rivaled his late father's, beneath that aura of dissipation there lurked an impression of coiled power, of lethal energy that Jillian sensed could be dangerous if ever unleashed.

"Far from gentlemanly behavior for a future viscount," he drew out in a silken purr. "Wouldn't you say, Stratton?"

The other man, whom Jillian now recognized as the eldest son and heir to the Viscount Lanscombe, fixed the earl with an ugly glower. "Here now. I don't see where this is any of your business, Hawksley. The girl was asking for it, otherwise she wouldn't have followed me out here unaccompanied. After all, all of London knows she's no better than her mother."

The cruel accusation wrung an outraged denial from Maura, and Jillian felt her cheeks heat with fury as she prepared to fling herself at the odious toad and wipe the superiority off that leering visage.

But once again, Lord Hawksley intervened.

"I'm certain you don't mean that, Stratton. Because if I thought you did, I might have to ask you to meet me outside. And we wouldn't want that." Despite the softness of his tone, there was a distinct hint of menace that vibrated just beneath the surface of his words.

A menace that had Stratton suddenly looking less than sure of himself.

Hawksley paused, then leaned forward the slightest bit, as if he were getting ready to impart something of great secrecy. "After all, all of London knows I'm no better than my father. And he was a murderer, remember?"

There was a second of stunned silence. Then Stratton flushed an unbecoming shade of crimson and drew himself up like a blustery gamecock. "Now see here—"

"No, *you* see here. You will beg the lady's pardon, and you will do so at once, before this entire situation becomes even more tedious than it already is. And I'm sure I needn't warn you that I tend to react badly when I find something—or *someone*—tedious."

"Bloody hell, very well!" Obviously, the mere possibility of coming to blows with the earl was enough to make Stratton back down. Bristling with displeasure, he faced Maura, gritting his apology out from between clenched teeth. "I beg your pardon, my lady. I'm afraid I lost my head. It won't happen again."

Hawksley arched an eyebrow. "Ah. Not very

graciously done, but there it is. Now, isn't there somewhere else you should be, Stratton?"

The young lord growled a savage imprecation under his breath, but he didn't argue further. Instead, he spun on his heel and stalked off down the corridor back toward the ballroom.

As soon as he was out of sight, Jillian pushed past Hawksley and rushed to Maura's side, throwing herself down on the bench and wrapping her arm around her sister's quavering shoulders.

"Maura, darling, are you all right?"

Her stare never wavering from Hawksley, the younger woman gave an almost imperceptible nod.

Jillian returned her attention to the earl as well, giving him a sincere—if a trifle shaky—smile of gratitude. "Thank you, my lord."

"You needn't thank me." His coolly perfect features an unruffled mask, Hawksley barely glanced at her before resting his unnerving green eyes on Maura. "I can assure you that if I'd realized who Stratton was accosting, I might not have been so quick to involve myself."

Maura's entire body stiffened and she lunged to her feet. It was only in that instant that Jillian realized that her sister wasn't trembling with fear, but with anger. "How dare you? And you just accused Mr. Stratton of lacking the manners of a gentleman!"

"But then, I never claimed to be a gentleman, did I?" Hawksley's mouth twisted into an almost self-deprecatory smile, and he offered both women a stiff, mocking little bow. "Ladies."

With that, he seemed to fade away, back into the shadows, and was gone.

Maura glared after him. "That arrogant, insufferable rogue!"

"Please, Maura." Jillian reached out to catch the girl's wrist, drawing her back toward the bench. "The last thing I'm interested in right now is Lord Hawksley's rudeness. The man has served his purpose, and that's all that matters."

"How can you say that when his father murdered our mother?"

"Perhaps."

Maura whirled, tugging free from Jillian's hold and gaping down at her as if she believed she had gone mad. "Perhaps? Oh, Jilly, don't tell me you still have doubts about that? Why, Hawksley just as good as admitted it."

Jillian sighed. She had no desire to get into a discussion about what she believed or didn't believe regarding the late Lord Hawksley's culpability in their mother's death. Her sister had never wanted to hear about it, and she doubted anything had changed. "Can we discuss this later? At this point I'm far more concerned about you."

"I'm fine." Maura lifted a hand to brush a few inky black curls that had tumbled free from her elegant topknot back behind her ear, then righted the sequined bodice of her pale blue ball gown, which was slightly askew. "You and Lord

Hawksley showed up before he had managed to do much more than paw at me. And before you say anything, I categorically deny that I followed Mr. Stratton out here. I was on my way to the ladies' retiring room when that . . . that bounder came up behind me and dragged me into this alcove. I had very little choice in the matter, as you could see."

"I never thought—" Jillian began.

But Maura cut her off, her piquant face suffused with dismay and pain as she began to pace in front of the bench, clearly agitated. "I'm so tired of it all, Jilly. Tired of being compared to her. It seems as if no matter how hard I try to behave as I should, to be circumspect and decorous and all of the other things society expects from a proper young lady, everyone insists upon eyeing me as if they are anticipating the moment when I shall finally do something outrageous and prove that I'm just like Mama."

"Oh, Maura, I'm certain that's not true. Just because one man—"

"Do you honestly think this is the first time something like this has happened? That I haven't been propositioned and groped by such barbaric louts before? I cannot tell you how many supposed gentlemen have approached me this Season, assuming I'll be only too willing to take up where the former Marchioness of Albright left off."

Jillian was overcome by a blinding rush of rage. "Who? Tell me who and I'll—"

"What?" Maura came to an abrupt halt and swung about to face her sister with her hands on her hips. "You'll what, Jilly? Do you truly believe that you haven't made matters worse with your own behavior? You may not have acquired it in the same way, but your reputation is almost as notorious as Mama's."

And that was nothing but the truth, Jillian conceded to herself, a sharp jab of guilt piercing her. "We could tell Papa. Maybe he could—"

"No, we can't tell Papa. All it would do is worry him more when he already has enough to worry about. And Aunt Olivia . . . well, we both know she wouldn't understand."

Feeling abashed, Jillian contemplated her hands clasped together in her lap. She hated that her own misadventures had added to Maura's burden in any way. Perhaps this was part of the solution to the mystery of why her sister had grown so aloof, so distant from her.

But it couldn't be helped. How could she possibly give up on her crusade when every instinct she possessed told her that something about the night her mother died wasn't right? She simply had to continue, no matter what.

Which reminded her of her plans for the evening.

Some of what she was thinking must have shown on her face, for Maura's eyes narrowed and she crossed her arms before her, looking much the way Jillian could remember their mother looking whenever she had scolded her daughters for some childhood transgression. "Just what were you doing out here anyway, Jilly?"

Jillian bit her lip. She would have to choose her words with great care. Alerting her sister to her scheme would cause no end of trouble. "Actually, I was looking for a servant. But I suppose now you can deliver my message to Aunt Olivia instead."

"What message?"

"I'm afraid I'm not feeling quite the thing. My headache has returned with a vengeance, and I thought I would return home a bit early and then send the carriage back for you and Aunt Olivia."

Lines of suspicion wrinkled Maura's forehead. "Jillian, if you are up to something that will cause trouble—"

"Don't be silly. What could I possibly be up to when my head is pounding so abominably? All I want to do is go home and go to bed." Eager to be on her way now that she knew her sister was going to be all right, Jillian rose from the bench, hoping that her expression conveyed an innocence that she was far from feeling. "Now, if you are sure you are fine, I need to find a member of the Hayworth staff to have the coach brought round and you need to return to the ballroom. Aunt Olivia will be wondering where we are."

"But—"

"We'll talk later, Maura. And I promise there's nothing for you to be concerned about. I'll be home, sleeping, by the time you and Aunt Olivia get there."

Without waiting for her sister to respond, Jillian pivoted and hurried off back down the hallway toward the front of the house, praying that she hadn't just told a blatant falsehood.

Chapter 17

When questioning a witness, make sure to use tact and diplomacy. An overbearing manner will gain you naught.

Jillian stood on the threshold of the late Wilbur Forbes's former residence, surveying a gruesome scene much like the one she'd viewed at Grayson and Monroe Shipping just a few short days before.

Lit by a single candle, the tiny room with its grimy window that overlooked a narrow, debris-scattered alley was obviously less expensively furnished than Stuart Grayson's office had been, with a small wooden table, a set of mismatched chairs, and a rather lumpy and uncomfortable-looking bed. But the blood that coated the walls and floor and that had left a large stain on the sagging mattress was exactly the same.

As was the overpowering stench of death that seemed to permeate the air, mixing with the foul smell of rotting garbage and the rank odor of unwashed bodies in a way that had Jillian's stomach revolting.

Covering her nose with one hand, she stepped into the room, giving herself a moment to take stock. Despite the fact that she'd been expecting such a sight, the grisly evidence of the crime that had been committed here had her closing her eyes for a fleeting instant in order to distance herself from the horror that surrounded her.

She didn't have time to nurse a case of jittery nerves. She had to get to work, for there was no telling how soon Maura and Aunt Olivia would return home from the Hayworth ball. By then, Jillian wanted to make sure that she was sound asleep in her own bed, just in case someone decided to check up on her.

Someone like her highly suspicious sister.

Her shoulders straightening with renewed purpose, she moved farther into the chamber. She supposed she could take some comfort in the knowledge that so far everything had proceeded according to plan. Back at the Albright town house, after her hasty departure from the ball, she had informed Iverson that she would be retiring for the rest of the evening due to a headache and had retreated to her room, where she had changed into the white lawn shirt, dark breeches, and coat that she had managed to appropriate from the stables earlier in the day.

From there, it had been a simple matter to shimmy down the trellis outside her window and make her escape out the rear garden gate and through the mews.

However, things hadn't progressed quite as smoothly upon arriving at her destination. The owner of the boardinghouse, a woman by the name of Mrs. Plimpton, had at first been resistant to the idea of letting anyone examine Forbes's room. But once a bit of monetary incentive had been thrown in, an avaricious glint had entered her pale eyes and she had allowed Jillian entry with the admonition that she was not to disturb any of the other boarders.

Not that there had been much chance of that, for it seemed the other inhabitants of the house were either out or already asleep. She had passed no one on her way up the creaking staircase, and the second-floor hallway had been surprisingly quiet. Almost eerily so.

And now, here she was, in the very room where a monstrous madman had murdered someone less than twenty-four hours before.

Alone.

It was enough to send a chill coursing through even the most stalwart person.

Jillian looked at the blood smeared across the floor. If Connor was right and his stepfather was responsible for this . . . well, the sooner they caught him, the better off the citizens of London would be.

Most especially Connor himself.

But where to begin? she mused, once again noting the lack of furnishings. She had to admit that her motive for coming here this evening had been twofold. She had hoped that in addition to furthering her investigation into Connor's case, she just might happen to stumble across some sort of clue that Forbes had left behind that would offer an explanation as to why he had disappeared on the very night his employer had supposedly killed her mother. But the more she studied the starkness of his chamber and the few personal effects that were displayed, the more she was coming to realize it was a waste of time to hope. It wasn't likely that he had kept anything that could tie him to Lord Hawksley.

And right now she had to focus on the far more urgent business of capturing a killer before he could strike again.

Nearing the bed, she let her gaze trail from the walls, to the rumpled sheets, to the pool of blood that had soaked into the dingy pillow and the mattress beneath it. Bow Street believed that Forbes had already been abed when the killer entered the room and had only awakened upon being attacked. Though he had apparently made a valiant attempt to fight back, he had been groggy and disoriented and far from an even match for a determined foe armed with a knife.

Unlike the other crime scenes Jillian had visited thus far, the signs of a struggle here were obvious. A chair had been knocked over next to the bed, and a mirror that had once hung on the wall above the headboard had been torn from its hook. The Bow Street officers who had inspected the room earlier must have moved it from where it had been found, for it had been propped on the floor against the overturned chair, its glass shattered.

Jillian felt her heartbeat pick up speed as she stared at the oval-shaped frame. For some reason, mirrors seemed to hold some special significance to the killer. If he had followed true to form . . .

Kneeling before it and taking extra care not to cut herself, she ran her hand over the mirror's backing, then over the outside edge of the frame, but felt nothing that seemed out of the ordinary. It wasn't until she inserted a finger between the glass and inside edge of the frame that she withdrew a tiny, folded slip of paper.

Another message!

Her mouth went dry with anticipation, but before she could even open the note to read it, a strident voice called out from behind her.

"What's this, then?"

Startled, Jillian shot to her feet and spun about to find a stick-thin whippet of a woman hovering in the doorway of the room, glaring at her in a less than friendly fashion. The plain gray gown and ragged apron she wore, as well as the mop she clutched in one hand, left little doubt that she was a servant of some sort, but her manner was far from deferential.

"This ain't a bleedin' museum, ye know!" she

continued accusingly, pointing at Jillian with the handle of the mop. "What the 'ell are ye doing in 'ere?"

Hastily stuffing the piece of paper into the pocket of her breeches, Jillian reached up to pull the bill of her borrowed cap lower over her eyes, making sure that her ebony curls were still tucked away out of sight. She could only pray that her unusual height, clothing, and husky voice, along with the dimness of the room, would contribute to the impression that she was a male. She certainly didn't want it getting out that a female had paid a visit to Wilbur Forbes's room.

It would take no time at all for Connor to figure out who the visitor had been, and that was the last thing she needed to deal with right now.

"I'm sorry," she ventured, deliberately keeping her tone low and raspy. "Mrs. Plimpton told me it was all right for me to come up here."

"Oh, she did, did she? Well, the old biddy might 'ave told me. She's been nattering on at me to clean this room, and now that I finally get time to do it what wiv' all the other chores she piles on me shoulders, she sends someone else up 'ere to traipse about and get in me way."

"I'm sorry—"

The servant waved her free hand in a dismissive gesture before Jillian could even finish her apology. "Never mind. It's not like I was looking forward to the job any'ow." She propped her mop against the wall and placed her hands on her hips, grimacing at the carnage around her.

"I'll be up until dawn cleaning this mess as it is, and then Auntie will expect me down in the kitchen to 'elp wiv' breakfast, never mind that I ain't gotten a wink of sleep all night."

The matter-of-fact way in which she spoke was off-putting, to say the least, but such bloody scenes were more than likely a matter of course this close to the rough environs of St. Giles and Seven Dials. Jillian supposed that being exposed to such violence on a daily basis would be enough to inure anyone sooner or later.

"Mrs. Plimpton is your aunt?" she prompted, ducking her chin into the collar of her coat and drawing back farther into the shadows as the woman took a step into the room.

"To me everlasting regret. She pays me to 'elp out around 'ere, but I'm beginning to think it ain't nearly enough to put up wiv' 'er. Me name's Pansy."

Jillian nodded an acknowledgment of the introduction, but didn't accept the obvious invitation to give her name in return.

When she remained silent, Pansy tilted her head, peering at her through strands of straggly light brown hair with narrowed eyes full of curiosity. "Are ye looking for a room to rent? As ye can see, this one ain't quite ready for a new boarder. Of course, Auntie never passed up a chance to make some blunt, never mind that the poor bloke what used to live 'ere was just offed. But then, I guess ye must 'ave 'eard about that."

"Yes. As a matter of fact, Mrs. Plimpton was

just telling me about it." Jillian hesitated, trying to think of a way to frame her next question that wouldn't arouse the maid's further suspicions. "Were you here when it happened?"

"Thank the blessed Lord, no. Last night was me night off. And from what I've been told, no one else 'eard or saw a thing except the old codger who 'as the room next door. Says 'e was awakened by some banging around at about two in the morning, but all 'e did was beat on the wall and go back to sleep."

"No one knows how the killer got in?"

"Could 'ave been any number of ways. Auntie never locks up. We 'ave too many people coming and going at all hours, and we don't 'ave much to steal."

"Did you know him well? Mr. Forbes?"

A saucy smile curved Pansy's mouth. "Oh, I suppose ye could say that. 'E was a bit of a brute, but sometimes 'e got lonely and needed some female companionship, if ye know what I mean." She shrugged. "Like I said. Me aunt doesn't pay much."

Jillian reminded herself to tread carefully. She didn't want to alarm the woman by pushing too hard, too fast. "Did he ever say much about his past?"

"Whenever 'e was in 'is cups, though a lot of what 'e said didn't make any sense." The servant crossed her arms over the practically nonexistent curve of her bosom and stared at Jillian in sudden distrust. "Why do ye ask?"

"I'm a friend of his."

"Wilbur never mentioned any friends."

"An old friend from long ago. Back when he used to work as a coachman for the Earl of Hawksley."

Pansy seemed to pale at Jillian's words, though it was difficult to tell in the dimness of the room. There was no mistaking the tension that seized that bony frame, however. It was instantaneous and almost tangible.

Every instinct Jillian possessed sprang to immediate attention at the telling reaction. Was it possible . . . ? Could Forbes have told Pansy about that night four years ago? she wondered.

"Something happened," she drew out cautiously, struggling to make out the maid's expression through the gloom. "Something to do with Lord Hawksley. Wilbur took off and I hadn't seen him since."

Pansy shifted her slight weight from one foot to the other in a restless motion. "I'm sure I wouldn't know about that."

"Are you quite certain?"

The woman paused for a moment, then sidled closer to Jillian, a rapacious gleam entering her eyes. "Well, it's possible Wilbur might 'ave mentioned something. But I would need a little . . . 'elp recalling the information."

Jillian barely restrained an exasperated sigh. After dealing with Mrs. Plimpton, she should have known. In the end, it all came down to greed.

Digging into the inside lining of her coat, she withdrew a few coins and pressed them into Pansy's outstretched palm, taking care to keep her face out of the flickering candlelight as much as possible. "Well?" she prompted, unable to quell the impatience that seethed within her.

The servant tucked the money into the pocket of her apron and glanced back over her shoulder toward the door, as if making sure no one lingered in the hallway, before speaking. " 'E didn't like to talk about it much. I know 'e was afraid. 'E'd 'eard that the law was looking for 'im for some reason, some bad business regarding 'is most recent employer. Said if they ever caught up to 'im, 'e'd 'ang for sure, because they'd never believe 'e was innocent after Lord 'Awksley's murder."

Jillian blinked. Murder? But the earl had killed himself. Hadn't he? "What did Forbes tell you?"

" 'E said 'e 'ad driven this 'Awksley to some ball or other one night, and when 'is lordship called for the coach afterward, Wilbur noticed right off that 'e was acting strangely, not like 'imself. Instead of going on to the next affair as 'e usually did, 'e asked to be taken to an address on Belgrave Square."

Belgrave Square? Jillian's hands tightened into trembling fists at her sides. Her family's town house?

"The earl told Wilbur to wait with the carriage out of sight," Pansy continued, "be'ind the 'ouse in the mews. But 'e 'adn't been waiting for very

long when 'Awksley came tearing out of the rear
gate like the 'ounds of 'ell themselves was at 'is
'eels. It was raining that night something fierce,
and there was thunder and lightning, so Wilbur
said 'e couldn't quite make out what was 'appen-
ing, but all of a sudden this dark figure appeared
out of nowhere and called out 'Awksley's name."

"A male figure?"

The servant nodded. " 'Awksley stopped and
turned, and the man pulled out a pistol and . . .
and shot 'im in the 'ead."

So there had been someone else there that
night, Jillian thought, her pulse pounding loudly
in her ears. Someone besides Hawksley. She had
known that there were too many things in Bow
Street's scenario of events that hadn't added up,
but now it was beginning to make sense.

Had this mysterious person had something to
do with her mother's death, as well?

"What did Forbes do?" she asked Pansy, keeping her voice calm and even despite her swiftly
growing excitement. As much as she had hoped
to find some answers tonight, she had never expected this. She was finally getting somewhere!

" 'E was terrified. The man aimed 'is gun at 'im
and started toward 'im, and Wilbur said a flash of
lightning lit up the sky and 'e saw 'is face."

"He recognized him?"

"Yes. 'E said 'e was sure 'e was going to die.
But instead the man just threatened 'im. 'E told
Wilbur to disappear, to never tell anyone what
'e'd seen, or 'e'd make sure that the law believed

'e 'ad been responsible for 'Awksley's death 'im- self and that 'e was 'anged for it. And Wilbur believed 'im. 'E said it would be a gent's word against 'is. So 'e ran."

When Pansy paused, Jillian leaned forward, struggling with the urge to reach out, catch the woman by those narrow shoulders, and shake the rest of the information out of her. "Who was it?"

"Wilbur wouldn't ever tell me 'is name. Just that 'e was a titled gent, someone 'Awksley knew. 'Wiv friends like that, Pans, who needs enemies?,' 'e used to say to me." The maid's mouth tilted upward at a cynical slant. "I guess the bleeding aristocracy ain't so much better than us low folk after all."

Jillian wet her lips, anticipation flooding through her veins with such force that she vi- brated with it. There was so much she wanted to know . . .

But before she could even begin to form a co- herent sentence, a sound from the direction of the door had the women looking up to find a large figure looming before them with such un- expectedness that they both gasped.

"What in sweet Christ are *you* doing here?"

It was Connor.

Chapter 18

A cool head should always prevail.

"Do you mind telling me what the bloody hell you thought you were doing?"

Connor knew almost as soon as the angry words left his lips that he had made a mistake.

From the moment he had discovered Jillian boldly questioning the maid in Wilbur Forbes's room, he had been struggling with the overwhelming urge to grab her and shake her until her teeth rattled. But he had learned through experience that losing his temper with her only served to make her that much more determined to go her own way. Confrontation was never the best course of action when dealing with this infuriating woman. So somehow he had managed to quell his initial fury, and they had made the carriage ride back from St. Giles in stilted silence.

Now that they were back at his town house, however, and safely closeted in the parlor, the inclination to deliver a tongue-lashing she wouldn't soon forget had once again begun to seethe beneath the surface of his deceptively calm façade like a bubbling cauldron ready to boil over. He had been so determined that he would present his grievances in a cool and rational manner, but the antagonistic looks Jillian kept shooting him as she paced before the fireplace—for all the world as if *he* had been the one who had done something wrong—had finally goaded him past all bearing.

So much for avoiding confrontation.

Halting mid-step, Jillian planted her hands on her hips and whirled to face him, her amber eyes blazing. "I was trying to help you. That's what I was doing."

Tossing back the last of the brandy he had poured to fortify himself when they had first entered the room, Connor slammed the glass down on a nearby table and prowled over to the window, where he stood with his back to her as he fought to rein in his rapidly rising ire.

You will not yell. You will not yell.

The mantra echoing in his head, he reached up to scrub at the back of his neck with one hand and spoke without turning around, his voice dangerously soft. "Yet I could have sworn that just this morning I forbade you to continue helping me. In fact, I believe that I said I would dispense with Tolliver's services if I found out—"

"Don't you dare blame Tolliver for this."

Jillian's voice came from close behind him, and he spun about to discover that she had followed him across the room and now stood less than a foot away.

Much too near for his peace of mind.

"He knew nothing about it," she continued, crossing her arms in a belligerent fashion. The movement pulled the material of her shirt taut against her breasts, and the men's breeches she wore hugged the curves of her hips and the long length of her legs in a way Connor found most distracting. "It was important that I examine the scene as soon as possible, but he never would have allowed me to even consider doing such a thing alone, and you know it."

"Then I must applaud Tolliver's good sense," Connor gritted out from between clenched teeth. This close, he could smell the lush jasmine scent of her skin, and ignoring its effect on him was becoming next to impossible. "Obviously that is something his partner is sorely lacking."

Jillian gasped, but he didn't give her a chance to say anything. Needing to put some distance between them, he brushed past her and marched over to the fireplace, his strides agitated as he took up pacing where she had left off. "My God, Jillian! Visiting St. Giles, by yourself and in the middle of the night? Do you have any notion at all of what could have happened to you?"

There was a moment of silence, and when she

finally spoke again, her tone was so humble as she acknowledged her folly that Connor froze and gaped at her in shock. "I'm well aware that it wasn't the most intelligent thing I've ever done. But it was something I *had* to do."

Her eyes were wide and serious, and the grief and pain that swirled in their depths told him there was something more at work here, something that went far deeper than mere altruism and an inherited interest in criminology.

"Tell me about it, Jillian. Make me understand why all of this is so important to you." He held her gaze with his own, willing her to confide in him. "And I'm not just talking about this obsessive need you seem to have to help me with my case, regardless of my wishes to the contrary. I'm talking about what it is that drove you to continue your father's work to begin with."

When she didn't answer, simply bit her lip and glanced away, he prompted gently, "This has something to do with your mother's murder, doesn't it?"

Her eyes flew back to his face in surprise. "You knew about that?"

"Everyone knows about that, Jillian."

"You never mentioned it before."

"I didn't want to bring up what must be a painful subject for you. But now I think I have to. That's why you do this, isn't it?"

She wrapped her arms about herself in a curiously vulnerable and childish gesture that made Connor want to take her into his own arms. "Yes."

He closed his eyes for a moment, lost for words. God, but what could he possibly say to get through to her without putting her back up?

"Jillian," he drew out slowly, carefully, "I know the loss of your mother, especially in such a violent manner, must have been a tremendous blow. But this path you have chosen isn't going to bring her back. Maybe you think that by dedicating your life to helping the law capture these criminals, you'll be punishing Lord Hawksley for his crimes against your family in some way, but—"

"No." She cut him off, her response vehement and unequivocal. "It's not that."

"Then what?"

There was a second's hesitation, as if she was unsure whether to answer him or not. Her reply, when it finally came, was not at all what Connor had expected. "I don't believe that Lord Hawksley was responsible for my mother's death."

Perplexed, he studied her in consternation. She sounded so certain, but Tolliver had told him that Bow Street had been positive of the man's guilt. "That doesn't make any sense. Didn't your father catch him in the act?"

"He found Hawksley standing over the body, yes. But it isn't that simple. Too many things seem off."

Connor was suddenly reminded of Tolliver's reaction to his queries regarding Lady Albright's death on the night he had first met Jillian. The Runner hadn't seemed entirely convinced of Hawksley's culpability in the crime himself, and now Connor had to wonder why.

He inclined his head, encouraging her to go on. "For instance?"

"For instance, Lord Hawksley's body was found in the study of his town house. He was slumped behind his desk with a gunshot wound to his head and a pistol in his hand. A pistol that he supposedly used to kill both my mother and then himself. Yet there was only one bullet missing from the chamber."

"There could be a perfectly logical explanation for that."

"Yes, but there are too many other things that seem wrong, Connor." Jillian took a step toward him, her expression earnest. "If my mother had chosen him, was running away with him as everyone believes, then why would he kill her? And there's something else that stumps me. As you mentioned, my father walked in on him in the midst of the act. But Hawksley only hit him in the head and ran. If the earl was already responsible for taking one life, why would he draw the line at doing away with Papa?"

Connor mulled over the details she had presented him with. He had to admit that she had a point. Several aspects of this case didn't seem to add up. But he wouldn't rush to judgment. "As I said, there could be any number of reasons for all of those things, Jillian."

"I know. That's what everyone told me whenever I expressed any doubts at all about the law's
conclusions. And I was never certain of anything. Until tonight." She lifted her chin, her eyes
filled with utter conviction. "But now I know,
Connor. Lord Hawksley didn't kill himself. He
was murdered."

"And how can you possibly know that?"

"The maid I was speaking to tonight? She
told me."

Jillian sounded tentative, almost guilty, and a
frown marred Connor's brow. Quite suddenly,
without a shadow of a doubt, he knew she was
keeping something from him.

"I don't understand. How would this woman
have come by such information?" he asked.

She shifted her weight from one foot to the
other, avoiding his gaze. "I'm afraid there's something I haven't been completely honest with you
about," she admitted. "It's part of the reason
I've been so adamant about involving myself in
your case. Wilbur Forbes was once the Earl of
Hawksley's coachman. He was there the night
my mother was killed, but he disappeared afterward, and I've spent the last few years trying to
find him."

For Connor, the light dawned. "So this is why
you took an interest in your father's work. You've
been investigating your mother's murder."

Jillian nodded and looked back up at him.
"The maid at the boardinghouse knew Forbes.
She said he told her that someone else was there

that night. He saw a man shoot Hawksley. A man he recognized. A titled gentleman."

"Gypsy, you must know you can't believe a thing that woman told you. She could have been lying. And even if she was telling the truth, do you know how far-fetched this would sound to anyone else? A titled gentleman shot your mother, then shot Hawksley and carried his body back to his town house to set things up so it would look like a suicide? Proving such a thing would be next to impossible."

Her mouth tightened into a resolute line at his words. "I won't just give up. Not now that I know I'm right. I have to keep looking. I can't let my mother's real killer go unpunished." Though her voice was strong and unwavering, something lurked just beneath the surface. A panicked desperation that Connor could read all too clearly.

Forgetting for the moment that getting too close to her never seemed to be a good idea, he moved forward to stand in front of her. Her hands were balled into tense fists at her sides, and he captured one of them in his.

"What about your father?" he suggested quietly. "If you told him what you've discovered, perhaps—"

"Papa has been through enough. He's just not the same without my mother. And he's not the only one." Jillian twined her fingers through his, her face pale and drawn. "My youngest sister, Aimee, was there that night. We think she saw what happened, but she doesn't remember any of it. Her entire recollection of the incident has been wiped clean. Yet she jumps at every loud noise, searches the shadows as if she expects someone to leap on her at any moment. It breaks my heart."

Connor felt his own heart squeeze at the tears pooling in her eyes. "Jillian—"

"And Maura and I . . . We found them, Connor. Mama and Papa. Lying on the library floor. Sometimes I think I'll never be able to forget the blood. The fear I felt when I realized my mother was dead."

"Jillian, please—"

"And Mama." She spoke over his soothing murmur, her tears overflowing to stream down her cheeks, though she appeared to be making a valiant effort to hold them back. It was as if a dam had burst somewhere inside her, and she couldn't seem to halt the flow of words and emotions that spilled out of her with ever-increasing speed. "She didn't deserve what happened to her, no matter what society believes. The woman they know is nothing like the woman I remember. The woman who used to sing me to sleep at night, who never hesitated to hike up her skirts and go wading in a stream or take part in an impromptu tea party on the front lawn. She was a wonderful mother and I never doubted that she loved me."

She peered up at him, her shoulders shaking with the force of her sobs, and all Connor wanted to do was sweep her into his arms. To protect and shelter her, to take away every cruelty she had ever endured and every hurt she had ever suffered.

"Do you want to know something I've never told anyone else?" she asked in a hoarse whisper. "I had a feeling that night that something bad was going to happen. If I had paid attention to it earlier, if I had gone downstairs sooner, I might have been able to stop it."

The self-blame written on her face was all too familiar to Connor. It was something he had lived with for most of his life. "Or you might have been killed, too."

"But I'll never know, will I? And it's the not knowing that haunts me. That's tearing me apart."

The agony that swam in her eyes, that choked her voice, was more than he could bear. Releasing her hands, he reached up to cup her chin in his palm, tilting her face to his.

"Hush, Gypsy," he murmured. "Hush."

Then he pressed his lips tenderly to hers.

Chapter 19

When emotions become involved, mistakes are made.

As always, Jillian's wits went begging the moment Connor's mouth settled upon her own.

Everything that had occurred that evening became nothing more than a hazy blur, and her tangled and troubled emotions seemed to fade away into the background of her awareness, for every particle of her being was focused on the man whose lips caressed hers with such exquisite mastery.

But even as she allowed herself to be swept up by the powerful undertow of their mutual ardor, she realized dimly that something about this kiss was different, that it wasn't at all like any of the others they had shared in the past few days.

Before, they had come together in anger and passion. This time, there was an underlying gentleness, a reverence that told her it meant something more, that this went much deeper than satisfying a lust aroused by mere physical attraction.

And suddenly the feelings that welled up within her were far too overwhelming for her to contain or deny.

She loved Connor Monroe. She loved everything about him. His strength and determination. His dedication to watching over and protecting the people he cared for. She even loved his moodiness and his stubborn refusal to back down in an argument. And despite the fact that it left her more defenseless than she could ever remember being, she no longer had any desire to fight the dictates of her heart.

So, throwing all caution to the wind, she returned his kiss without restraint or inhibition.

Encouraged by her fervent response, Connor wrapped his arms around her waist, pulling her closer to him, and she reveled in the warmth of his big body pressed against her. He nipped at the satiny surfaces of her lips, tracing their lush outline with the tip of his tongue and making sounds of enjoyment deep in his throat, as if he were savoring the last bite of a ripe and succulent fruit.

"Do you have any idea," he murmured between kisses, his voice husky, "just what I want to do to you, Gypsy? I want to strip off these clothes and bare every inch of your body. To touch and taste you all over."

Jillian gasped at the sensual images his words evoked. "Connor, I—"

"Shhh," he hushed her, lifting his head to brush his mouth over each of her eyelids in turn, gathering up the last of the moisture that lingered on her lashes before skimming along the line of her jaw to the patch of skin just below her ear. "No more tears, love. And no more dwelling on past tragedies. I don't want to think about anything else. I only want to make love to you."

Jillian let her head fall back, giving him better access to the slope of her neck, and he nibbled delicately, his teeth raking over the flesh there in such a titillating manner that she couldn't hold back a shudder of pleasure. "I want that, too, but . . ."

He looked up when she paused. "But?"

In the lamplight, she could see the hectic color that stained his cheekbones, the heated glitter in his eyes, and it made it difficult to concentrate on putting her thoughts into any semblance of order. But somehow she managed a halfway coherent reply. "I want you. I do. But if you're going to start making love to me, only to push me away again and go to someone else . . ." She recalled the crushing weight of betrayal she had felt earlier that day, when Connor had confessed to her that he had visited his mistress the night before. Just imagining him in bed with another woman left her feeling shattered. "I don't know if I could bear that."

His harsh visage softened, and he reached up

to tuck a stray tendril of ebony hair back behind her ear. "Nothing happened between Selene and me, Gypsy. I swear. Yes, I went to see her hoping to forget about you, but the second she kissed me I knew it was no use. And before I left, I informed her that I wouldn't be calling on her again. The only woman I want in my arms is you."

"That's not what you led me to believe this morning." His rejection of her was still a raw and painful wound that hadn't even begun to heal, and she couldn't keep the hurt out of her voice.

"I know, and I'm sorry. Behaving so coldly toward you was the hardest thing I've ever done. My only excuse is that I was trying to protect you."

"You were trying to chase me away."

He grimaced, but made no attempt to refute the truth of her accusation. "Yes, that too. But no more. I'm tired of fighting the desire I feel for you. So, if you want me, I'm yours. For tonight."

For tonight.

His words echoed in her head, their implication clear. He was telling her that he could give her nothing beyond this night. There would be no promises, and no guarantees that what was between them now could ever become anything more. Not that she would have expected a happily-ever-after. She was well aware that too many obstacles stood in their path for them to ever have a permanent relationship.

But was she brave enough to seize what he was offering? He had already touched her in ways that no other man had, both physically and emotionally, and she didn't think she would ever again be the same. Could she bear to risk her heart any further, to discover what it was like to be with him, to feel him moving inside of her, becoming a part of her, only to be forced to let him go afterward?

"Jillian?"

Connor's whisper was thick with need, and for an instant he looked unsure. Almost as if he was actually afraid that she was going to refuse him.

And that was when she knew. If this single night was all she could have with him, she would take it and be grateful for it.

Smoothing her hands up the solid wall of his chest, she gripped the lapels of his coat and met his somber gaze with utter certainty. "Connor, please make love to me now."

A triumphant light flared to life in his eyes, and this time when he kissed her, it was with a scorching demand that turned Jillian's knees to water. If she had any more doubts that he wanted her, they disappeared right then. The proof of his desire was in the rough cadence of his breathing, in the hungry sweep of his tongue as he plundered her lips before plunging deep into the moist recesses of her mouth.

And she was lost.

Caught up in the fevered intensity of their embrace, Connor himself was swiftly losing control of the emotions he usually held under such tight rein. Jillian's honeyed flavor was intoxicating,

and when she tentatively met his invading tongue
with her own, engaging him in a teasing game
of thrust and parry, he felt his manhood stir to
rigid, aching life.

Sweet Christ, but why had he waited so bloody
long to give in to this?

Trailing the hand he had splayed across her
back down the ridge of her spine, he palmed the
taut curve of her derriere and fit her intimately
against him, then nudged his hips forward until
his heavy, swollen erection nestled into the val-
ley between her thighs as if it had found its way
home. A groan broke from him at the tantalizing
contact, and she gave an answering whimper of
delight that was muffled by their still-dueling
tongues. He could almost feel the damp heat of
her feminine core through the material of her
breeches.

He tore his mouth from hers and closed his
eyes for a fleeting instant, struggling to go more
slowly, to keep from rushing her. This wasn't
enough. Not nearly enough. He wanted to be
inside of her now. Wanted to lay her down and
thrust all the way to her womb, to carry her off
to a world of sweet oblivion where nothing and
no one else mattered except the two of them.

And before this night was over, he planned on
doing exactly that.

Reaching up, he tore off her cap and tossed it
aside, then threaded his fingers through the midnight strands of hair that tumbled free, relish-
ing their silken texture and the scent of jasmine

before sliding his hand down over her shoulder to cup the firm globe of her breast through her shirt.

Jillian let out a moan and arched her back, her nipple instantly hardening and stabbing into his palm, and even through the thin barrier of fabric he could tell that she was wearing nothing underneath.

When his brows rose at the discovery and he looked down at her, she sank her teeth into her kiss-swollen lower lip, avoiding his stare.

"I was in a hurry," she mumbled.

"I'm not complaining," he told her quietly, eyeing her rounded curves with predatory intent. "In fact, I'd wager a guess that after this evening I'll have an all-new appreciation for men's fashions on a woman."

As if to emphasize his point, he flicked his thumb over the engorged tip of her nipple, wringing another quavering moan from her.

Leaning forward, he spoke close to her ear, his voice hoarse with anticipation. "I want to put my mouth there, Gypsy. To kiss and suckle you. To taste your sweetness. Tell me you want that, too."

He heard the gust of her indrawn breath and watched as she nodded, her eyes dazed and drowsy.

But when he released her breast and his fingers went to the buttons of her shirt, she suddenly caught him by the wrist, halting him with a single word. "No."

Connor froze and his gaze flew back to her

face, scrutinizing every inch of her features, searching for some sign of fear or hesitancy. Had she changed her mind? he wondered. Did she want him to stop?

"Jillian, I—"

She interrupted him by covering his mouth with her palm, and though she flushed rather shyly, the glance she cast up at him from under lowered lashes was far from frightened or hesitant. In fact, her expression was so unexpectedly seductive and inviting that it set his heart pounding at a rapid tattoo.

And when she spoke, her voice was a velvety purr. "Let me."

The boldness of her statement stunned him. He had suspected that his gypsy witch would be no blushing, stammering miss when it came to making love, but her transformation from innocent to temptress left him confused and intrigued in equal measure. What was she up to?

He stood like a statue as she backed out of the circle of his arms and moved a short distance away. Surely she wouldn't . . . She couldn't . . .

But she did.

With a lift of her chin, she started right in on the fastenings of her shirt, the visible trembling of her fingers on the buttons the only outward sign of her underlying nervousness. Slowly but surely, bit by bit, the material parted, revealing dusky, soft-looking skin that gleamed with a warm golden sheen. And with each inch of flesh she exposed, Connor's tension increased until he felt as if he was hanging on to his sanity by a thread.

On the very last button, she paused for what seemed like a small eternity, and the slight upward curl at the corner of her mouth told him that she was being deliberately enticing. Determined not to let the brazen minx know it was working, he waited with bated breath, his forehead practically dripping with sweat, until she finally shrugged out of the shirt and let it drop to the floor.

The sight of her bare breasts—full and plump and topped with delectably rosy crests that puckered even more under his avid stare—had a growl rumbling in Connor's chest, and he took a step toward her.

Only to have her throw up a hand to ward him off.

"Not yet, Mr. Monroe." She pursed her lips in a sexy pout. "I'm not quite done."

His hands clenched into fists at his sides. "Not done with what? Driving me bloody mad?"

"Is that what I'm doing?"

"You know you are."

She gave him another knowing smile, tucking her thumbs in the waistband of her breeches. With a sensuous wriggle, she eased them down over her ample hips and the long length of her legs until they pooled at her feet.

Then stepped out of them to stand naked before him.

Connor's mouth went dry. With her long, blue-black hair framing her exotic features in tousled disarray and her abundant curves gilded by the lamplight, she resembled some fey, wild creature from his most lustful fantasies, a pagan goddess of the moon.

And it was at that moment that his patience snapped, like a rope strung too tautly.

Crossing the space that separated them in a few long, purposeful strides, he scooped her up into his arms and bore her from the room. He couldn't wait any longer. But she deserved better than to be ravished on the parlor floor, and he had to admit to a rather urgent longing to see what she would look like stretched out amid satin sheets and silk pillows on a big, comfortable bed.

Preferably his own.

Caught off guard by Connor's unexpected action, Jillian clung tightly to his wide shoulders as he carried her out of the parlor and proceeded up the winding staircase that led from the foyer, bearing her weight with casual strength. The spark that smoldered in the depths of his eyes as he stared down at her left her speechless, unable to speak even if she had known what to say.

She had taken off her clothes for him! A shocking thrill raced through her veins at her own daring. Never had she believed herself capable of behaving in such a wanton manner, and she couldn't help but wonder what Thomas would think if he could see her now. More than likely he would have been scandalized, but she found that she didn't care. Perhaps it was wicked of her, but if this was the only night she would ever share with the man she loved, she intended to take what she could from the experience, to be bold and reckless and worry about the consequences tomorrow.

It seemed she had far more of her mother in her than she had ever dared dream.

At the end of the second-floor hallway, Connor came to a stop and used his booted foot to nudge open a door that already stood ajar, then stepped into a large and airy chamber done in varying shades of blue and gold.

The master suite, Jillian surmised. But she had little opportunity to take in the surrounding décor. Depositing her on the high mattress of the canopied bed, Connor shed his shirt and breeches with a swift economy of motion and turned to face her, driving every other thought from her mind.

He towered over her, his nude form a vision of utter masculine perfection, and Jillian let her gaze trail from his broad, sculpted chest, to his lean hips, to his tautly muscled flanks with something close to awe.

But it was the bold jut of his hard male arousal from the thatch of dark hair between his thighs that had her suddenly feeling more than a bit intimidated.

As if reading her mind, Connor lowered himself to sit on the side of the bed, his mouth curving into a lazy grin. "Don't turn shy on me now,

Gypsy," he rasped, the gruff quality of his tone sending shivers through her.

Then, bending over, he cupped her face in his hands and captured her mouth with his own.

His musky male scent and the devastating power of his kiss combined to cloud her senses once again, sweeping all of her misgivings aside as if they had never been. With a languid thoroughness, he explored the satiny contours of her lips, testing and tasting before he stroked his tongue deep into her mouth, plumbing its depths with a lick of fire.

Raising arms that were weak with desire, Jillian wound them around his neck, tangling her fingers in the shaggy strands of auburn hair that curled at his nape. Their tongues entwined hotly, and she was only vaguely aware when he moved to stretch the full length of his body out over hers—until the solid breadth of his chest came into contact with her already sensitive breasts.

The soft abrasion of his coarse chest hair against her tender, aching nipples had her breaking away from their kiss with a sobbing gasp.

"Connor," she pleaded, looking up into aqua eyes that regarded her with absorbed intentness. "Please . . ."

"Please what, Gypsy? What do you want?"

Oh, the maddening man! She had no doubt he knew exactly what she wanted, what she needed. He was just tormenting her. And how dare he do it now, when she could barely remember her own name, much less put a coherent sentence together?

Some of her frustration must have shown in her expression, for he gave a low, seductive laugh and leaned forward to nuzzle the soft hollow of her throat, his tongue flicking out to lave the pulse that beat there before gliding down over the indentation of her collarbone.

"Is this what you want?" he husked. "Do you want me to kiss you here?"

She could only nod in reply, flinging her head back on the pillow.

"Or perhaps you want me to kiss you here?"

It was the only warning she had before his mouth latched onto the pointed tip of one breast. Heat arced through her, and she let out a wavering cry as his tongue lashed the stiffening peak, suckling and tugging with insistent need. Her nerve endings hummed in exultation, and each hungry pull at her nipple set off a resultant twinge within her womb.

Pressing her back against the mattress, Connor carefully straddled her legs and sat back on his haunches, looming over her like an avenging Greek God, his craggy visage fierce. His palms cupped and molded her breasts, then skimmed down over her rib cage and the curve of her hips with a light touch designed to titillate.

It worked. With a sigh, Jillian parted her thighs enough to allow him to sift through the ebony nest of curls at their juncture, seeking the treasure hidden there. Her head rolled from side to side, and a strangled moan escaped her as he separated her feminine folds, two of his fingers inserting themselves into the opening of her damp, velvety channel.

"I'd much rather kiss you here, Gypsy," he told her, his thumb circling the tender nub of her clitoris, beginning a rhythmic stroking that caused her to rock her pelvis against his hand in time to his caress. The tight muscles of her passage flexed and contracted, squeezing in an attempt to capture some elusive feeling that hovered just out of her reach.

Then she felt him slide downward, felt his fingers withdraw and his warm breath fan over her most secret place. Dear God, he had said he wanted to kiss her there, but she hadn't thought he would actually do such a thing. It was sinful! It was wicked! It was . . .

Heavenly.

She cried out and arched upward as Connor grasped her hips, holding her steady for the penetration of his tongue.

"Easy, sweet," he crooned against her honeyed entrance. "Easy. Let me love you like this. Let me taste you. I'll bet you taste so good."

Accepting no denials, he stabbed his tongue deep, laving, sipping, licking, driving her to heights she had never before imagined existed. A slow, spiraling pleasure began to build, and she closed her eyes, her fingers gripping his hair as the sensation gradually grew and strengthened until the ecstasy overtook her and she finally exploded in a burst of white-hot radiance, screaming out her completion.

She was still convulsing and panting with the aftermath of her climax when Connor rose above her, the hunger and ferocity etched into his features almost frightening. But he gave her no chance for second thoughts, for he fit the swollen tip of his manhood to the cradle of her thighs and, with an upward thrust of his hips, plunged home.

Jillian's muscles clenched at the invasion and she clutched at his shoulders, her nails digging into his sleek skin. He was huge and hot inside of her, and she was cognizant of a burning sensation, an unaccustomed feeling of pressure and fullness. But as Connor continued to move within her, going deeper and deeper with each slow, steady stroke, the discomfort lessened, and she began to move in counterpoint, the delicious friction restoking the flames of her previous passion.

They ascended the peak together, and when they leaped from the precipice, it was in tandem. Connor's seed erupted within her, his harsh groan torn from him at the same time as Jillian orgasmed for the second time in as many minutes, calling his name.

And as he collapsed on top of her and they floated back to earth in each other's arms, she knew that her life had been forever altered.

Chapter 20

Never assume you know the whole story.

Connor lay with Jillian cradled in his arms and her head resting on his chest, listening to the sound of her soft, even breathing and staring up at the canopy overhead as he attempted to sort through the confused tangle of his wildly seething emotions.

He had done the one thing he had promised himself he would never do. He had given in to temptation and made love to a woman he could never have a future with. A woman who had already managed to work her way past his defenses and burrow far too deeply under his skin for his peace of mind.

Yet he couldn't seem to find it within himself to regret one moment of the experience.

Jillian had been a revelation. Responsive,

passionate, and every inch the gypsy witch he had compared her to so often. She had cast her spell on him the moment she'd stood so bravely before him and divested herself of her clothing in such a coquettish and seductive manner. And if he were truthful with himself, he would have to admit that he was still feeling the effects.

He closed his eyes, picturing the look on her face when he had brought her to completion that first time with his mouth. The echo of her cries of pleasure, the musky sweet taste of her on his tongue, were forever imprinted on his memory, along with the way it had felt to finally sink deep inside of her, to become one with her. The tight, moist walls of her feminine passage had sheathed him like a glove, the tiny muscles contracting and gripping him, milking him dry and lifting him to heights he had never before attained. The force of the orgasm that had ripped through him had left him utterly drained, both physically and emotionally.

Sweet Christ, but he didn't think he would ever be able to forget any of it.

"Connor?"

The sound of Jillian's whisper close to his ear startled him. He'd been sure that she had fallen asleep, but when he craned his neck to look down at her, it was to find her amber ayes staring back at him, wide and alert.

Propping herself up on her elbow, she ran her palm over the tense muscles of his chest in a motion she may have meant to be soothing, but was actually anything but. The tantalizing sensation was enough to have his manhood stirring to life once again.

"What are you thinking?" she asked quietly.

He lifted a hand to brush a strand of hair back from her face. He had no intention of discussing the chaos of his thoughts with her, so he gave her only one small portion of the truth when he answered her. "I was wondering if you were all right."

"I'm fine." A knowing smile curved her lips. "Perfect, in fact. So don't you dare feel guilty."

"How can I not, Gypsy? It was your first time. It should have been with the man you intend on spending the rest of your life with. I—"

She hushed him by pressing the tip of one finger against his mouth. "Don't. This was my choice, and I'm not sorry for any of it."

He gave her a lazy grin. "I've said it before, my lady, and I'll say it again. Lord Shipton has no idea what he walked away from. The man was a bloody fool."

To Connor's surprise, Jillian's own smile vanished and she sat up, facing away from him and drawing the sheet up to cover her naked breasts.

"No. He was no fool." She cast a brief glance at him over her shoulder, her expression shuttered. "To be honest, I can't blame him for changing his mind about wedding me. I certainly gave him ample reason."

"What do you mean?"

"My family was never what you would call conventional, Connor, and there were always wagging tongues. Rumors about my mother's former life as an actress and my parents' marriage. But Thomas never let it sway him. I'd known him from the time we were children, and he was a good friend."

Connor felt a surge of anger on her behalf. "Not such a good friend, if he abandoned you when you needed him most."

"You don't understand. It wasn't until later, after Mama was killed and I became so wrapped up in Papa's work, that he began to draw away from me a bit. And it was the scandal that resulted from my involvement in the Ranleigh jewel theft case that finally ended things. Looking back on it now, I can't blame him. It all happened right around the time Thomas inherited the title from his late father, you see, and his family was pressuring him to make a good match."

Jillian paused for an instant, then shook her head. "I'm afraid I'm far from that. And I suppose it was naïve of me to believe that he would continue to stand by me in the face of such adversity."

Connor's heart contracted with sympathy at the resigned note he heard in her voice. Regardless of whether she would acknowledge the fact or not, Shipton's defection had hurt her a great deal.

Reaching out, he caught her by the arm and drew her back to lie beside him once more.

"You're wrong, sweetheart. You had every right to expect the man you loved to stand by you, no matter what."

"That's just it." Curling into his side, she wrapped her arms about his waist with a sigh. "I don't think he ever loved me. And sometimes I wonder if I ever really loved him. We cared for each other. But love . . . ? I know I never came close to feeling for him what I feel for you."

And what do you feel for me?

The question reverberated in his head, but Connor didn't dare ask it out loud. He wasn't sure he was ready to hear the answer. And he certainly wasn't ready to examine his own feelings too closely when it came to this maddening woman.

He might never be ready for that.

Burying his nose in her jasmine-scented hair, he let the silence linger for several long seconds before speaking again. "I'm sorry about your mother, Gypsy."

Jillian's voice was muffled against his shoulder when she replied. "I am, too. She was a good woman, Connor. Yes, she did some things that were wrong and far from wise. But she loved me. I never doubted that."

"You know, sometimes it's the people who have been hurt the most who can be the most hurtful to others. I learned that from Brennan. He was my twin, the other half of me, yet toward the end he seemed intent on striking out at me at every turn."

At his words, she peered up at him curiously. "Brennan was your twin? The way you spoke of him, I assumed he was younger."

"He was. By about eleven minutes. But sometimes it seemed more like eleven years." Connor hesitated again, trying to think of a way to phrase what he wanted to say that wouldn't offend her or start an argument. "Jillian, have you ever considered giving all of this up? Putting it behind you?"

When she pulled back to arch an inquiring brow at him, he explained. "Your work with Bow Street, I mean. Your quest to find out whether or not Hawksley was falsely accused of your mother's murder."

Her gaze was serious and never wavered from his. "Tell me, Connor. What if someone asked you to quit looking for the man who murdered Stuart, Peg, and Hiram? Could you do it?"

"This is a different situation, Jillian. There are other people in immediate danger—"

"Perhaps. But let's say for the sake of argument that this murderer stopped killing tomorrow. That you never got another letter from him or heard another word about him. Would you ever be able to stop looking for him?"

There was no need for him to even respond. He knew everything he felt must be there for her to see in the abrupt hardening of his visage, the tightening of his jaw. No, he would never stop searching for this sick bastard. Never. Somehow he would find the man and make him pay.

As if privy to his innermost thoughts, Jillian inclined her head in a nod. "So you see how impossible it would be for me to ever forget about any of this. I'm the only one who suspects that there was more to my mother's death than meets the eye, and if I don't do something, no one ever will."

Connor could understand her need for answers. But the mere thought of the risk she was taking by continuing on this path was enough to strike terror into the depths of a heart that he had believed was far too battered to ever feel such things again.

His hold on her tightened, but she went on speaking as if unaware of his trepidation. "This man, whoever he is, robbed me of my mother and tore my family apart, and I don't know why. My father and sisters and I deserve to know the truth." A militant light entered her eyes. "And so do Lord Hawksley's wife and son. My God, Connor, can you imagine the pain they must have gone through the last few years? Believing that the earl was a murderer when he might have been innocent? I can't let that stand."

No, Connor mused wryly, he didn't imagine she could. He had come to know his intrepid little investigator well enough to realize that she would never be able to turn her back on an injustice. She was so damned stubborn, so set on doing what she believed was right, that the danger she could be placing herself in was of little consequence to her.

Part of him longed to sweep her up and carry her away from it all, whether she willed it or not. To wrap her in cotton wool so that nothing and no one could hurt her. But he was well aware that he had no right to do so. Never mind that he had just made love to her, that they had been closer than any two people could be. In the end, it changed nothing.

And yet, it changed everything.

It had been a mistake to allow this woman to come to mean so much to him, he concluded, studying her drowsy and sated features in the pale glow of moonlight that spilled in through the bedroom window. In the heat of their passion, he had not only let himself forget the insurmountable differences in their backgrounds and stations, but he had nearly forgotten that caring for someone—especially someone who seemed determined to repeatedly place herself in harm's way—was a dangerous proposition. And where Jillian was concerned, he was obviously already far too vulnerable.

Connor settled back against the pillows with a weary exhalation. It was apparent that she would not be swayed from her self-imposed mission, and he couldn't afford to let her into his heart and life, only to lose her as he had lost so many other people he had cared for and failed to protect.

Somehow, he would have to figure out a way to nip these inconvenient emotions in the bud, to separate himself from her, before it was too late.

But he had no doubt that such a feat was going to prove far easier said than done.

Long after Connor had drifted off to sleep, Jillian remained wide awake and restless, cuddled close against him as the events of that day replayed themselves over and over in her mind.

So much had happened. In the span of just a few short hours, her life had altered in totally unexpected ways. Not only had she finally managed to stumble upon a lead regarding the night of her mother's death, but she had just given herself to the man she loved in a tender, exquisite, passionate exchange that had far surpassed her most cherished fantasies of what making love could be like.

A tingle of excitement raced through her as she recalled the way Connor's mouth and hands had explored her body. The way it had felt to have him moving deep inside of her. It had been so perfect.

But afterward, she had sensed his withdrawal, the distance he had placed between them once more. And despite herself, she had been hurt by it, even though it hadn't surprised her. Connor was a very controlled man who would find it difficult to ever completely let down his guard.

Even with the woman who shared his bed.

She bit her lip. She knew that their lovemaking hadn't meant nearly as much to him as it had to her. And she also knew that he didn't approve of her involvement in her father's work and the investigation she had been secretly conducting. Oh, he might not have said anything out loud, but she had recognized his expression. It was one she'd seen all too often before.

The sound of a grandfather clock striking the hour somewhere in the farthest reaches of the town house pulled her from her musings and reminded her that she should have dressed and headed for home long ago. She certainly didn't want any of her family members discovering she wasn't asleep in her bed. But somehow, even with that threat hanging over her head, she couldn't quite seem to make herself move. There was a part of her that feared leaving Connor's side. As if by staying here with him, she could hang on to whatever small amount of closeness they had managed to forge between them this night.

Dear God, she wanted to believe that everything could work out for them, that there might actually be a chance that they could have some sort of future together. But how could she when so much seemed to be against them?

Softly, so as not to awaken him, she pressed her lips to the satiny flesh of Connor's muscled shoulder, then snuggled as close as she could get without burrowing under his skin. The strength of his arms around her made her feel so safe. Perhaps if she continued to lie here for a while longer, she could eventually convince herself that she could be happy with whatever small part of him he was willing to give her.

And that she hadn't once again made the mistake of giving her heart to a man who was incapable of standing by her.

Chapter 21

Sometimes a single clue can open doors you never expected.

"Jillian Daventry, you'd better have a very good explanation for where you've been all night!"

The strident voice rang out in the early morning stillness, startling Jillian just as she was clambering back in through her bedroom window shortly before dawn. Her heart flying into her throat, she teetered precariously on the ledge for what seemed to her like an eternity before she finally managed to regain her balance and scramble the rest of the way over the sill.

With her feet planted firmly on the floor of her room, she took a moment to steady her wildly racing pulse, to school her features into some semblance of control, before turning to face the person who stood behind her, arms crossed in an imperious manner.

"Maura. What are you doing in here?"

"Waiting for you, of course." Her sister's blue eyes narrowed in a frosty glare. "I suspected you were up to something when you left the ball early last night, and when I returned home and peeked in here to find you gone, I knew for certain. I wasn't about to miss the chance to catch you sneaking back in, so I slept in here."

Jillian took note of the displaced throw pillows on the chair next to her bed, the book that lay open on its seat, and doubted that her sister had done much sleeping.

She glanced in the direction of the door, a bit surprised that the rest of her family hadn't already come bursting in. "You didn't . . . tell anyone?"

"No. But I should have. I decided to give you the opportunity to explain yourself, even though you don't deserve it."

Jillian stifled a weary sigh. She supposed she had no one to blame for this confrontation but herself. She had known there was a possibility of something like this happening, yet she had chosen to linger at Connor's side until almost morning, when she had finally slipped from the bed they had shared, dressed, and left the town house without waking him.

As she had made her way back to Belgrave Square through the quiet, empty streets, she had debated in her mind how she would deal with it if someone at home had discovered her absence. But now that it had come to pass, she was at an utter loss.

"I really don't see that what I do is any of your business—" she began.

Maura cut her off with a furious stamp of her foot. "Don't you dare try to fob me off with that. It most certainly *is* my business when what you do reflects upon this family. Do you care nothing for our reputation?"

She gave Jillian no time to answer, but whirled and began to pace, the ruffled hem of her night-dress frothing about her ankles with each agitated stride. "What am I saying? Of course you don't care. I had forgotten that you are the one who seems to take such delight in deliberately flouting convention and blackening the Daventry name at every turn."

The accusation had Jillian's own temper rising to the fore. "That's not true. How can you believe that of me?"

"How can I believe anything else? Do you have any idea what could have happened if anyone we knew had seen you wandering about out there at this hour, dressed like that?" Maura gestured contemptuously at the breeches Jillian wore. "After years of being whispered about, of being snubbed and slighted, we are finally starting to be accepted by the *ton* again. Aunt Olivia thinks my prospects for making a good match this Season are excellent, and you know how important that is to me. Yet you seem set on ruining it all."

Pierced by a sudden shard of guilt at her sister's words, Jillian felt some of her indignation subside and bowed her head. It was true. Regardless of whether or not she felt that her actions were justified, she was well aware that she was jeopardizing her family's standing in society every time she thumbed her nose at their strictures.

"Maura, I'm sorry," she said softly. "I know that my behavior in the past few years has made things worse for you in so many ways. If nothing else, I realized that at the ball last night, after coming across you with Lord Lanscombe's son. But I swear, it isn't my intention to hurt you."

Her sister came to an abrupt halt and spun about to face her once more. "Then what *is* your intention? Make me understand why you seem to have so little regard for those you are supposed to care for."

Jillian hesitated at the honest bewilderment and pain that marked her sister's heart-shaped face. She hated being at odds with Maura, missed the days when she had been able to confide in her, and she had to admit that the thought of unburdening herself to at least one of her family members was tempting . . .

Perhaps it was time for her to try being honest. Or at least, as honest as she could be in the circumstances. She wouldn't mention Connor or the specifics of his case, but she could reveal what she had learned from the maid at Wilbur Forbes's boardinghouse. Maybe once Maura knew everything, she would see that Jillian had sound reasons for her suspicions.

She took a deep breath. There was only one way to find out, and no other way to do it than to just come right out and say it.

Seizing her courage in both hands, she blurted, "I've been helping Tolliver."

There was a long, taut silence as her sister gaped at her, obviously stunned. Then, enraged color flooded into Maura's cheeks and her hands balled into fists at her sides. "You've been what?"

"Maura, if you would just listen—"

"Listen to what? There is nothing you can say that could possibly excuse this! How could you involve yourself with that man again after what happened before? Especially now, when it is more important than ever that we all remain above reproach?"

"I had to. He came to me with information about a suspect in one of his cases. A man who may have had ties to what happened to Mama."

Looking as if someone had struck her, Maura sank down onto the foot of the bed. "Is that what this is all about? You're still set on proving that Lord Hawksley was innocent?"

"Just because the rest of you refused to see the inconsistencies in the law's investigation doesn't mean I forgot about them," Jillian defended herself. "And now I have more reason than ever to doubt their conclusions."

She quickly filled her sister in on Wilbur Forbes and what she had been told by Pansy, pointing out all the ways in which the maid's story fit her own theory of events as she did so.

Then, she patiently waited for Maura's verdict.

When it came, it wasn't at all what she had hoped it would be. "Do you have any idea how mad this sounds? Lord Hawksley *had* to be guilty. He was there that night. He was standing over the body and he struggled with Papa."

Jillian had to resist the urge to gnash her teeth in frustration. She should have known that convincing her sister wouldn't be easy. "Yes, but there could be another explanation for his presence."

"The only explanation is that Mama chose the wrong man to have an affair with." Maura's voice was cold, almost brittle. "Jilly, it's been four years. When are you going to let this go? Can't you put it behind you so that we can all move on with our lives?"

"Not as long as there are so many unanswered questions. My God, Maura, someone else was there! If that person was responsible for killing Mama instead of Lord Hawksley, don't you want to know?"

"No. No, I don't, because I don't care. Do you hear me? *I don't care!*" It was the cry of a wounded child, and the grief that lurked in the depths of Maura's eyes belied the bitterness of her outburst.

Going to her knees next to the bed, Jillian met her sister's gaze unwaveringly. "I don't believe that."

"Believe it. She was leaving us, Jilly. She was

running away with another man and leaving us."

"Maybe."

"What do you mean maybe? We found Lord Hawksley's note to her."

"That doesn't mean she was taking him up on his offer. And notes can be forged."

"What possible reason could anyone have for doing such a thing?"

Jillian shook her head. "I don't know, but don't you think it's at least worth looking into? Why is it always so easy for you to believe the worst of her?"

"And why is it so hard for you?" Maura rose and moved over to the window to stare out at the rosy dawn sky. "You were so willfully blind where she was concerned, Jilly. You act as if you never saw the way she hurt and humiliated Papa. But I saw it. And I hate her for what she did to him."

She glanced back over her shoulder, her expression tense, as if she were remembering things she would rather not. "You know, I heard them arguing that night. Their voices woke me, and I was out in the hallway when Papa came storming out of their suite on his way to the guest room. I'll never forget the agony on his face, the tears in his eyes." Her own eyes sparkled with sudden moisture. "*She* made him cry, Jilly. And I can't tell you how many nights since then that I've walked by the library door and seen him sitting behind his desk, clutching that miniature of her he keeps in his top drawer, looking so sad and alone I want to die for him."

Jillian's heart broke at the mental image of her father, slumped at his desk, clinging to the one last thing he had that still made him feel close to his lost wife.

Poor Papa.

Maura swung away from the window, her delicate frame rigid with fury. "She was going to abandon him, abandon all of us, and I can never forgive her for that."

Jillian got to her feet with a sigh. She had known that Maura nursed a certain amount of anger toward their mother, but she had never realized before just how deep that anger went. "He left her, too, Maura. Long before she left him."

"What are you talking about? He never left her. He was right here."

"No he wasn't. Not really. He might have been here in body, but he started retreating from us in spirit the moment Grandfather died and he became the Marquis of Albright."

When Maura simply set her jaw and looked away, Jillian took a step forward, reaching out to catch her sister by the arm. She had loved both of her parents, and she had no desire to point accusing fingers. But she also wasn't about to stand here and allow all of the blame to be heaped on her mother's head. Not when she knew the truth.

"Papa was just as responsible for the strife that existed between them as Mama was, and you know it," she said, her tone gentle. "After he took on the title, he changed. He became distant and retreated into his work. And the more he withdrew, the more frantic Mama became to gain his attention. She went about it in the wrong way, yes, but she was desperate. Mama needed him to defend her against the whispers of society, to stand by her, and he didn't do it."

Maura tugged free of Jillian's hold, then wrapped her arms about herself, as if trying to ward off the sting of a blow. "Even if that's true, don't you see that all you're doing by raking up the past is causing us all more pain? Regardless of who killed her and why, knowing the truth won't bring her back."

"I wish I could remember."

The tiny voice came from the doorway, and both Jillian and Maura whipped about to find a waiflike figure clad in a long, white nightgown, standing just inside the room, watching them.

"Aimee!" Concern for her youngest sibling overwhelming everything else, Jillian hurried toward her. "How long have you been standing there?"

"Long enough to know that you still believe that someone other than Lord Hawksley killed Mama."

Jillian winced. The last thing she wanted was to upset Aimee by reminding her of the night that had left her so traumatized that she had wiped it from her memory.

Placing her arm around the girl's frail shoulders, she steered her back in the direction of the door. "Darling, you should still be in bed. It's far too early for you to be up and about, and—"

"You needn't treat me like a child, Jilly."

Taken aback, Jillian glanced over at Maura, who looked equally shocked. It wasn't like their youngest sister to speak so firmly, so unequivocally.

Aimee went on, staring up at her with wide, serious amber eyes. "I know you do it because you love me, but I don't need you to protect me. I'm not a little girl anymore, and I have just as much right as the two of you to know what's going on."

Jillian considered her words. She supposed there was a certain amount of truth to them. She couldn't deny being overly protective where her little sister was concerned. Because Aimee's small stature and shy, timid nature made her seem much younger than her thirteen years, people had a tendency to treat her accordingly.

She pulled the girl close in a tight hug. "I'm sorry, lamb. I truly don't mean to leave you out of things. It's just that you've already been through so much."

"I wish I could remember what I saw that night." Aimee's voice was muffled, sounding wistful in her ear. "If I could just remember, we would finally know the truth and you wouldn't have to fight anymore."

"Oh, sweetheart."

Aimee lifted her head from Jillian's shoulder and looked over at her other sister, who was watching them with an unreadable expression. "Jilly's right, you know."

Maura's brow furrowed in puzzlement. "Right about what, darling?"

"About Mama not wanting to leave us. That's one thing about that night I *do* remember. She came into our room while you were sleeping."

Jillian was unable to smother a gasp at the revelation. Understandably, her youngest sister had always seemed reluctant to speak about what had happened four years ago, and she had never before mentioned their mother making a visit to the room she shared with Maura that evening.

"The storm frightened me and I called out to her," Aimee was saying, her gaze never wavering from Maura. "She sat down beside me on the bed and kissed my forehead, and she told me . . . She told me that she loved us all so much and that she was sorry for the way she had been acting. That from that moment on she was going to try to do better."

She paused for an instant, her countenance solemn, before she continued in a choked voice. "And she was crying, too, Maura."

A lump swelled in Jillian's throat. And suddenly Maura's expression wasn't quite so unreadable. Her face crumpled and the tears she had been holding back started to stream down her cheeks, the force of her sobs shaking her delicate shoulders.

Reaching out with one hand, Jillian drew her other sister into the huddle with her and Aimee. And in one another's arms, the three Daventry sisters cried together for the first time over the night that had robbed them of so much.

Chapter 22

An investigator must be prepared to resort to whatever means are necessary.

"So Maura has agreed not to mention my most recent exploits to anyone. At least for the time being."

Turning away from her contemplation of the busy street outside the big bay windows, Jillian faced the Dowager Duchess of Maitland across the width of the parlor, having just finished telling her friend about the events that had transpired the evening before.

"Of course, she isn't completely convinced I know what I'm talking about," she went on, "but she's considering the possibility. Which is more than I had ever expected from her."

Regally ensconced on a brocade-covered love seat, Theodosia smiled and set aside her steaming cup of tea. "I'm glad you were able to confide in her, dear. I know how much you have missed being close to Maura, but now you have a chance to mend things. You mother would have wanted that for her daughters."

Jillian felt her own lips curve upward as she recalled the hours she had spent with both Maura and Aimee that morning, talking and taking the first tentative steps toward rebuilding a sisterly bond. It wasn't going to be easy and they had a long road ahead of them, but they were well on their way.

"I know," she murmured. "I only wish we had been honest with one another long ago. I never realized Aimee felt so smothered by our constant coddling. And if I had known how much anger Maura still harbored toward Mama—and why—I could have better understood the distance she kept between us."

She crossed the room to stand before the duchess, her hands clasped before her in an almost convulsive grip. "But as happy as I am that my sisters and I have come to some sort of accord, there's another reason I'm here."

The elderly woman's smile faded and she sighed. "Your mother."

"Yes."

There was a long, drawn-out silence. When it became obvious Theodosia wasn't going to speak, Jillian prodded her gently. "You never did tell me what you thought about what I learned from Pansy."

The dowager's plump countenance creased with sudden displeasure. "I'll tell you what I think, young lady. I do not approve of what you did last night. St. Giles is a very dangerous place at the best of times, but especially so after dark. You should have waited for Tolliver."

"Perhaps. But I can't be sorry for it. If I hadn't gone, I might never have met Pansy or found out what I did." Jillian sank down on the love seat next to the duchess, her gaze imploring. "Please. Is there anyone you can think of who was close to Hawksley who might have been . . . acquainted with my mother, as well? A titled gentleman?"

Theodosia's brow furrowed in concentration, as if she were giving the matter considerable thought. "There were Lords Lanscombe and Bedford, of course. They went drinking and gambling with Hawksley quite often, and they both had a mild flirtation with Elise. Dissolute rakes, they were. Though I must concede that Bedford has mellowed in recent years." She shook her head. "But I'm afraid I can't see either one of them killing your mother and setting up Hawksley to take the blame."

Jillian bit her lip. "Whoever it was, it must have been someone with a great deal of power. Pansy said Forbes seemed terrified of him."

The duchess touched her arm in a gesture of sympathy. "I'm so sorry, dear. I wish I could be of more help, but a titled gentleman . . . ? It could be anyone."

"I suppose. But at least I finally have *some*

details to work with. More than I had before, anyway. I know that I'm on the right track." With a lift of her chin, Jillian rose again and began to pace before the love seat. "Right now, however, I need to try and put this aside and give my attention to Connor's case. With the only other suspect in these murders dead, I'm afraid Bow Street has focused their investigation on him. If I can't stop this killer, and soon, not only could more people die, but Connor could wind up going to jail for something he didn't do."

"Connor, is it? You truly care for this man, don't you?"

There was a sly note in Theodosia's voice, and when Jillian stopped pacing and glanced over at the woman, she was greeted by a calmly knowing expression.

"Yes, I do," she admitted. There was little use in denying what she was certain was written clearly on her face. "More than I should."

"You're in love with him."

It wasn't a question, and Jillian nodded.

"I don't know how it happened so quickly," she whispered, pressing one hand against her chest in an effort to quell the ache that seemed to grow stronger every time she thought of the man who held her heart. "Just a week ago I didn't even know he existed, and now I can't imagine my life without him."

With a cluck of her tongue, the duchess held out a hand to her. "Come here, dear."

There was no refusing that no-nonsense tone, Jillian mused with a hint of humor, returning to Theodosia's side and accepting her hand.

"I'm not going to ask you what happened between you and Mr. Monroe," the duchess assured her, giving her fingers a gentle squeeze. "But I will say this. From what I have observed of him, he seems like a good man. A very strong man." An understanding light shone in her eyes. "He is not Thomas, dear. I don't believe he is the sort who would abandon you when you needed him most."

Jillian took a shaky breath. She had always known that Theodosia could read her far too well, but hearing her fears spelled out in such a stark fashion was unsettling. It made them seem far too real. "I can only hope you're right. Because it's far too late to guard my heart."

At that moment, there was a tap at the door, and the butler poked his head into the room at the duchess's summons.

"Your Grace, a rather strange, er . . . parcel has been delivered to the door by a street urchin. For Lady Jillian. Shall I bring it in?"

"Yes, please do, Fielding." As the servant departed, Theodosia looked up at Jillian. "That's odd. Who on earth would send something to you here?"

Intrigued herself, Jillian waited until the butler reappeared in the doorway before she came forward to take the small package he held out to her. "Thank you, Fielding."

He bowed with his usual stiff formality and departed.

The box was long and flat, roughly battered and tied with a frayed cord, and Jillian turned it over, examining it curiously. There was no card attached, though her name was printed on the outside in scrawled letters.

Lady Jillian Daventry

Theodosia heaved herself to her feet with the aid of her cane and shuffled over to peer over her shoulder. "Is your Mr. Monroe sending you jewelry already?"

It was true that the box was about the right size for such a thing, but its condition convinced Jillian that she wasn't going to find a diamond necklace or matching earbobs inside. "I don't think so."

Her heart skipped a beat as she stared down at the package in her hands. It was so innocuous-looking, but something about it . . .

Without another second's hesitation, she yanked the cord loose and lifted the top.

Nestled within were several locks of flaxen-blond hair.

Stunned and confused, it took her but an instant to realize that the strands were matted with a rust-colored substance. The brassy smell that drifted to her nostrils was unmistakable.

Blood.

A small scrap of paper lay atop the tangled mass. It was torn and stained, but despite its bedraggled state, the handwriting on it was still legible, and hauntingly familiar.

You'll regret the day you ever met Connor Monroe. Just ask Selene Duvall.

Jillian didn't even wait for the driver to open the door when the carriage came to a halt at the curb in front of Grayson and Monroe Shipping. She had already flown from the conveyance and was rushing up the steps of the building before the poor man could even climb down from his perch.

The macabre package she had received was tucked under one arm.

From the moment she had opened the box, Jillian had been aware of nothing but an all-encompassing urge to find Connor. Theodosia had been far from happy when she had insisted on going to him at once instead of waiting to alert Tolliver. But upon realizing she would not be dissuaded, the duchess had relented with the stipulation that she take the Maitland coach and driver.

Jillian hadn't argued. All she could think about was Connor. If something had truly happened to his former mistress, if the woman was dead, there was little doubt that Bow Street would be knocking on his door before too long.

He would need her, like it or not.

Entering the lobby, she saw that it was empty except for a tall, almost cadaverously thin man with a balding head and spectacles seated behind a high desk in the corner. He looked up as she approached.

"May I help you?" he asked, eyeing her askance.

"Yes. I need to speak with Mr. Connor Monroe."

"Do you have an appointment?"

Something about the man's patronizing tone rubbed Jillian on the raw when her nerves were already strung much too tautly, tempting her to reach across the desk and shake him by his scrawny neck. But she remained calm with an effort. "No, I don't. But I really do need to see him. If you could just tell him I'm here?"

"He's in his office, but he's with someone rather important at the moment." He gave her a patently false smile, then gestured toward a logbook on a pedestal a few feet away. "If you would care to sign in and wait. Or perhaps come back later? *Much* later?"

Jillian fumed. The odious little weasel sounded almost hopeful that she would give up and go away! "You don't understand, sir. This can't wait. It's urgent that I see him at once."

"I'm afraid that's not possible."

"Well, we'll just see about that," she gritted out, then marched past him up the stairs, taking great satisfaction in the sputtering that came from behind her.

"Wait!" he called out, sounding panicked. "You can't do that!"

But she ignored him and kept going. If he wanted her out, he would have to bodily throw her out.

It didn't take long for her to reach the landing, and as she made her way along the second-floor hallway toward Connor's office, she swept by several people bustling in and out of the other rooms that lined the corridor. Unlike the last time she'd been here, when the building had been eerily silent, the hum of voices could be heard. She also noticed in passing that the door to Stuart Grayson's office stood ajar, and all signs of what had occurred there over a week ago had been scoured clean.

It seemed that things were once again all business at Grayson and Monroe Shipping.

Connor's own office door was shut, and she stopped only long enough to give it a short, sharp rap before swinging it open and stepping into the room.

And into the midst of what was obviously a heated discussion.

Hat in hand, Tolliver hovered just inside the doorway, surveying the scene taking place before him with visible dismay. Connor stood behind his desk, his hands braced on its polished surface as he glared across the room at the two Bow Street Runners who had questioned him at his town house the day before.

Ah. It appeared she was not a second too soon.

All eyes flew to her, and the sudden tightening of Connor's jaw told her that he was most decidedly not pleased to see her.

"What are you doing here?" The words were

enunciated, drawn out from between his clenched teeth.

Jillian didn't take offense at his harsh greeting. After all, she was well aware that she had walked in at a less than convenient time, and when he glanced back in the direction of the Bow Street Runners, she knew that his anger hid a very real concern for her.

He didn't want her dragged into the middle of things.

Her heart filled with warmth, and her first instinct was to race across the office and throw herself into his arms. But she managed to stifle the inclination. While she more than appreciated his worry on her behalf, at the moment she was far more frightened for him.

Straightening her shoulders, she hurried over to Connor, speaking softly once she reached his desk. "I had to come. I know about Selene." She paused, licking her suddenly dry lips as she searched his rigid features. "Is it true? Is she . . . ?"

He inclined his head in a stiff nod.

When it became apparent that he didn't plan on elaborating any further, Jillian looked back at Tolliver over her shoulder. "How?"

The Runner met her gaze, his countenance troubled. "The same as Mr. Grayson and Wilbur Forbes."

So, Selene's throat had been cut.

"I beg your pardon."

This came from the intimidating Officer Albertson, who had moved to join them at the desk and was peering at her suspiciously. "Just how is it that you know about what happened to Miss Duvall, Miss . . . ?"

Jillian ignored his obvious attempt to draw her name from her and instead chose to address Connor, holding the package she had brought with her out toward him. "This was delivered to me at Theodosia's home."

Connor took it, one eyebrow winging upward in question. But when she said nothing further, merely watched him with trepidation, he shrugged and removed the lid.

There was absolute silence. Each tick of the clock in the far corner could be heard as he stared down at the box's contents. The curling flaxen hair. The bloodstained note.

A muscle started to work in his jaw. When his eyes met hers again, there was an anguish, a helpless rage in their depths that she immediately recognized, because she felt the same way herself.

Connor had been right all along. Not only did the killer know her name, but he knew exactly where she was. Had even known when she would be at Theodosia's.

He had been following her.

"See here." Albertson broke into the silent communication between them with his peremptory demand. "I want to know what's going on here. What is that?"

Connor shoved the box into the Runner's hands.

"Now do you see?" he rasped, leaning forward over the desk, his big body practically vibrating with tension. "Now do you see why you must take what I say seriously? Why you must locate my stepfather as soon as possible?"

Albertson assessed what was in the box with narrowed eyes, swiftly scanning the note before handing it to his partner and turning back to Connor. "Monroe, I can assure you we will leave no stone unturned in this investigation. But you must admit that this isn't precisely compelling evidence in your favor. You could have written these notes or sent this package yourself, to divert suspicion. And if this Trask fellow is responsible, why would he have waited all these years to gain his revenge on you?"

Connor raked his hands back through his hair in an aggravated gesture, making the russet strands stand on end in a way that enhanced his already dangerously feral appearance. "Damn it, man, I don't know! He's a criminal, and he's not quite sane when it comes to me. Who knows how he thinks?"

"We'll look into it. But in the meantime I need to know what you did last night. Where you went and who you were with."

Jillian felt her stomach flutter in distress as she took in the Runner's officiously superior expression. Dear God, he didn't believe a word. She could read it in the condescending curl of the man's upper lip. He was simply humoring them.

Her gaze locked with Connor's, and she knew right away what he was thinking. If he told the truth about what he'd been doing and who he'd been with the night before, it would be all over London before the sun went down. The Daventry name would be dragged through the dirt, and she would once again become the subject of speculation and scandal.

And if she didn't act quickly, she had no doubt that Connor would sacrifice himself for her reputation.

In that split second, she made a decision. As much as she cared for her family and had no desire to expose them to further gossip or pain, she couldn't stand by and do nothing when she could save an innocent man from hanging.

The man she loved.

Clearing her throat, she took a resolute step toward the Runner. "Excuse me, sir. I believe I can provide you with the information you seek."

"Jillian, don't."

Connor's vehement protest rang in her ears, but she brushed it aside and focused on Albertson as he studied her with calculating interest.

Screwing up her courage, she took a deep breath and sealed her fate. "My name is Lady Jillian Daventry, and I was with Mr. Monroe at his town house last night. All night."

Chapter 23

Persuasion is an art an investigator would do well to perfect.

"I'm sorry."

At the sound of the quiet voice, Connor glanced up from his brooding contemplation of the floor of the jostling coach to find Jillian watching him with wary intentness from her perch on the very edge of the opposite seat. With her hands folded tightly in her lap and her shoulders set and stiff, she held herself with such rigidity that she could have passed for a garden statue.

"I didn't mean to make you angry," she continued, holding his gaze without flinching despite her obvious anxiety. "I was only trying to do the right thing."

Reaching up, Connor gave his cravat a sharp tug, loosening the knot before allowing himself to relax back against the velvet squabs of the Maitland carriage with a weary sigh. "I'm not angry."

Doubt seeped into her expression. "You certainly behave as if you are. Except for insisting on seeing me back to Theodosia's house, you've barely spoken a word since I told Albertson I was with you last night."

He supposed that was true. But that was because he'd been too stunned by her confession to string a coherent sentence together. All the while the Runners had been questioning her, he'd been struggling with the chaos of his thoughts, trying to understand why she'd done it.

Now, not only had she been targeted by a killer, but she had once again exposed herself to the gossip and innuendo of the *ton*. And this time, her reputation could be besmirched beyond repair.

All because of him.

None of it made sense, but somehow he couldn't quite bring himself to question her about it. Even after Tolliver had departed with a still skeptical Albertson and his partner to do some further checking into the whereabouts of Ian Trask, Connor hadn't asked Jillian for explanations.

He was far too busy trying to figure out how he was going to keep her safe from his stepfather.

"Connor?"

Her gentle prompting had him looking back up to meet her eyes once again. "It's not that I'm

angry," he said, removing his hat and raking a
hand back through his hair in a frustrated gesture. "I'm exhausted and at the end of my rope,
and your interference has complicated things.
You were already far more involved in all of
this than I ever wanted, and now . . . All right,
yes! I *am* angry! Why did you do it?"

Jillian's chin rose in direct proportion to the
volume of his voice, and by the time he had finished speaking she was glaring down her up-
lifted nose at him. "I was trying to help you.
And the least you could do is thank me. I did
save your life, after all."

"I don't know about that. What's the difference between meeting my maker with my neck
in a hangman's noose or at the business end of
your father's hunting rifle?"

"My father doesn't own a hunting rifle. And
he won't be upset with you. He'll be upset with
me. It was my choice."

Terror for this woman who had come to mean
so much to him flooded through Connor's
veins, stark and undeniable, and a mental image
of Stuart slumped over his desk, blood pouring
from the wound in his throat, sent a chill racing
up his spine. God, if something like that happened to Jillian . . . "Damnation, Gypsy, you are
so stubborn. You just won't let anyone protect
you, will you?"

She turned away to stare out the window at
the passing scenery, her expression shuttered.
"I didn't ask to be protected."

"Nevertheless, you need a keeper. You seem determined to put yourself in the middle of dangerous situations, time after time. If you won't think of yourself, think of your family. You've dragged them into the muck right along with you."

Jillian bit her lip at his words, but didn't turn to face him. "I realize that, and I'm sorry for it. I never wanted to hurt them. But when weighed in the balance, an innocent man's life is much more important than a reputation, and I'm certain my family would agree. I couldn't let them arrest you."

"Why the bloody hell not?"

Amber eyes that glowed molten gold in the dimness of the carriage swung back in Connor's direction, pinning him in place with their piercing and incisive gleam. "Because I love you, you exasperating oaf!"

It was the last thing Connor had expected to hear, and it echoed in his ears, stunning him. The truth was, as perfect as their lovemaking last night had been, as much as he had relished every moment of it, he had begun to fear that Jillian herself might have had feelings of regret. She had slipped away without waking him before the morning sun had touched the sky, and when he had opened his eyes to find her gone, he hadn't been certain whether to be relieved or disappointed that he wouldn't be able to make love to her again.

But he couldn't let himself believe what she

was saying. She couldn't love him. It was impossible.

Struggling to find the right words, he spoke slowly, cautiously, loath to hurt her, but determined to make her see reason. "Jillian, I know last night was your first time. But don't let yourself confuse sex with love. You—"

"Don't treat me like a child, Connor," she interrupted him, her cheeks flushing with angry color. "And don't tell me what I feel. Last night wasn't just about sex. At least not for me. I never would have let you touch me to begin with if I didn't love you."

"I don't deserve your love, Gypsy. You'd be far better off with a wealthy young lord. Someone of your class and station who still has a heart left to give you. My own was torn out of me long ago."

"I don't believe that, Connor." Jillian's countenance suddenly softened and she leaned forward in her seat, her gaze steady and earnest. "You're not nearly as unfeeling as you pretend you are. I've seen the way you care for the people closest to you. Stuart, Peg, Hiram. You loved them, whether you will admit it or not."

"And you see what happened to them. You may have noticed that I have an unfortunate tendency to let down the people I care about. They all seem to wind up dead."

"That's not your fault."

"It *is* my fault. I should have been able to protect them." Desperate to get through to her, Connor reached out to grasp Jillian by the shoulders, giving her a little shake for emphasis. "What about Selene, Gypsy? I was enough of a bloody fool to think that she was safe just because I had stopped seeing her, and look what happened. And Brennan. The one person I cared for more than anyone else in the world, and he's dead because of me."

"Connor—"

"No. Don't love me, Gypsy. I can't ever love you back. I can't afford to let myself care that much for anyone ever again."

She stared into his eyes for a long, drawn-out moment, the only sound the muffled clop of hooves as the carriage horses wended their way through the crowded London streets. Tension hovered in the air around them, almost palpable. And just when Connor thought he was going to explode if she didn't say something, she smiled.

It was like the sun coming out after the rain, so warm and bright and beautiful that it robbed him of speech.

"Connor," she murmured, lifting her hands to cup his face, her palms cool against his heated skin. "It's too late. I love you and there's nothing you can do about it."

"Gypsy—"

She stopped the movement of his mouth with the tip of a finger, shaking her head at him. "I'm not asking you to love me back, but I'm not going to let you convince yourself that what I feel isn't love. And you might as well save your breath, because I'm going to kiss you now."

And letting one arm slide up over his shoulder until she could wind it around his neck, she did just that.

She tasted so sweet, so pure, and Connor couldn't stifle a soul-deep groan as her lips moved over his in a feather-light caress, her tongue darting out to tickle and tease the corners of his mouth. He knew he should push her away, that he should be fighting the overwhelming desire she aroused in him with such little effort, but he seemed incapable of doing so.

And instead of setting her from him, he wrapped his arms around her waist and pulled her even closer, their swiftly increasing passion spiraling out of all control.

"Jillian," he muttered between their deepening kisses, his hands knocking her bonnet to the floor of the carriage and tangling in the falling tendrils of her hair. "Jillian, this isn't a good idea."

She evaded his mouth long enough to nuzzle the strong column of his throat, wringing a shudder from him as she skimmed her tongue over the salty flesh just above his cravat. "I happen to think it's a very good idea." Tugging at the already loosened knot with her teeth, she peered coyly up at him when the material parted and she pressed a kiss to the golden wedge of muscled chest that was exposed. "A very good idea."

Her sensual purr stroked over his nerve endings with the smoothness of silk, her breath wafting against his skin tantalizingly, and he was so lost in the pleasure of it that at first he didn't notice when her fingers went to the waist-band of his breeches and began to undo the fas-tenings.

Until his rigid and aching maleness sprang forward into her eager palms.

A growl rumbled in Connor's throat and his eyes fell shut, his fingers tightening almost con-vulsively in her hair as she worked his stiffness, exploring him with tentative, yet agile fingers. She coasted her thumb over the swollen, plum-shaped head, gathering up the moisture at the very tip and spreading it over his length with a surprisingly expert touch that had him finally jerking from her hold with a panting gasp.

"That's enough, Gypsy," he rasped, nipping at the delicate shell of her ear. "I don't want to come until I'm inside you."

Gliding his hands downward over Jillian's rounded curves, he briefly molded the volup-tuous mounds of her breasts through her bodice, then shaped her ample hips before cupping her bottom to pull her onto his lap. The skirts of her gown were shoved up out of the way so she could straddle him.

Through the material of her drawers, he could feel the heated core of her come into contact with the hardness of his manhood.

"Are you sure you want this, Gypsy?" he asked huskily, his finger finding the slit in her under-garments, testing the readiness of her feminine channel.

She gazed up at him from under lowered

lashes, her eyes so full of love that he almost had to look away from it. God, he didn't deserve her.

"Connor," she told him throatily, "I will always want this."

It was all the answer he needed. He sank deep, and a moan escaped Jillian before she began to ride him, her palms braced on his shoulders and her head thrown back as she slid up and down along his length.

Connor lifted his hips to meet her, his hands on her waist guiding her slow, steady movements. He pumped into her wet heat in counterpoint to the rocking of the coach, his ecstasy building with each thrust, carrying her with him until she finally cried out and convulsed around him.

The velvety contractions deep in her womb sent him over the edge, and his own climax pulsed over him in powerful waves, leaving him weak and gasping.

Jillian collapsed against his chest, and for long seconds neither of them said a word. They merely held each other, spent and sated.

Then her voice drifted up to him, muffled but firm. "I can take care of myself, you know."

She raised her head, her eyes troubled and serious as she searched his features. "And you can't blame yourself for the choices other people make, Connor. We are responsible for our own decisions. Brennan made the decision to get involved with your stepfather again, to turn to a life of crime. *He* made the decision to struggle with the Runner, and his death was the result of that decision. It wasn't your fault."

Connor cupped her chin, tilting her face up to his. "Jillian, if I told you that what happened to your mother wasn't your fault, that your chances of finding her real killer were so minuscule as to be nonexistent, and that you can't spend the rest of your life tracking down criminals as some sort of penance for your supposed sins, would you listen?"

She didn't answer, simply bit her lip and looked away.

"Then you can understand why I can't be swayed," he said gently. "As much as I enjoy making love to you, this doesn't change my mind. I won't let myself love you. Especially not when you feel compelled to put your life at risk at every turn. You need someone who is capable of protecting you, of keeping you safe."

He paused, then drew her head back to his chest with a soft, regretful sigh. "And as much as I hate the fact, Gypsy, I'm afraid I'm not that man."

Chapter 24

Sometimes a re-examination of the evidence is called for.

Later that evening, Jillian sat before the dressing table mirror in her bedchamber, brushing her hair with slow, meditative strokes as she went back over the events of the past few days.

So much had occurred, she mused. Within the last week, she had made a momentous discovery about the night Mama had died, forged a fragile peace with her sisters, given up her virginity, and fallen in love.

With an infuriating, insufferable man who seemed determined to fight her at every turn.

She sighed and set aside her brush, propping her chin on her hand as she stared wistfully at her reflection. Why couldn't she have given her heart to someone less obstinate? Less set on taking the weight of the whole world onto his shoulders?

Because then he wouldn't be Connor Monroe, her mind answered.

After dropping her off at Maitland House earlier that day, Connor had pressed a soft, soul-stirring kiss to her lips before leaving to catch a hackney back to the Grayson and Monroe Shipping offices. There had been no getting through to him. The man was certain that what was between them could never work.

And she was just as certain that it could.

Jillian felt her cheeks heat and her pulse speed up as she recalled how they had come together in the carriage, the way he had touched and kissed her. The wanton way she had ridden him to her utter fulfillment. And afterward, he had held her as if she were some precious treasure he couldn't bear to let go of.

No matter what he said, she knew he loved her. Now, she just had to convince him of that.

Getting to her feet, she wandered over to stare out the window at the darkness that was just starting to descend over the landscape. She had no doubt that a relationship between the two of them would be difficult. A marquis's daughter marrying a tradesman would have the *ton* agog, and whispers and innuendo would follow them wherever they went. But she was used to such things, after all. And yes, Papa would be furious at first. At least, until he saw how happy Connor made her. In the end, that would be all that mattered to him.

With the mistakes of her parents to show her which pitfalls to avoid, Jillian knew that she and Connor could have a wonderful life together.

But right now, she had a killer to help catch. Perhaps once the law had apprehended his stepfather and the danger of being with him was removed, Connor would be ready to listen to her arguments.

At that moment, there was a soft tap at her bedroom door, and Jillian glanced back over her shoulder before calling out to whoever it was to enter.

The panel eased open a small crack, and the housekeeper poked her head into the room.

"Dinner is being served, my lady," she announced. "I know you said you had another headache and didn't wish to eat with the family this evening. But I thought I would check to see if you would like a tray brought up."

Jillian smiled at her. She was fond of the matronly Mrs. Bellows. In fact, in the last four years, the woman had been more of a mother to her than Aunt Olivia had ever been. "No, thank you. I'm truly not hungry."

The housekeeper's plump face was wreathed with obvious concern. "If you're sure, my lady."

"I am. And you needn't look so worried. I'm fine. Just a bit of a headache, as I said."

Mrs. Bellows nodded, but she still seemed less than convinced as she backed out of the chamber and closed the door behind her.

Once the housekeeper was gone, Jillian reached

up to rub at her aching temple with a grimace. The woman knew her far too well. This time, her headache wasn't a complete fabrication, but the truth was that she simply had no desire to see anyone right now. Though it appeared that word of her confession to Bow Street hadn't yet made the rounds, she was well aware it was only a matter of time before it did. And she had no intention of being anywhere near her family when it finally reached their ears.

She would give them a while to get over their initial anger before she attempted to explain things.

In the meantime, she would occupy herself by setting her mind to the task of trying to figure out where Ian Trask might strike next.

Fisting a hand in the window drapes, Jillian leaned her head against her arm and let her thoughts drift back, over the pieces of the puzzle they had gathered so far. For some reason, something was troubling her, but she couldn't quite put her finger on what.

As much as she hated to admit it, that bore Albertson had a point. It did seem odd that after being free from Newgate for almost five years, Trask would choose now to seek his revenge on Connor. And other than the message repeated by Elmer Patchett, there had been nothing in the cryptic letters or clues left behind to indicate that his stepfather was the culprit.

From the very beginning, Jillian had been

positive that the killer's actions were deliberate, that he was trying to tell them something.

The man wanted Connor to know who he was.

So what was the significance of the mirrors? It made little sense if Trask was their murderer. If the mirrors themselves were actual clues—

Wait a minute. Mirrors . . .

Jillian's heart flew into her mouth, practically choking her. Dear God, she had forgotten the message she had found in Wilbur Forbes's room!

Whirling away from the window, she hurried over to the wardrobe to swing open the door, digging through the discarded clothes at the bottom to find the lad's breeches she had worn the night before. She had tucked the note into her pocket . . .

Yes, here it was.

Withdrawing the small scrap of paper from the depths of the pocket, she unfolded it, her hands shaking with anticipation.

I'm the other half of you.

And in that instant, it all became appallingly clear. The pieces of the puzzle that didn't fit. The details at the crime scenes that had been nagging at her for days.

Snippets of past conversations with Connor blazed across her brain.

The force of it knocked him off the edge of the dock

*and his body wound up in the Thames. Unrecover-
able. I don't even have a grave to mourn over.*

He was my twin, the other half of me . . .

Jillian's gaze went to the mirror over her dressing table. That would explain it all, she thought
with slowly growing excitement. It would explain why there had been no signs of struggle at
most of the crime scenes. Why the victims had
apparently trusted the killer enough to let him
get close to them.

Because they had believed he was Connor.

Ian Trask wasn't the killer. It was Brennan
Monroe.

Balling the note into a crumpled wad in her fist,
she wrapped her arms about herself, trying to
calm the pitch and roll of her stomach. She couldn't
believe she had forgotten this. It had contained a
vital clue and it had been languishing here in her
room for over twenty-four hours. Of course, in
her own defense she *had* gotten a bit sidetracked
with other things, but that was no excuse.

A good investigator would never have forgotten.

There was no telling how Brennan Monroe
had survived his brush with the business end of
a pistol, followed by his dunk in the river. No
knowing where he had been for the past six
years, and no time to wonder. The fact was that
somehow he *had*. And now he was back in London, apparently blaming his brother for the fate
that had befallen him.

She had to get to Connor and warn him.

Returning to the window, she peeked around the curtain, waiting for the brief flash of movement that she had seen out of the corner of her eye when she had been standing here earlier. It only took a second and . . . Ah-ha, there it was.

A man slunk into view from around the corner of the garden wall, staring up at the windows on the upper level of the Daventry town house before once again disappearing into the gathering darkness that shrouded the mews.

It didn't surprise her at all that Connor had posted a guard to look after her. In fact, she had been halfway expecting it. She recognized the man as one of Tolliver's comrades, and she had no doubt that if he caught her slipping out of the house, he would march her right back to the front door and hand her over to her father. His instructions were more than likely not to allow her off the premises. For any reason.

It had just gone seven, and she was relatively certain that Connor would still be at Grayson and Monroe Shipping, as he had told her he would be working late for quite some time in order to get caught up with everything that had been neglected while the offices had been closed. All she had to do was change into her male disguise, figure out some way to get past the guard, and hail a hackney to get her to Fleet Street before it was too late.

She could do it. She wasn't Elise Daventry's daughter for nothing.

But dear God, don't let her be too late.

* * *

Connor was seated behind the desk in his office, trying to concentrate on the mound of paperwork he had yet to complete, when a loud knock sounded on his closed door and Tolliver stuck his head into the room without even waiting for permission to enter.

"I just had a message delivered to me from Albertson," the Runner announced, his lined face flushed with excitement as he hurried forward. "He has managed to locate Ian Trask."

A wave of relief washed over Connor, and he lunged to his feet, reaching for the coat draped over the back of his chair. His entire body hummed with expectation. "Where?"

"A tumbledown shack on the outskirts of London. We're to meet Albertson there."

This was it. Finally.

For the past few hours, Connor had been attempting to keep himself busy, to focus on the affairs of Grayson and Monroe Shipping and forget about his earlier encounter with Jillian in the Maitland carriage. It hadn't been easy, for the feel of her in his arms seemed permanently imprinted on his senses, and the words she had uttered with such certainty kept echoing in his head.

I love you.

Getting it out of his mind had been next to impossible, especially as he was so confused about his own feelings. He knew he cared for Jillian. But how could he let himself love her when the very thought of losing her was enough to incapacitate him with grief?

This was just what he needed, however, to forget about all of this. Once the law had Trask in its grasp, perhaps then he could take the time to look into his own heart and consider what it was he really felt for her.

Right now, he had a killer to catch.

"Let's go, then." Shrugging into his coat as he went, Connor led the way out of the office and down the stairs to the lobby, where Lowell Unger occupied his usual place behind the main desk. Though the rest of the shipping company's employees had gone home over an hour ago, Connor's new assistant had stayed behind in order to finish up a few things.

"Unger?" he called out as he strode forward.

The thin, bespectacled man peered questioningly at him over the tops of his wire-rimmed glasses. "Yes, sir?"

"I'm afraid a bit of an emergency has come up and I need to leave early. Do you mind making sure everything is locked up before you go?"

Unger's narrowed, inquisitive gaze went back and forth between the two men standing before him several times before he gave a sharp, affirmative nod. "Of course, sir."

"Good. Thank you." Connor didn't hesitate any longer, but stalked toward the door with Tolliver trailing in his wake.

By the time this night was over, he intended to make sure that the man who had been tormenting him for over a month, who had killed Stuart and Peg and so many others, finally received his comeuppance.

Jillian surveyed the weathered façade of Grayson and Monroe shipping from under the lowered bill of her cap. It was fully dark now, but she could see from her position on the sidewalk that the light of a lamp still shone in the window of Connor's office.

Thank heavens he was still here!

Her escape from Belgrave Square had gone much more smoothly than she had hoped. Having dressed in her borrowed outfit of men's breeches and shirt, she had chosen to sneak out the servants' entrance of the Daventry town house rather than attempt to climb from her window in plain view of the guard. By mixing and mingling with several stable lads in the vicinity of the carriage house, she had walked right past the man without him blinking an eye, and she had to pat herself on her back for her ingenuity.

And now it was time to reveal to Connor that his dead twin brother wasn't quite so dead after all.

It was a task she wasn't looking forward to.

With one last glance up at Connor's window, Jillian turned to the jarvey and briefly considered whether or not she should ask him to wait. But realizing that there was no telling how long this would take or what was going to happen as a result of her revelation, she went ahead and paid him before sending him on his way. Then, taking a deep breath, she climbed the steps to the front door.

The inside of the lobby was dimly lit, and it took a moment for her eyes to adjust to the change in lighting. When it did, she noticed Connor almost immediately, standing with his back to her in front of the high desk in the corner. No skinny, weaselish-looking man occupied the chair behind it this evening, and she could only be happy about that. She certainly didn't need an audience for what she was about to tell the man she loved.

"Connor."

He whirled about when she called his name, and she swept off her cap and hurried forward, reaching out to seize his hands as she drew near.

"Please hear me out before you get angry," she rushed to explain before he could say anything, taking in the tight set of his features. "I know I shouldn't be here, but there's something you need to know. I found another note in Wilbur Forbes's room last night. I'm sorry. I had forgotten about it, but tonight I remembered and read it and . . ." She paused, licking suddenly dry lips, then blurted, "Your stepfather isn't the killer, Connor. It's Brennan."

There was dead silence.

And it was at that moment that Jillian caught sight of the legs on the floor, sticking out from behind the desk.

Her eyes flew back to Connor's face in alarm,

and this time she noticed the subtle differences she should have seen before. This man had the same thick russet hair and towering height, the same aqua eyes. But his shoulders weren't quite as broad, there was no off-center cant to that blade of a nose, and his face was substantially thinner.

And the look in those eyes as they glittered down at her was maniacal and not quite sane.

She swallowed and tried to back away, but the man tightened his grip on her hands and refused to let her go.

"Y-you're not Connor," she managed to squeeze out from between bloodless lips.

An evil-looking smile curved that wide mouth. "I'm afraid not."

In a move that was so lightning swift it caught her off guard, the man whipped out a knife and spun her about, clamping her back against his chest and pressing the sharp blade to her throat.

"Allow me to introduce myself, my lady," he purred near her ear. "Mr. Brennan Monroe, at your service."

Chapter 25

An investigator must learn to think fast in any given situation and never panic.

Connor knew the moment he and Tolliver stepped down from the carriage in the rutted lane and saw Albertson waiting for them in the weed-infested yard of the old shack that something wasn't right.

The Runner stood on the front stoop. The look on his face as they approached was strangely shuttered, and his eyes were narrowed and full of a curious sort of watchfulness that immediately put Connor's sixth sense on alert.

"Tolliver says you've located my stepfather," he prompted as he joined the man. "Have you questioned him yet?"

"Oh, we've located him all right," Albertson

drew out slowly, shoving his hands deep into his coat pockets before peering up at Connor from under lowered brows. "But we won't be questioning him anytime soon."

"What's that supposed to mean?"

"He's dead. Has been for some time, by the looks of him. And a right mess it is, too. Worse even than your partner or Wilbur Forbes."

"That's not possible."

"Well, you can tell that to his corpse."

Connor pushed past the Runner into the shack, and the smell hit him almost immediately. It was a smell that had become all too familiar to him during the course of the past week.

Blood.

Once again, it was everywhere. And the crumpled heap in the middle of the room, beaten and battered and carved to ribbons, was barely recognizable as a human being.

"I'd say that rather lays waste to your theory that Ian Trask is our man," Albertson said dryly from the doorway.

Connor was stunned. This made no sense. He'd been so certain that the killer *had* to be Trask, and without that certainty to hold on to he was left reeling.

"I don't understand," he muttered, reaching up to scrub at the back of his neck in bewilderment and frustration. "If not Trask, then who?"

"Whoever it is," Albertson said, moving forward to stand at his side, "he left another message for you." He gestured toward the far corner of the shack.

Connor jerked his head in that direction. There, on the rotting plank wall, words had been written in blood that had long ago dried.

You can't hide from your reflection.

And below that, in larger, sprawling letters:

Grayson and Monroe Shipping.

Bloody hell, was the bastard threatening his company now?

"Any ideas?" Albertson asked with an arched eyebrow. "Does the message mean anything to you?"

Connor shook his head and his jaw set as he struggled to sort out the confusion of his thoughts. Another reference to mirrors. Jillian had been insisting for quite some time that the mirrors meant something to the killer, but what?

You can't hide from your reflection . . .

A sudden possibility slammed into him with the force of a blow, so staggering that it nearly paralyzed him. Surely it wasn't possible. And yet . . .

Turning, he strode from the shack and started toward the waiting hackney.

"Monroe?" Tolliver called out from behind him. "Where are you going?"

"Back to the shipping offices," he tossed back

over his shoulder without slowing down. "And once you're finished here, you might want to meet me there. I have a bad feeling . . ."

His mind awhirl, he issued instructions to the jarvey and climbed back into the coach. Oh, yes, he had a very bad feeling. Because what he was thinking was impossible.

Wasn't it?

As Brennan Monroe dragged Jillian up the staircase to the second floor of Grayson and Monroe Shipping, she struggled to look back over her shoulder at the man who lay slumped on the floor behind the desk in the lobby, praying to see the rise and fall of his chest, some small indication that he was still alive.

"You don't need to worry about Mr. Unger, Lady Jillian," Brennan told her as if reading her mind, his voice sounding vaguely amused. "He still lives. I only rendered him unconscious. My brother cares nothing for him, so he's in no danger from me right now. Though I can't promise that will continue to be the case."

Terror such as she had never felt before raced through Jillian's veins, chilling her blood and prickling her skin with gooseflesh. She was in the hands of a madman and she had no idea how she was going to get away.

But she had no intention of letting this bastard know just how scared she was.

"I suppose you let the poor man believe you were Connor," she said with false bravado, doing her best to ignore the sharp prick of the knife at her throat.

She was pressed so close against his chest that she felt him shrug as they moved down the hallway. "Having a twin can prove most useful at times. People can be so damned trusting, and they never look deeper than the surface."

"You mean like Stuart Grayson?"

Brennan pushed open Connor's office door and shoved her ahead of him into the room, then slammed it closed behind them with a booted foot. His narrowed, malicious gaze never wavered from her for a second as she faced him. "Yes, like Stuart Grayson. Or Peg Ridley. Or Selene Duvall. I had me a piece of that one before I did her, you know. My brother has good taste."

Jillian shivered with revulsion, feeling the heated touch of his eyes trailing over her in a lascivious caress. She quickly moved to put the solid bulk of Connor's desk between them. It would offer no real protection if Brennan decided to attack her, of course, but it made her feel a bit better.

He laughed, as if he found her ploy humorous, then waved his knife in the air before him, seeming to relish the frightened intake of breath the action elicited from her. "They all just let me right in, never the wiser for their mistake until it was too late. It's funny. That old codger Ledbetter was the only one who knew I wasn't him. Wasn't fooled for a moment, so I had to get a bit rough."

Swallowing, Jillian forced herself to work past her fear, to think clearly. That was what a good investigator would do. Disassociate himself. Use his brain to get out of this situation.

She had to keep him talking. She had no idea where Connor had gone, but she had to believe he would be back soon.

If not, she was doomed.

"Why, Brennan?" she asked softly. "Why would you do this? Connor is your brother. He loves you."

"Loves me?" He shook his head, his expression one of incredulous disbelief. "That's right, my brother loves me. The brother who turned me in to the law and watched me get shot without blinking an eye."

"That's not true. He regrets what happened to you, and he blames himself for it."

Brennan's cheeks suddenly flushed crimson and his eyes turned wild as he shouted, spittle flying from his mouth. "Spare me the bleeding-heart drivel! He *should* blame himself! If he loved me so much, where was he when our stepfather was selling me to his friends for a poke?"

"He didn't know it was happening."

"He should have." His voice choked, his face contorting into a mask of pain and grief, and for a fleeting instant Jillian caught a glimpse of the hurt, lost, scared little boy Brennan Monroe had once been. "He should have known. He was my twin brother and I needed him and he wasn't there!"

He spun, knocking a brandy decanter and several crystal glasses off a nearby sideboard, sending them crashing to the floor, where they shattered into pieces.

"Everything was always more important than me!" he raged, pacing like a caged animal in front of the desk, continuing to brandish the knife as if for emphasis. "Hiram, Peg, Stuart. This damned company." He scowled at her. "And now you."

Jillian lifted her chin, though it was a struggle to keep it from quivering. Brennan was so unpredictable, his temper so uncertain, that there was no telling what he would do or how he would react to anything she might say. She had no desire to provoke him. "You're wrong. He doesn't care about me. Just ask him. I handed him my heart this afternoon and he told me he could never love me back."

"Oh, he might not want to admit it, but I've seen the two of you together. I've seen the way he looks at you." His features twisted into an expression of predatory intent, Brennan leered at her. Seeing such a look on the visage of someone who so closely resembled the man she loved was chilling. "I know Connor and he loves you. I'd be willing to lay a wager on that."

Circling around the side of the desk in swift strides that covered the distance between them before she could avoid him, he came to a stop at her right elbow, a little behind her and just out of her sight range. She hated not being able to see him, but there wasn't any way she was going to turn to face him when he was so close.

"But you see, his sins are catching up with him," he murmured, leaning in close to her, his moist breath brushing against her ear in a way that had her stifling the urge to retch. "He has to be punished, and I've come up with a brilliant plan. I'm going to take away everybody he has ever cared for, one by one, until he's left all alone. The way he left me."

There was a long pause, and when he spoke again, a note rang in his voice that raised the hairs on the nape of Jillian's neck. "And I'm afraid, my lady, that you're next on the list."

Something hard slammed into the back of her head with punishing force, and she knew no more.

Chapter 26

An investigator's most formidable weapon is his brain.

Grayson and Monroe Shipping looked dark and still, the only light coming from the lamps left burning in his office window and on the desk in the lobby as Connor let himself into the building. Everything was peaceful, and Lowell Unger appeared to have already gone home for the evening.

Lingering just inside the door, Connor took a moment to let his gaze travel over his surroundings, straining to hear any sounds that seemed strange or out of place. Though the trace of an odd scent tickled his nostrils, he noticed nothing amiss. Yet he couldn't shake the feeling that something was wrong.

You can't hide from your reflection . . .

It was as if someone had whispered the words in his ear, and it was at that moment that he saw the faint outline of a body lying stretched out on the floor behind the desk.

Lowell Unger.

His heart skipping a beat, Connor went swiftly to the man's side, taking in the blood that matted his thinning hair with concern. Bending over, he pressed his fingers against the artery in Unger's neck, feeling for a pulse.

It was there. Weak and thready, but there.

"Hello, Connor."

The voice came from behind him, low and stark and somehow familiar.

Straightening with slow, deliberate movements, Connor turned around just as a large figure stepped out of the shadows of the lobby and into the pool of light cast by the lamp.

Recognition was instantaneous.

"Brennan." Despite the chill that settled over his skin at the sight of his supposedly dead twin, Connor managed to speak with a steadiness that belied the turmoil going on inside him. "It's been a long time."

His brother lifted a careless shoulder. "Over six years."

Perhaps he should have been surprised, but somehow he wasn't. He had been halfway expecting the appearance of his twin ever since the meaning behind the message at Trask's shack had registered with him. But he hadn't wanted to believe that Brennan could be the killer.

Taking a deep breath, Connor fought to rein in the feelings of shock and confusion that threatened to overwhelm him. "Where have you been?"

"Oh, here and there." Brennan waved a hand in a matter-of-fact gesture, the lamplight glinting off the sharp blade of a knife. "You see, after the little incident with the Bow Street Runners, I managed to drag myself from the Thames and luckily collapsed in the yard of an accommodating widow who possessed a bit of medical knowledge. Of course, when you've been shot in the chest and dumped in the filthy waters of the river, it can take months to heal. And then, when infection sets in . . . well, let's just say it was at least a year before I was fully recovered."

He took a step toward Connor, his mouth curving in a smile that held not a trace of humor. "About that time, I decided it would be best if I made myself scarce from the city for a while. I did quite a bit of moving around. All over England, as a matter of fact. But I've been back in London for almost a year now, and I've been watching you." He raised a brow. "You didn't know that, did you, brother? Thanks to you, I've become very adept at skulking about without being seen."

Connor felt as if his brother had just plunged the blade of the knife into his heart. The pain was almost unbearable. This was all because of him. "I'm sorry, Brennan."

"I'd say it's too late to be sorry, Connor. Wouldn't you?"

"I never would have let Bow Street arrest you. You have to know that. I was trying to save you from Trask."

"Trying to save me?" Brennan's aqua eyes narrowed into slits and the icy rage that filled them was chilling. "Well, that was a noble sentiment. But where was it when we were boys and I *needed* you to save me? While you were out gadding about the docks, I was being punished because of you. Beaten because of you. I was being . . ." The words ended in a strangled hiss.

"I know." In agony, Connor moved forward an inch or two, being careful not to make any sudden moves that might alarm his twin. "I know, Brennan."

"You know nothing. You have no bloody idea!"

"Yet after what he did to you, you went back to the man."

"Only after you proved you had no use for me. There were too many other things that were more important. You never cared."

"That's not true." Connor shook his head. "Time and again, I tried to reach out to you, but—"

"You didn't try hard enough, did you?"

None of this made any sense. Pain, fury, grief welled up just beneath the surface of Connor's calm demeanor, threatening to explode. It seemed he had never really known his brother at all. Brennan had killed the people he cared about. Brennan had set out to hurt him. It was a nightmare, yet he held on to his control with an effort. "Why? Why are you doing this? Hiram and Peg and Stuart. They were good people and they didn't deserve what you did to them."

"Well, that's a matter of opinion, isn't it?" Brennan stepped up to the desk, studying Connor across its surface with a flint-hard expression. "Actually, I didn't plan on killing anyone. Not in the beginning. But like I said, I've been watching you, and you have it swell here, brother. A partnership in a company that has made you wealthy. A nice home and plenty of material possessions. While I've been sleeping in alleyways and gutters because of you."

One corner of his mouth twisted in self-righteous wrath. "Can you blame me if I decided I deserved something for myself and I was going to take it?" He looked down at the knife in his hand, turning it over, running his thumb over the tip of the blade in an almost absent fashion. "Hiram was the first. You see, I remembered that watch he always prized so highly, and I figured it must be worth a little blunt, so I went and knocked on his door one night. The codger wouldn't hand it over, so I had to do some convincing. Got carried away, I'm afraid."

Connor's last bit of hope that Brennan was innocent was thoroughly extinguished. He could see the relish on his brother's face, the madness in those eyes so like his own, and knew there was no saving Brennan this time.

And as his anger slowly overtook him, he realized that he no longer had any desire to. Because of this man, too many innocent people were dead, and he allowed himself a brief second to be grateful that Jillian wasn't with him and that she wouldn't be exposed to this, that he had made sure she was safe and well guarded.

"But once I took the watch and left," his twin was saying, "I realized how much I had enjoyed the power I felt. The power of life and death. Like the Sword of Damocles, I could decide who lived or died, and I could mete out the punishment. Your punishment."

His gaze went back to Connor. "And that's when I came up with the most brilliant plan. To make you pay by taking away the people who mattered to you the most. And with each person I rid you of, the more I enjoyed my work. The more I enjoyed the feel of their blood on my hands."

Out of the corner of his eye, Connor sighted the door. He could run for it, he knew. Or grapple with Brennan. But he didn't want to take a chance on letting his brother get away. He had to keep him talking until Tolliver and Albertson arrived. "You left me messages. You wanted me to know it was you."

"Of course. What was the point of it all if you didn't realize I was the instrument of your torture? Though you were a bit slow, weren't you? Thinking it was that fool Trask, when I took care of him right after I did away with Peg. After all, he had to pay, too. And killing Forbes set you up all too perfectly as a suspect in the crimes."

Brennan leaned forward and Connor tensed. But instead of attacking him, his twin lifted the lamp from the desk with his free hand and held it aloft, letting the light play over his features and giving himself a rather satanic appearance.

"That's at an end now, though," he said, wandering over toward the stairs. "I've taken care of the last person on my list, and all that's left is this company and you. Do you smell something, brother?"

The abrupt change of subject threw Connor off balance. But after a second, he recalled the strong odor he had smelled when he had first stepped into the building. "Kerosene."

Brennan's grin was evil personified. "That's right. You see, before you showed up, I took the time to douse the lobby, the stairwell, and the upper-floor hallway with lamp oil. All I need to do is drop this lamp right here, and before you know it, the entire place will go up. Twin brothers, each the other half of the other, perishing together in the inferno."

He held the lamp out from his body, lifting a brow at Connor, as if daring him to try and take it from him. "A brilliant ending, wouldn't you say?"

And with that, he opened his fingers and let the lamp fall to shatter on the floor.

Jillian fought her way back to consciousness to be greeted by the smell of smoke.

Rolling over with a groan, she blinked her

eyes open to find herself on the floor of Connor's office. The memory of what had happened washed over her like a tidal wave, and when she tried to sit up, a shaft of pain shot through her head, forcing her to remain perfectly still until it passed and she could push herself to her feet in an unsteady manner.

She supposed she should be thankful she was alive, she thought, reaching up to probe gingerly at the tender knot on the back of her head. A mental image of Stuart Grayson's office the way it had looked the first time she'd been here flashed through her mind, and she shivered. If Brennan had decided to take his knife to her, it could have been so much worse.

But why hadn't he?

She glanced about her, ignoring the blurred quality of her vision, to assure herself that the madman was no longer with her. But even as it registered that she was alone in the room, she caught another whiff of smoke.

Something was burning.

Wobbling on weak legs over to the door, Jillian tried the knob to find it locked, and sheer terror streaked through her when she felt the heat against her palm and saw a puff of grayish smoke float upward from underneath the panel to hover in the air before her.

Good Lord, it was the building! Connor's twin had set it on fire!

Whirling about, she closed her eyes until the dizziness caused by the sudden movement passed, then began to think frantically. She had to get out of here. But even if she could manage to get the door unlocked, she knew that wasn't the way to escape. Already she could hear the crackle of flames out in the hallway, and the smoke was thickening as she stood there, choking her.

Hurrying over to the window that overlooked the main street, Jillian tugged and pulled at the sash. Another jolt of fear shot through her when she realized it was stuck, it wasn't going to budge.

Use your brain, Jillian, she told herself firmly, fighting to keep her panic at bay. *You are not going to die like this. There is too much left for you to do, and you can't leave Connor alone. Not when he needs you.*

Through the haze, her eyes fell on the chair behind Connor's desk, and she bit her lip as she contemplated it. It looked a bit heavy, though she believed she could lift it. But how on earth would she get down safely to the ground?

There was no time to plot and plan. She would simply have to use her instincts.

Getting a firm grip on the draperies hanging at the window, Jillian tore them loose with a mighty heave and went to work.

Flames immediately shot up from the floor of the lobby and blazed a trail up the stairs as Connor looked on in disbelief. But he had little time to come to grips with what he was seeing, for Brennan suddenly lunged at him, knocking him backward. Recovering quickly, he squared off with his fists raised, and when his brother flung himself forward again, he was ready.

The fight began in earnest.

The two of them were rather evenly matched with their similar height and build, and at first neither could get the upper hand. They grappled amid the blaze, and smoke filled the room. Connor's eyes began to tear and his lungs burned, but he wouldn't allow himself to weaken. He was determined not to give in.

A picture of Jillian flashed across his inner vision as a silent reminder of how much he had to live for.

At that moment, Brennan suddenly shoved him away and slashed out with his knife. The blade sliced across Connor's abdomen and he let out a hiss at the pain. But his brother's action as he drew back the weapon gave Connor the opening he needed to strike.

He swung a fist upward, hitting Brennan under the jaw with a force that snapped his head backward. There was an instant of absolute silence. Then his twin toppled to the floor.

Pressing a hand to his midsection to staunch the flow of blood from his wound, Connor stared down at his brother for a second, then took in the conflagration that surrounded him before turning to stride through the growing smoke to the still unconscious Lowell Unger's side. There was no time for indecision. He had to get his assistant out of here.

With a heave, he lifted the man up over his shoulder, clenching his teeth when the motion wrenched his injury, and made his way to the door and outside into the fresh air. Its coolness struck his face, and he breathed it in gratefully as he carried Unger down the steps to the sidewalk, just as Tolliver and Albertson stepped from a hack at the curb.

"What the hell is going on here?" Albertson bellowed, hurrying forward to help him lower the man to the ground.

Connor sent another glance at the shipping office. Smoke was beginning to pour from the cracks in the windows, and even from this distance the roar of the fire could be heard.

Brennan was in there. And no matter what he had done, he couldn't let his twin die in such a way.

"Wait here and I'll tell you when I get back."

Ignoring Tolliver's shouts behind him, he raced back into the building.

The interior of the lobby was practically engulfed in flames, the smoke thick and black and impossible to see through, and Connor felt as if it took a small eternity to locate Brennan, still spread out on the floor at the foot of the stairs. His twin wasn't nearly as light as Lowell Unger, and when Connor was struck with a sudden fit of coughing and wheezing, he was forced to drag Brennan's bulk one step at a time toward the door.

By the time he had managed to get them both out onto the steps, he could barely speak due to the rawness of his throat.

"Now, will you tell me what the hell is going on here?" Albertson asked as he and Tolliver aided him in getting Brennan a safe distance from the building.

He collapsed to the pavement, sucking air into his lungs in great gulps. He could feel the sweat dripping down his face, and reached up to wipe it away with the sleeve of his coat. "This is your murderer, Albertson," he gasped. "My twin brother, Brennan Monroe. He planned on burning Grayson and Monroe Shipping down with both of us in it."

The Runners gaped at him in astonishment.

"Mr. Monroe?"

A hand landed on Connor's shoulder, and he looked back to find the guard he and Tolliver had assigned to watch Jillian earlier that day. For some reason, a sudden icy chill crawled up his spine.

"What is it?" he asked, unable to hide his anxiety.

The man glanced from him, to the burning building, and back, his eyes wide. "Where is Lady Jillian?"

"At home, I should hope."

Blanching at Connor's reply, the guard shook his head. "I'm afraid not, sir. She slipped out a couple of hours ago, and by the time I realized she had managed to get by me, she was way ahead. When I finally caught up to her, she was entering Grayson and Monroe Shipping, so I figured she was safe with you. I've been out here watching and she hasn't left the building."

Connor's horrified gaze went to the flames he could see dancing just behind the glass of the structure's windows. No. It wasn't possible. Jillian wasn't in there. She couldn't be.

He must have uttered the words aloud, though he didn't remember doing so, for someone suddenly spoke over the growing hum of muted conversation from the people who had started to gather in the street to watch the blaze.

"Oh, she's in there, all right."

Connor pushed himself to his feet and turned to find that his brother was conscious, sitting up on the sidewalk as Albertson bound his hands behind his back.

"I knocked her out and left her locked in your office," Brennan went on, his eyes gleaming with malicious glee. "I could have carved her up, you know, but I thought it was a fitting end that the woman you loved should die with you in the same way."

The woman he loved. In that moment, it all became agonizingly clear. He *did* love Jillian. With all of his badly battered heart and every bit of breath in his body. Maybe he had loved her all along, but he had been too afraid to admit it. She had come into his life like a ray of light, occupying his every thought and refusing to let him hide from his feelings. And now it was too late to tell her.

Never had he felt such anguish, such a grinding sense of loss and despair. His knees went weak and he was certain that his heart would be ripped right out of his chest from the twisting, tearing grief. Jillian had been everything bright and beautiful to him and now she was gone.

No, he wouldn't accept that! He would not lose someone else he loved!

With a roar, he lunged toward the building like a man possessed, determined to get to her, to save her. But hands pulled him back, overpowering him when he would have raced headlong into the inferno, and dragging him to the ground.

"It's too late!" Albertson yelled in his ear, barely able to hold on to him, even with the help of Tolliver and the guard. "Look at it, man! No one could survive that!"

Then, as if to punctuate his statement as well as prove the inaccuracy of it, a chair came crashing through Connor's office window, barely missing a group of merchants who milled about just below it.

A second later, a line of knotted material was slung over the sill, and a female figure dressed in men's breeches and coat began to shimmy down it.

A very alive Jillian.

"Gypsy!"

Connor's voice was so hoarse it was barely audible, but he managed to wrench free from the hands that restrained him and ran forward to catch her as she dropped to the ground. She landed in his arms with a soft *oooph*, and he savored the feel of her, despite the jab of pain he felt as the curve of her hip prodded the knife wound in his midsection. It was like heaven to him. A heaven he'd never thought to know again.

She blinked up at him owlishly, tears caused by the smoke streaming from her eyes. Her face was streaked with grime and her ebony hair was a nest of wild tangles about her shoulders, but she had never looked more beautiful to him.

"There, you see," she croaked. "I can take care of myself just fine."

Her words startled a laugh from him, and he hugged her close, his heart too full for him to speak for a second. She returned his hug, but when she started to draw back, he tightened his hold.

"No, Gypsy, don't let go," he said huskily in her ear. "Please don't ever let go."

Their lips met in a long, slow, melting kiss that tasted like kerosene and smoke.　●

Connor had never tasted anything so good.

"*No!*"

It was a wild, keening cry that rent the night, prompting Connor to tear his mouth from Jillian's and raise his eyes just in time to see

Brennan go running past him. His twin looked frenzied, almost crazed, as he evaded the hands that tried to stop him, dashing up the steps and into the blazing building.

A second later, his anguished screams echoed from inside.

Chapter 27

For every case that is solved, another waits just around the corner.

Jillian sat before the window in the parlor of the Daventry town house, elbow propped on the sill and chin resting on her hand as she gazed out at the traffic on Belgrave Square.

It had been three days since her nightmare confrontation with Brennan Monroe and the fire at Grayson and Monroe Shipping. And while it seemed that almost every person in London had paid a call on her at least once in those three days, she hadn't seen Connor since the night it had all happened.

Of course, she was well aware that his time was limited. Not only did he have to contend with the fact that the shipping offices had been almost completely destroyed, but she was certain the law was keeping him busy answering questions about his twin.

But, oh, how she longed to see him.

She sighed. Perhaps she was hoping for something that wasn't going to happen. He'd been so caring that evening, holding her close, kissing and touching her as if she were utterly precious to him. But maybe she had read something more into it than what it was.

After all, he had never actually told her he loved her.

"Thinking of Connor?"

At the question, Jillian looked back over her shoulder to find Maura watching her from her place on the nearby love seat, her expression concerned.

"Am I so horribly obvious?" she asked.

"I would say so." A faint smile curved her sister's mouth. "That's the fourth time I've heard you sigh in the last quarter hour."

That was something else that had happened in the last few days, Jillian mused. When the story of her involvement with Connor and a murder investigation had finally swept through the *ton* and the whispers had started, her family had rallied around her in ways she had never expected. Though her come-out hung in the balance, Maura hadn't outright condemned her. On the contrary, her sister had been surprisingly understanding. Especially once Jillian had explained to her about her feelings for Connor.

And their father . . . well, he'd been shocked

and angry at first and had given her quite a lecture about the danger she had exposed herself to, but he had gotten past it for the most part. And though he still seemed a trifle short-tempered, that was mostly because he was incensed on her behalf at Connor's continued absence.

"He ought to be brave enough to come and ask me for your hand," the marquis had grumbled to her just the day before. "What with all the trouble he's caused and the tongues he's set to wagging by seducing you, it's the least the chap can do. I've a mind to call him out right now."

Jillian had pressed a kiss to her father's head, brushing back a lock of hair with a gentle hand. "He didn't seduce me. And you won't call him out, Papa, because you know I love him. He *will* be here. Just give him some time. So much has happened . . ." She had let her voice trail away, praying she was right.

"No excuse. No excuse at all. But I'll give him the benefit of the doubt, since you say you love him." He had paused for a moment, studying her with tired eyes, then reached up to caress the curve of her cheek. "I know you think I was weak when it came to your mother, darling. That I should have stood by her instead of retreating the way I did, and you're right."

Dismayed that he had read her innermost feelings so accurately when she thought she'd hid them so well, she had stared at him with her mouth agape for several seconds before finally managing to protest. "No, Papa. I don't think that."

"Ah, but you do. You're your mother's daughter, Jilly, and that's a compliment. I admire that strength and independence in you just as I admired it in her. If you feel so strongly about the night she was killed, perhaps it's worth looking into."

Remembering his words caused Jillian's heart to speed its pace even now. He hadn't promised anything, but at least he had shown her that he took her suspicions seriously and offered her some hope. If her father said he would look into it, he would. She had no doubt of that.

Yes, it meant everything to her that everyone in her family so obviously loved and supported her.

"I must say, I find it disgraceful that you show no regret at all for your deplorable behavior."

Well, almost everyone.

Jillian glanced over at her aunt Olivia, who had just entered the room and stood with her hands on her hips and a frown marring her forehead. Her contemptuous blue eyes raked over her oldest niece with displeasure and scorn.

The marquis's sister had been far from supportive. But that was no less than Jillian had expected. The woman had often accused her of being no better than her mother, and she supposed she had only proved the accusations to be true. At least in her aunt's eyes.

"Of course, the scandal you've caused means

nothing to you," Olivia went on, her tone waspish and full of venom.

Maura spoke up before Jillian could even open her mouth to defend herself.

"Don't be silly, Aunt Olivia." Her sister's voice was light, her manner careless as she got to her feet and crossed the room to stand next to the older woman. "Oh, perhaps there have been a few who have been cruel, but most of the people who have visited in the past few days believe that Jilly is quite the heroine. After all, she did foil a murderer. It makes for a rather juicy tale."

It was true. To Jillian's astonishment, the current gossip appeared to be favorable rather than derogatory. Theodosia had filled her in on some of the varied accounts that were making the rounds about the part Jillian had played in the apprehension of Brennan Monroe, and they were almost laughable in their depiction of her as a veritable Athena. Not even her apparent romance with a tradesman had dimmed the enthusiasm, and everyone who had stopped by had been most kind and eager to hear about her adventure.

Of course, well she knew how easily and swiftly the tide could turn. Society had a definite tendency to be fickle.

"This family needs no more juicy tales told about it," Lady Olivia was saying with an exasperated huff. "And if you think that—"

She was interrupted when Iverson suddenly appeared in the doorway.

"The Viscount Shipton and Lady Gwyneth Wadsworth," he announced.

Jillian barely stifled a groan. Of course. The very last two people she wished to see.

Rising from her position on the window seat, she shook out her skirts and smoothed her features into a polite mask just as the pair swept into the room.

"There you are, you poor dear," Lady Gwyneth gushed, barreling toward her like a ship at full sail. "I have heard the most appalling stories about you and I just had to come and see for myself."

Arching a brow at her, Jillian tilted her head in inquiry. "See what?"

"Why, if you were all right, of course. Some of the tales are simply beyond belief. But then, we *are* talking about you, aren't we?"

"Gwyneth," Thomas began warningly, but Jillian halted him with a wave of her hand.

"No, Lord Shipton, it's all right. I'm certain Lady Gwyneth only meant her comment in the best possible way." She narrowed her eyes at the blonde, resisting the urge to bare her teeth. "Isn't that right, Gwyneth?"

"Of course. Now come, you must tell me all about it. Is it true? Did you really have an . . . association with a man in trade?"

The impertinent question shouldn't have shocked Jillian, but it did, and she had to struggle to answer in a coolly controlled voice. "I don't believe that's any of your business."

"Well, it's not as if it isn't already all over London. Everyone has heard about it. Surely you can fill me in on just a little gossip."

"To be truthful, Lady Gwyneth, I find I have no interest in telling you a thing."

From across the room, Lady Olivia gasped in outrage, but Jillian ignored her. She kept her entire focus on the dainty blonde before her. She had long ago recognized this woman for the predator she was, and she had no intention of showing her any weakness.

"My, my." Lady Gwyneth peered up at her knowingly from under lowered lashes, her smile more closely resembling a smirk. "Your manners certainly do leave something to be desired, don't they? But then, I've always known that. Your mother was an actress, after all."

"Actually, Lady Gwyneth, I would say you're the one whose manners could use a bit of work."

The deep voice came from the direction of the doorway, and every eye in the room went to the tall, broad-shouldered man who loomed in the opening, practically filling the space with his imposing breadth.

Jillian's heart flew into her throat. "Connor."

His eyes blazed at her with a fierce light as he strode forward to join her. When he reached her side, he turned to face Lady Gwyneth, his visage stern.

"The Lady Jillian," he told her, his tone dangerously soft, "happens to be the most beautiful, the most brilliant, the most wonderful woman I have ever met. And in my opinion, my lady, females such as yourself only pale in comparison. Now, I think it's time for you to leave."

Gwyneth drew herself up with haughty aplomb, her cheeks turning bright pink. "Well, I never. That's what I get for trying to extend an olive branch to the likes of anyone in *this* family. Come, Thomas."

Whirling, she marched stiffly from the parlor without looking back.

But Thomas didn't immediately comply. Instead, he paused, the tiny quirk of his lips as he met Jillian's gaze sad and regretful. "I'm sorry, Jillian. For a lot of things."

In that moment, she saw Thomas for who he really was. A man who had truly cared for her, but who had simply been too weak to withstand the pressure put on him by his family and society.

Her mother had been right. He never would have made her happy.

With a short bow, the viscount followed his fiancée from the room.

There was a taut silence. Then Maura ventured into the breach, sounding amazingly cheerful. "Well, I suppose we should leave you two alone."

"Alone?" Lady Olivia stared at her niece as if she had lost her mind. "I hardly think so. It wouldn't be proper at all. Especially after—"

"Come, Aunt Olivia. I doubt we have reason to be concerned when the damage has already been done. Wouldn't you agree?"

It was the second time that day that Maura had come to her aid, and Jillian couldn't help but be astounded by that fact as her sister winked at her, tucked her arm through her aunt's, and drew a protesting Olivia from the room, closing the door behind them.

Once the two women had departed, an awkward hush descended once again, and it seemed like a small, painful eternity before Connor finally cleared his throat and spoke. "I'm sorry I haven't been to see you sooner. I wanted to come, but things have been . . . rather hectic." He hesitated, scrutinizing every inch of her features, as if intent on assuring himself of her well-being. "How are you?"

Surreptitiously wiping her damp palms on her skirt, Jillian told herself that she wasn't going to rush to any conclusions, that she wasn't going to let herself assume, simply because he had championed her with Lady Gwyneth, that he was here for any reason other than to inquire after her welfare. "Tired. Better than I expected, however. I was certain I would be a pariah, and instead it appears I'm the new toast of the *ton*."

"Yes, I heard. You're the heroine of the hour, it seems."

Her own gaze took inventory of the dark circles under his eyes, the exhaustion that marked his countenance, and her heart ached for him. "And what about you, Connor? I'm so sorry about the shipping offices."

"It's all right. It will be difficult, but I can run things from the warehouse for now. We'll rebuild. It will take time, but Stuart showed me that you can do anything if you put your mind to it."

"Mr. Unger?"

"Recovering."

Jillian paused, licking her lips before broaching the subject that she knew caused him the most pain. "And Brennan?"

A shadow passed over his craggy face, and there was no mistaking the grief that flashed in the aqua depths of his eyes, though he offered her the suggestion of a smile. "It's been difficult. It hurts. After all, he was my twin. But I've finally come to realize that it's not my fault. It took seeing what he had become for me to understand that."

Unable to keep from touching him for another instant, Jillian placed a comforting hand on his arm. "I'm glad you finally do." As always, a tingle raced through her at the contact, and she curled her fingers into the material of his coat sleeve, savoring the warmth. "What changed Brennan happened when you were both little more than boys. There was nothing you could have done then. And afterward . . ."

"Afterward it was too late. I know. I just wish . . ."

When his voice drifted off into nothingness, she gave his arm another squeeze. "Ian Trask was the one responsible, Connor. Blame him, if you must blame someone. But never yourself."

Connor peered down at her inscrutably for several long seconds. Then, in an unexpected motion, he reached up to cover her hand on his sleeve with one of his own. "Thank you."

"For what?"

"For helping me see that. For caring. For being there for me in the last week, even when I fought you every step of the way."

Jillian felt her cheeks heat with embarrassment. "I'm afraid I wasn't much help at the end. If I hadn't forgotten that note, we might have known it was Brennan sooner and—"

"No." Connor cut her off with a shake of his head. "You helped me more than you will ever know. And it goes much further than just catching a killer or saving my sanity. It goes soul deep, Gypsy."

Something in his deep, gravelly tone sent a shiver coursing throughout her body, and she had to take a deep breath before she could ask him the question she'd been dying to ask since he'd sent her unwelcome visitors on their way with his impassioned defense. "Did you mean all those things you said to Lady Gwyneth?"

"Every one. But there was one thing I forgot to say." Twining his fingers through hers, he lifted her hand from his sleeve and brought it to his lips so that he could press a tender kiss to the back of it. Quite suddenly, he looked far from inscrutable. The gravity of his expression, the scorching heat in his eyes, took her breath away.

"I love you, Gypsy," he said, genuine emotion suffusing every word. "I know I said I couldn't, that I wasn't capable of it. But I lied. You've held my heart almost from the beginning. And I hope you never give it back."

So much joy welled up within Jillian that she could barely contain it all, and she felt the smile that stretched over her face like a ray of sunlight. "Oh, Connor, I love you, too."

Pulling her close, Connor wrapped his arms about her and whispered in her ear, "Will you marry me, Lady Jillian Daventry?"

"There is nothing I want more."

Their lips met in a slow, sweet, blissful exchange that left them both trembling and aching with need by the time they finally pulled apart.

"I must warn you," Jillian managed to inform Connor breathlessly, "that my father expects an official request for my hand."

"Then he shall have it." A momentary frown marred his brow. "There's just one thing. I couldn't take it if you ever regretted marrying me, Jillian. Will your family mind that I am not a titled aristocrat?"

Jillian rolled her eyes and wound her arms around his neck. "As if I could ever regret being your wife, darling. And my mother was an actress, remember? As long as I'm happy, that's all my family cares about."

Chuckling, Connor swept her up and swung her about, grazing her temple with another kiss before regarding her seriously once more.

"You proved something to me the other night, Gypsy," he told her. "You are an independent and capable woman who can take care of herself, and I want to be with you, no matter what that entails. So if you need to keep working with Bow Street, keep searching for the truth about what happened to your mother, I'll help you. I would never ask you to give that up. Though you'll have to forgive me if I tend to be overbearing when it comes to your safety. I will more than likely always worry. But it's only because I couldn't stand to lose you."

Never could Jillian remember feeling so happy. Her life with this man would be far from trouble-free, but she knew they were perfect for each other. Connor Monroe would never abandon her. He had proven that today with Lady Gwyneth. She knew he would stand by her, supporting her, no matter what. "You won't lose me. I promise."

"Good, because I never again want to feel the way I felt when I thought you were in that burning building. It was like my worst nightmare realized." Connor nuzzled the top of her head, one corner of his mouth curving upward in a wry manner. "Ahhh, Gypsy. I love you so much. But I have a feeling my life will start swiftly spiraling out of control from the minute we wed."

Tightening her arms around his neck, Jillian smiled, her entire countenance aglow with the strength of her love for this man.

"You don't need to worry, darling," she promised him teasingly. "I'll protect you."

Author's Note

During the early half of the 1800s, crime scene investigative procedure was—for all intents and purposes—nonexistent. Techniques such as fingerprinting and blood analysis didn't come along until much later, and many times simply being accused of a crime was enough to ensure a conviction.

It was a nineteenth-century crook-turned-law officer named Eugene Francois Vidocq who eventually pioneered a change in the way police work was done. The first chief of the elite French Surete in 1811, Vidocq introduced such innovations as the science of ballistics into police work, was the first to make plaster-of-paris casts of shoe impressions at crime scenes, and was a master of disguise and surveillance. He is considered by many to be the father of modern criminal investigation and one of the world's greatest detectives.